The
CENTAURESS

Kathleen Jones

Kathleen Jones is a biographer and poet whose short stories have won several awards including a Cosmopolitan fiction prize and a Fay Weldon award. Kathleen's biography of Catherine Cookson was in the top 10 best-seller racks in WH Smith for 8 weeks. Her first novel, The Sun's Companion, was short-listed for the Kindle Review best historical novel of 2013. Born and brought up on a hill farm in the Lake District, Kathleen currently spends a lot of time in Italy with her partner, sculptor Neil Ferber and runs a creative writing course there every September. She is a Royal Literary Fund Fellow and, in 2012, was elected as a Fellow of the English Association.
Further information at: www.kathleenjones.co.uk

"Down from the waist they're centaurs, / Though women
all above"
King Lear, Act IV, Scene vi, ln.124–125:

Introduction

This is a work of the imagination - you won't find the Kaštela exactly in Istria, although you will find places just like it. Motovun has an old citadel and a village around it, and you can watch the sun set in the Adriatic from the terraces of Grosjnan. The hill village of Buje is also beautiful. In Rovinj you will discover apartments just like the one Zenia and Lucia rented. You can drink in the Viecia Batana, pass through one of the ancient gateways and sit on the rocks beside the sea just as Alex and Gianfranco did.

The ravages of war have now been repaired and, since Croatia joined Europe, all the locations are thriving and just as beautiful and atmospheric as they were before. Istria is now open for business and welcomes tourists of every nationality.

All the characters are fictional and bear no resemblance to anyone living or dead. Any similarities are entirely accidental.

Zenia's voice is beautiful on the MP3 file. I sometimes switch the laptop on just to listen to her speaking, in the interviews she gave me, three years ago, on that first, tentative visit to the Kaštela Visoko in Istria. She talks with a painter's eye for visual detail and her voice in the headphones is vibrant, husky, and challenging – just as Zenia was in life. But as I listen, I often wonder just how much of the truth she told. Does memory lie, or does it just accommodate itself to the conventions of story-telling? Or does it, as in dream, create narratives of its own?

The first recording is one of my favourites. We were sitting in the shade of the loggia on an airless autumn afternoon with a bottle of wine open on the table. It was one of Zenia's bad days. I had asked about her childhood, her family, her home, and found her evasive and uncooperative. Zenia had retreated into some small internal space and closed the door. Even encouraged by Freddi, she could not, or would not, answer my questions, turning her face obstinately away, talking about the olive harvest, the problem of finding girls to work for the tourist season, Concetta's marital difficulties. Anything but the one subject I wanted her to talk about – herself. Then, almost out of desperation, I asked, 'What's the first thing you remember?'

For a moment Zenia picked at the hem of her linen tunic with her fingers in an angry kind of way, and I thought she was going to ignore this question as she'd ignored all the others. But then her face changed; her eyes began to flicker with images that only she could see and her mouth relaxed, beginning to shape the words to fit. It was like turning the key to an ancient lock. I could almost hear the stiff tumblers clicking over, one by one, until the door unlatched and you could walk through. Zenia's voice on the recording is deep, almost masculine, but also musical, every syllable separately pitched and accorded its own variations of tone and colour. When she talks it's as if she's dreaming aloud. When I close my eyes it's as if I'm inside Zenia's memory.

When I wake up in the dark the first thing I see is the mirror. This one not very special, just a long thin glass on the wardrobe door beside my bed. As soon as I open my eyes I can see my hunched-up body under the bedclothes, then the enamelled bedstead. You have seen those old Italian beds? Painted with flowers and scrolls of gold leaf – very beautiful. On the other side of the room I can see the thick brocade drapes across the windows, flared with the shadows of the night-light my nurse has left on the bedside table. Even then, I was fascinated by the play of the light, how it shaped and sculpted and told different stories. There is a wash stand against the wall and a little chair beside it. In the mirror I can see the line of light that marks the edge of the door. It opens into a corridor and at the end of the corridor is the room where my mother is entertaining friends. Tap, tap, tap. Their heels echo on the marble floor. People are coming in and out of the room and as the door opens and closes, there are little pulses of music and laughter. I can't bear to be alone here in the darkness. Basta! I say to myself. I can't stay here.

It's a great distance from my bed to the floor. Slowly I slide down until I can just touch it with the tips of my big toes. My nurse used to put me in a long cotton nightdress and it has coiled itself round my armpits, stringing me up like a criminal. I tug myself free and lower myself onto the marble floor. How cold it is! How well I remember that feeling on the soles of my feet.

Zenia paused here, running her tongue over her dry lips. I thought she was going to stop and opened my mouth to prompt her, but Zenia had already begun again, lapsing into Italian, speaking fluently and fast, her beautiful eyes flashing. I had to struggle to keep up with the flow of language.

In the corridor the lights were flickering in their bronze sconces. In my mother's day there were Venetian mirrors in ornate frames on each side. These were fascinating for a child. In daylight they showed a series of paintings. Nature Morte, I suppose I would call them now. But I had already begun to suspect that behind their surfaces lurked other worlds, with different perspectives. It was as if the glass was a sheet of water, changing whatever you could see under it. I used to stare into them for hours. Reflections of ordinary things, a lamp or a vase of flowers, everything became magnified into something wonderful and strange. Even my own image came back to me altered. That was when I first knew that I was a twin. In the mirror was my other self; a changeling child, my face angelic and obedi-

ent, hair curled and be-ribboned by my nurse, clothes im-maculate – only my eyes were mine, dark, fierce eyes staring at me out of the glass.

But at night, these mirrors became a terrible ordeal, showing terrible things – distorted fragments – mutilated faces – images of hell. I knew I must avoid them, or they would steal my soul as I passed.

And then, suddenly, I am outside my mother's door and I think – how am I to open it? I am too small to reach the handle and this makes me angry. I lean against it in a temper and push. Like magic the heavy door swings open and I am there in all the warmth and the light. Eccomi! My mother is leaning against the piano with her head thrown back. Signor Puccini is sitting on the piano stool with his hands on the keys and another man I do not know is playing the violin.

'Ah! Bambina!' someone calls and the music stops. They all turn to look at me. My mother's head swivels towards me and her face is cross. 'I can't get her to stay in her room,' she says angrily. 'What am I to do?'

'So sweet!' One of the ladies leans forward. 'What's your name?'

'Zenobia,' I tell her.

'What a strange name,' she says. It is what every-one says. The cook says it is like an illness, or a foreign plant. But of course it was my grandmother's name they had cursed me with. My father's mother.

'They call me Zenia,' I whisper. She offers me a sweet. And then I am allowed to sit on her lap and listen to the music. I fall asleep with my face pressed against the hard sequins of this lady's dress. The dangling glass beads of her cap glitter above me in the light and, as they glance against each other when she moves her head, they sound *like someone laughing.*

And then suddenly Zenia stops. I remember that she looked dazed and disorientated. I can hear her voice on the recording asking, 'Who is this woman? What is she doing here?'

'She's come to write your life into a book,' Freddi says in very literal, awkward Italian, as if explaining to a child. 'She's the biographer.'

What did it mean to Zenia at that moment? The biographer? A collector of gossip, of memories, an assortment of facts, tossed together in a matrix of words, printed on paper, bound between glossy covers.

After a pause I can hear my own voice again, soothing, non-committal, hoping to restart the flow of recollection. 'Did you have a good relationship with your mother?'

'I was a difficult child,' Zenia replies, almost sulkily. She shrugs her shoulders and raises her hands. 'My mother could do nothing with me.' Then there's a brief silence on the recording as she looks at me with those penetrating, disconcerting eyes, almost as if she knows what's in my head. 'It is the most difficult relationship, is it not?'

It was an unusually cool September day. London felt tired. The view from the restaurant window was grey – grey pavements, grey buildings, grey water.

'So, how would you feel about writing this book?' Jane asked, a forkful of spinach and mozzarella pizza poised halfway between plate and mouth.

Alex liked Jane; she was sharp and funny and would probably have been a friend if she wasn't Alex's agent. They hadn't been in touch for a long time – it had been a bit of a surprise when Jane had rung yesterday and invited Alex to lunch. She'd felt wary, a little defensive, but had eventually accepted and now they were sitting opposite each other in a restaurant on the South Bank.

It was only when Jane had suggested a pizzeria, rather than one of the smart bistros and wine bars she usually favoured, that Alex realised how far down the ratings she'd sunk. But, considering Alex's own long silence, the unanswered emails and the abandoned book contract, it was a miracle that Jane was still speaking to her at all.

'Zenia's marvellous,' Jane put down her fork. She

was almost bouncing on the chair with enthusiasm. 'So articulate! And only the tiniest bit ga-ga – she's so eccentric you don't even notice. But apparently she's very ill and it's going to be vital to get everything down quickly before she deteriorates.'

Even before the menus arrived, Alex had realised that this lunch was simply an excuse for Jane to sell the notion she'd had on her recent holiday in a fortified hill village in Istria, owned by someone Jane described as 'the most extraordinary person I've ever met'.

'Zenia lived in England and America, knew Lucian Freud and Francis Bacon, stayed in Paris with Picasso. She even painted Marilyn Monroe for God's sake!'

Zenobia de Braganza, one of the most famous living European painters, the grande dame of the Veneto, who owned an entire Istrian hill village which she rented out to tourists like Jane in the summer, but in the winter filled with her friends, creating a colony of artists and simpatici.

'She seemed to like the idea,' Jane said, pushing a strand of blonde hair back from her face. 'Wants to tell the truth while she's alive so that people can't tell lies after she's dead. And I've talked to her London agent – no problems there. It would be a good excuse for a retrospective in the Tate Modern, which of course would help to sell the book. Bloomsbury might be interested, and Harper Collins, providing I can get a good writer. So I thought of you. A spell in Istria might cheer you up.'

Alex suppressed a sudden impulse to hit Jane hard across the face. The surge of anger was so strong and physical, Alex could taste the bile in her mouth. The violent reflex shocked her, but, thanks to the little blue capsules of anaesthetic, prescribed by the doctor, Alex managed to contain her rage. Why Jane should think a holiday would cure what she'd just been through was incomprehensible. Alex could only assume Jane had never experienced any kind of family tragedy or real pain in her entire life. Alex's whole world, her way of seeing everything had been irrevocably altered. It was like going back to the Tate Gallery after having become colour blind; the paintings would be there, still the same, but all the colour and life would have gone out of them. There would be no point. Alex hadn't written a word in almost two years. The grief counsellor she'd been assigned afterwards, had recommended that she kept a journal to record her thoughts and feelings, but the pages had remained obstinately blank. The feeling still persisted that there was no point in anything anymore, but the grant from the Royal Literary Fund was almost spent and her small legacy down to single figures.

The flush of anger receded, leaving Alex feeling slightly shaky. She held her tongue between her teeth for a moment longer and then asked, 'What sort of advance are you thinking of?'

Jane shrugged. 'We'll have to negotiate that. But Zenia's agent seems to think they can cover all your expenses to go out there on an initial visit – see how you get on with her, whether you like the idea. Get a synopsis together based on the published material – there's loads apparently. Then I'll try to sell it while you're out there. You speak Italian don't you? Of course it's Croatia now, but Istria used to belong to Italy before it was Yugoslavia and a lot of people still speak the language.'

Alex looked out of the window. It was a cold, bleak day with persistent drizzle. Pedestrians in gloves and scarves were scurrying along the concrete walk-way of the South Bank. An unkind wind was whipping the Thames into spiky waves. Jane had just been talking about Istrian sunshine, the citrus odour of the lemon tree below her window, describing the sunset in the Adriatic. Alex was conscious of a great longing for warmth, colour and light. Could she write this book? Was she actually still capable? It was the first time in two years that Alex had felt even the stirring of an inclination.

Alex spent the rest of the afternoon in the National Portrait Gallery looking at likenesses. There was a canvas by Francis Bacon, early work but still with the characteristically dramatic strokes, the cruel drawing out of the figure. Zenobia de Braganza's name was on the label, but the painting didn't give any clues to the reality of her appearance or character. In another room was a photograph of her aged twenty-five by Man Ray – a dark unruly head sculpted by light, jutting, furious brows, half-closed eyes and the most beautiful, androgynous face Alex had ever seen. The strong bone structure, voluptuous lips and brooding eyes could have belonged to either sex. This was no ordinary person. It was that face that decided Alex to write the biography.

Alex flew Ryan Air to Pula and picked up a hire car. It was raining as she heaved her suitcase onto the back seat and began to investigate the unfamiliar controls.

'Don't hire a big car,' Freddi's email message had advised. 'The road to the Kaštela is narrow and twisting and dangerous.'

Alex obeyed the detailed directions meticulously, following the signs north towards Rovinj, through lavender fields and vineyards, before she turned onto a small side road to drive up into dome-shaped hills covered in scrubby vegetation. Beyond them she could occasionally glimpse a blue line of mountains whose summits were shrouded in cloud. The road began to wind upwards towards a group of buildings huddled around a central tower on the top of a hill. The strip of tarmac was potholed and narrow, fenced on one side by trees in vivid autumn colours and on the other by the bare rock of the hillside. The distance to the valley floor, glimpsed through the trees, became more spectacular and unnerving as the road narrowed even further and the tarmac was replaced by gravel. Occasionally there was a wilting bouquet of flowers tied to a tree trunk with ribbon. Alex drove cautiously, peering past the windscreen wipers to find the almost non-existent road signs and land-marks Freddi had told her to look out for. 'Left past the Quick Bar; right at the shrine set in the wall; left where the track forks – there'll be a board that says 'Kaštela'.'

As Alex turned her head to look for it, a four-wheel drive loomed suddenly in the middle of the road. Instinc-tively she swerved away from it, hearing the screech of metal as the front bumper made contact with stone. The vehicle surged past with a blast of the horn but without slackening speed. Alex had a glimpse of camouflage jacket and American-style military cap. For several minutes she sat there trembling until she plucked up the courage to put the car in gear again and drive on – even more slowly. The wing mirror brushed the plants growing out of the rock. Alex wondered why Jane hadn't warned her about this road. And then wondered what else she hadn't told her.

The gradient had become so steep the bonnet sloped up, restricting the view of the left hand hairpin bend ahead. Alex took it too cautiously, trying not to scrape the car on the wall of the house that had suddenly come into view, and the engine stalled. Her hands were slippery with sweat as she let the car slide gently back to get a better run at it. Surely cars weren't meant to come this far up? The second time the car stalled again and she almost panicked, but at the third attempt she managed to wrench the car round the corner, clutch smoking, tyres screaming on the gravel. To Alex's profound relief there was a level space in front of her where two very battered cars with Croatian number plates were parked. She pulled up next to them and got out to inspect the damage. A slightly dented and scraped bumper. But when she looked at the scoured doors and scratched paint of the cars next to hers, she felt she'd got off lightly. It was only a hire car after all and she'd ticked the collision damage waiver box on the car insurance as instructed.

A girl in a dark blue dress had come out of the house Alex had just narrowly missed, holding an umbrella. She came towards her smiling and said, '*Dobrodošli!*' Then, seeing Alex's puzzled expression, she greeted her again in Italian, '*Benvenuto alla Kaštela.*'

'Thank you,' Alex replied in the same language. 'That road is unbelievable. How do you drive it and stay alive?'

The girl laughed. 'It's not for the faint-hearted. We have people who come in the summer who turn around and drive away again because they do not want, ever, to have to drive that road again.' She spoke Italian well, but with a strong accent. 'We tell Zenia that she should make a car park further down, but she just shrugs and says, "I do not want such cowardly people to stay in my house." So you see, it is a test.'

The girl was wiry and quick, with lively eyes and very black, springy hair. 'I am Lenka,' she said. 'And you must be the Signora Forbes?'

'Alessandra. But everyone calls me Alex.'

'Leave your suitcase in the car and Martin will bring it later.' She held her hand out for the car keys and Alex gave them to her meekly. 'Come with me and I will show you where you are staying.'

Lenka led her through an archway and paused beside a gate that led into an immaculate courtyard tiled in terracotta. Old stone steps led up to a blue doorway. There were pots of geraniums on the steps and tea towels hung out to dry on the railings.

'That's Concetta's house,' Lenka said. 'She is the

housekeeper for Zenia.'

The pathway ramped up into the citadel. It was flagged with a mixture of marble off-cuts and stone cobbles, beautiful, but slippery underfoot in the aftermath of rain. Then, another archway and the path opened out onto an avenue of cypresses, framing a view over the olive groves and the roofs of village houses in the valley below, swirling in cloud. Alex could see across the valley to where the sea glittered as the descending sun broke through the cloud. There was a terrace with a low wall and a pergola of wisteria still dripping from the rain. Music was coming from an open doorway in a single-storey building with a misshapen pantiled roof.

'Martin!' Lenka bellowed and a man poked his head round the door. Alex glimpsed ginger hair and beard. 'Suitcase for the Signora Forbes!' The car keys were thrown in a bright arc and expertly fielded. The ginger hair disappeared back inside.

'Who is Martin?'

'*L'uomo tutto fare*. The man who does everything.' There was a slightly mocking edge to Lenka's voice. 'He came from Canada some years ago to pick the olives, backpacking round Europe. Zenia liked him and so he stayed.' She shrugged as if it was a matter of indifference to her whether he came or went.

Her keys jingled in her pocket as she led Alex swiftly up a series of stone stairs, past stuccoed buildings, terraces edged with rosemary, paths shaded by pomegranate trees, round a corner where an encroaching persimmon was laden with perfumed yellow fruit. There were doorways everywhere.

'We've put you in the Casanova house,' Lenka said, pausing beside a green door and taking out a key. 'Each of the apartments is named for a famous person from Istria. You're in Casanova Uno.' She opened the door into a low ceilinged room with a tiled floor. The window looked out across the valley and a wood burning stove in the corner had already been lit. A tiny bedroom opened off the sitting room, white-plastered walls and terracotta floors. The bed was enormous, with a painted wooden frame and a white cotton counterpane. Another door opened into the smallest shower room Alex had ever seen. She would practically have to stand in the loo to get under the shower.

Back in the sitting room Lenka pointed to a table where a kettle sat beside a small fridge. 'We've left you wine and coffee. If you want anything else, just ask. At eight o'clock you're to go up to the house to meet Zenia and have dinner.' She was gone before Alex could ask how she was supposed to find it among this maze of paths and buildings.

Martin, when he arrived with the luggage, was rather more personable than he'd appeared at first. Thirty something, well groomed, with a slim muscular frame and vivid blue eyes. He had oil under his fingernails, but smelt of soap.

'Where d'you want this?' he asked in North American accented English, sizing Alex up so frankly she could feel goosebumps pricking on her forearms.

'Just leave it there. I'll sort it out later.'

'Lenka says you've come to write a book about us all.' His tone was brusque.

'Not necessarily.' Alex wasn't sure why she felt so defensive. 'I might be writing a biography of Signora de Braganza, but it depends whether we get on with each other.'

He laughed sardonically. 'You don't need to worry

about that. She'll be nice to you. If she wants something from you, she'll be nice. Next thing you know, you'll be joining all the other hangers-on round here.'

'Are there many?'

'The place is full of freeloaders. You'll meet some of them tonight. I don't have any time for them myself.'

He turned abruptly and went out, closing the door firmly behind him.

Alex showered and changed into a loose silk shirt and trousers, hoping that they were appropriate for such an important first meeting. She wondered whether to twist her hair up into a business-like knot, but in the end brushed it down to her shoulders. It had begun to curl at the ends with the water from the shower, making dark tendrils around her face. Alex's nerves were still frayed after the journey, so she opened the bottle of wine and drank a glass, wanted to pour another, almost did and then resisted, remembering that she was not supposed to mix alcohol with the little blue pills. By five past eight Alex was beginning to think that she had been forgotten. The familiar hollow feeling that precedes panic had begun to flutter just below her ribcage. She wondered if she should try to find the way by herself in the dark and then suddenly there was a light knock on the door before it was opened and a woman's head appeared in the gap. Seeing Alex she smiled and came into the room. She looked very young, but there were frown lines on her forehead that suggested that she was older than she looked – perhaps in her early thirties. She had bobbed black hair and a heart-shaped, delicate face devoid of make up. Her large, grey eyes were full of anxiety. She was wearing washed out jeans, a black shirt and a pair of rather grubby sneakers.

'Gosh, you do look nice,' she said holding out her hand and smiling. 'I'm Freddi Baker-Thompson. We've exchanged emails.'

Alex allowed her hand to be shaken.

Freddi's fingers were surprisingly tentative, rather shy. 'Did you have a good trip? Have you got everything you want?' She whirled nervously around the room, rattling out questions without pausing for answers. 'Zenia's really looking forward to meeting you. Jane and I went to school together. Cheltenham. Did you know that?'

Alex didn't, but it explained a great deal.

'Come and meet everyone.' Freddi was already half out of the door. 'We don't eat until nine o'clock, sometimes later, but it'll give you a chance to get to know everybody. Tomorrow Zenia's cousins are arriving. They thought you'd like to talk to them too. Her memory's a bit shaky these days so you're going to need a lot of corroboration.'

'I haven't actually got a contract to write the book yet, you know. This is supposed to be a kind of exploratory visit. Didn't Jane tell you?'

Freddi waved it aside as she galloped up a set of slippery marble steps. 'I'm sure everything's going to be fine. If you waited for a contract you might not get to talk to Zenia at all. She's determined to tell her story and the doctors have said there isn't a lot of time left to tell it in. If she has another stroke that could be it.'

Zenia's house was at the highest point in the citadel, at the base of the tower, up a series of narrow paths and steps illuminated by low level lights set in a long stone wall colonised by ferns and mosses. At the top of the steps, a stone figure confronted them in the semi-darkness, the figure of a woman, naked to the waist, her breasts hanging free, holding out arms that contained a limp child. It was such a stark image that Alex halted in front of it, her breath stopped in her throat.

'That's Zenia's Pieta,' Freddi said. 'A tribute to the grieving mothers of the civil war in Croatia.' She put her hand on Alex's elbow, as if to encourage her to move on. 'It's quite brutal, isn't it?'

On Alex's left there was a carved gate in the wall and then a courtyard with lots of plants in containers and a big bronze statue that resembled an upside-down tree, then more marble steps and another door. The room inside was large, dominated by a gigantic manorial fireplace made of slabs of marble with an elaborately carved lintel. There were windows on two sides looking out over the valley. Alex had a brief impression of marble mosaic on the floor, a painted ceiling of vines and other trailing plants, walls crammed with paintings, tapestries, kilim rugs under and over everything. But her attention was focussed on the people in the room, whose faces turned towards her as she entered.

Alex had already met Lenka but the others were strangers. There were two men; one very old, one very young. It was the younger of the two who got up from his chair and came towards her. He was ash blond, almost albino, with pink, polished skin and very blue eyes. His manner, not to mention his lavender-coloured silk shirt, was quite definitely camp despite the strong Australian accent.

'Hi. I'm Toby, Zenia's assistant.' He didn't ask any questions but his eyes were full of undisguised curiosity. Alex held out her hand to him and murmured a greeting.

'And this is Ludo,' Freddi said, indicating the elderly man in the high backed chair next to the fire. 'Ludovico

Babic. He's known Zenia forever. They were at art college together in Venice.'

Ludo nodded and gave Alex a brief, appraising glance as he took her hand.

The two women sitting side by side on the sofa stood up briefly as Freddi introduced them. 'And this is Jolene and Kelly who run our painting courses.' Alex noticed that Freddi's voice changed slightly as she spoke. There was a new note of constraint.

Kelly was young, probably in her early twenties, tall and restless, dressed like a Goth in loose black cotton with lots of embroidery and layers of silver jewellery. She giggled as she held out her hand to Alex and said, 'So you're the one who's come to pry into all our dirty little secrets.' Her mid-Atlantic English had a faint Celtic lilt.

'Don't be silly, Kelly!' Jolene looked about ten years older, much shorter and plumper, and she was wearing sweat pants and matching top. She held Alex's hand a little longer than was necessary and said in a slow, North American drawl, 'We're all friends here. No-one's hiding anything.'

'Everyone has secrets,' Kelly said, looking directly at the other woman, her chin raised as if she was taunting her. 'All of us have things we'd prefer other people not to know.'

Jolene flushed. 'Personal things, OK. But not big, earth shattering secrets. We're not terrorists, or spies.' She sounded furious.

There was a brief awkward silence. Alex was appalled at the direction of the conversation. Was this what they were all thinking? 'Look, I've come to do some preliminary research for a biography of Signora de Branganza, not to interrogate anyone!' She tried to speak lightly, make a joke of it. Everyone laughed. But not Freddi she noticed.

Alex could understand their concern. She had come into their community as an incognita, to observe and record, and they were worried that they might be mentioned unfavourably in the book of Zenia's life. About hers, they had no curiosity at all. They saw only the biographer, a literary lace curtain twitcher whose presence caused a frisson of excitement and apprehension.

Alex felt a sense of relief to be among people who didn't know her, who reacted only to her presence as a writer and not as a person. Back in England at social gatherings people had begun to treat her as if she had an infectious disease. What her friends referred to behind her back as 'Alex's Loss' had become as much an actual person as she was, a kind of horrific, invisible dopple-ganger. People never knew whether it was better to talk about it or ignore it. Alex could almost hear people crunching eggshells underfoot. Even her own family didn't know how to deal with it. Alex hadn't seen her parents for nearly a year. Not since her mother, after one of those agonising Sunday lunches, had turned to her in the kitchen and said, 'Your father and I think it's time you pulled yourself together and got on with your life. It's time you started trying to get over it.'

Alex had stared at her smooth, practical face with its carefully arranged expression of concern, her neatly bobbed hair, her immaculate Marks and Spencer's two-piece and realised that her mother was uncomfortable because Alex's grief disturbed the tidiness of her life. She also realised the impossibility of making her mother understand that it could not be folded away at the back of the cupboard like an unwanted gift. Nor could it ever be 'got over' like an illness. She had been permanently maimed and the wound

– Alex couldn't even think in terms of a scar, which implied healing – the wound was something she would have to live with for the rest of her life. From now on her life would always have to include this absence.

That Sunday was also the first time that Alex had realised that her way of dealing with difficulties had been learned from her mother. If you don't remember things they don't exist. Her first and only attempt at fiction, a short story she'd written at university, had been sent back to her with a suggestion that it might be 'improved', but it was torn up, put in the bin and never mentioned again; the first signs of flakiness in a boyfriend resulted in his number being deleted from her diary. Her husband had been excised from her life in a similar fashion, though it was her own flakiness that had been the problem there. She was still haunted by the thought that if she'd been more tolerant, more flexible, they would still have been together and the tragedy would never have happened. But, Alex told herself, such thoughts were useless. What happened had happened; and for the first time in her life this was something she couldn't just slam a door on and walk away from. To do so would have been a betrayal of a relationship, a denial of love.

Alex was glad, very glad, that these people didn't know anything about her.

'Come and meet Zenia,' Freddi said, taking her by the elbow.

Alex didn't have to ask who Zenia was, she had noticed her the first moment she entered the room, standing at the back looking out of the window. Zenia was tall, about six feet or perhaps a little less, with square shoulders and long powerful arms. When she put out her hand it was as big as a man's, with a strong grip and long misshapen fingers like a manual labourer's. She was wearing trousers and half-length suede boots with a matching suede tunic belted just above the hips. Her hair was white and thick, almost electric with energy, her brows black and shaggy like the dark moustache that shadowed her upper lip. All this Alex noted to write up later, but at the time it was Zenia's eyes that mesmerised. They were the most turbulent, tragic eyes Alex had ever seen. Zenia sat down on a bench beside the fireplace opposite Ludo and patted the chair beside her. Alex obeyed, dropping her eyes from Zenia's intense scrutiny.

'And are you going to tell the truth?' Zenia asked abruptly, as if carrying on the conversation Alex had just been having with the others.

'If that's what you want.' Zenia's directness caught Alex momentarily off balance.

'Of course! What would be the point if you did not? My life will have been wasted if all I leave behind are lies. Other people will tell you stories about me – they will say, "Ah! Zenia! She was so… this and so… that". And they did not know me at all. But you and I, we are going to tell this big story, the story underneath all the other stories. Are we not?'

Alex nodded. This was the first time she had ever been asked to write an authorised biography of a living subject and she'd expected Zenia to be selective about what she wanted to reveal. Alex wondered whether her wish to be completely frank was genuine. Perhaps the carte blanche would be qualified when Zenia realised what writing a biography involved.

'Do you have children?' Zenia asked, leaning closer. Alex didn't know then that she asked everyone that.

'No.'

Zenia put her hand over Alex's, where it lay on her knee and said, 'I am sorry,' as though she really was. And then she turned away to pick up a large pack of Italian Antico cigars. 'You smoke?'

Alex shook her head, and watched fascinated as Zenia took one out and poked a spill of paper through the bars of the fire and lit the cigar in a cloud of burning paper and tobacco smoke.

'You have a lover?' Again those cosmic eyes, like black holes, sucking you in.

'No.' Alex felt her cheekbones tauten with strain.

'You will,' she said. A statement.

'Zenia!' Freddi's voice was at Alex's shoulder. 'You mustn't ask her such personal questions. It's very rude.'

'Why?' She put her hands palm upwards and shrugged like a child. 'She has come here to ask me these things. Why should I not ask her?' Her head swivelled towards Alex. 'You don't mind do you?'

Alex did, terribly, but she had to shake her head and give Zenia the answer she wanted.

An elderly woman came out of a door in the corner that, from the rich smell of cooking that drifted out, seemed to lead to the kitchen. She was wearing a black dress with a maroon cardigan, her dark, greying hair brushed back from her ears to reveal big, gold-hoop earrings. Her ankles were swollen and she was wearing the kind of easy shoes bought by women whose feet hurt.

'Ah, Concetta,' Freddi said, putting her hand on Alex's elbow to usher her across the room. Freddi's Italian was fast but not very accurate as she began the introductions and Alex could feel her hand trembling. 'This is Alessandra who's come to write Zenia's life story.' And then turning to Alex, 'This is Concetta who looks after us all so marvellously.'

Alex was conscious that an air of appeasement had crept into Freddi's manner as she faced Concetta, which puzzled her. Freddi was apparently in charge of things here, so why should she be nervous of Concetta?

'*Buona sera, signora. Piacere.*' Alex held out her hand but found it was ignored. Concetta inclined her head to acknowledge the greeting, but looked at Alex without smiling. For a moment Alex felt quite shaken by her rejection and then recovered herself enough to give a little answering nod. She realised that if the others merely regarded her with suspicion, here was real hostility.

They sat at a long table that would have seated twenty with comfort. Zenia sat at the head of it with Alex on one side and Freddi on the other. She had Ludo beside her and Freddi had Toby, then Concetta and Lenka opposite each other in the middle, with Kelly and Jolene like bookends at the bottom.

Concetta and Lenka went backwards and forwards to the kitchen bringing dishes and platters of antipasto and a basket with chunks of rather tough-looking wholemeal bread. There was ravioli filled with wild boar and porcini mushrooms in a cream sauce with whole sage leaves. Then huge sausages and chunks of grilled meat Alex couldn't identify, with rocket salad and a local sheep's cheese flavoured with truffles to follow. The conversation around the table wandered from English to Italian and back again. Alex noticed that neither Toby nor the two women at the foot of the table spoke Italian well enough to hold a decent conversation and Concetta, apparently, did not speak any English, though as Alex watched her eyes flickering from face to face, she wondered how much of what was said she understood.

At dinner, Alex watched Zenia reach out to pour herself a glass of red wine and saw Freddi snatch it away.

'Not that one, Zenia, this one.' She turned round and picked up another bottle from the sideboard. 'It's better for you.'

She glugged some dark red liquid into the tumbler and Alex read the name 'Chianti' on the label and under it, just a fleeting glimpse, '0%' .

Zenia sipped it and pulled a face. 'I do not like this wine,' she said to Freddi. 'It does not have much grade. Why can we not drink proper Istrian wine?' And she threw the contents of the glass into the fire and filled it up again from the other bottle. Freddi was crushing pills between two spoons but she sighed and gave a little shrug of resignation.

'She's not supposed to have any alcohol at all,' Ludo whispered in Alex's ear. 'Freddi has to go to great lengths to keep it down.'

'I didn't think you could buy non-alcoholic Chianti.'

'Freddi imports it from London. We have no use for such a thing in Istria. What is the use of wine if it does not make you drunk?'

Freddi offered the spoonful of crushed white powder to Zenia.

'What is this?' she asked. 'Why do I have to have this?'

'Just swallow it, Zenia,' Freddi pleaded, with just a touch of exasperation in her voice. 'It will make you feel better.'

'Will it?' Zenia raised her eyebrows. Her eyes expanded. She was suddenly meek and childlike. Then she shrugged. 'OK darling. I will do it for you.' There was a playful gleam in her eye as she looked at Freddi who blushed and smiled back, suddenly looking ten years younger, her pale face illuminated by affection and pleasure.

Then Zenia was talking again, leaning across the table. 'Do you remember that time, Ludo, when we went to Paris just after the war and they wouldn't let us back across the border? They thought we were *banditti*.'

Ludo laughed. 'They wanted to take Zenia off to interrogate her,' he said to Alex. 'I had to give them two hundred cigarettes and tell them she was my mistress – that was to explain why she was dressed as a boy. I pretended to have a jealous wife.'

'Of course it was very difficult then,' Zenia said, 'after the war. People were still fighting, fascists and communists. I was captured by them once in the woods when I was taking messages for my brother Bernardo. They kept me overnight but they did not watch me very carefully and, next morning when I went out into the woods to make pee-pee, I was able to run away.

'Poor Bernardo.' She was quiet for a moment, staring at the darkness of the window. 'He was not so lucky.'

There was a silence round the table. Then Freddi jumped up. 'Come on, let's sit on the comfortable chairs and talk about something more cheerful.'

'I will make the coffee,' Lenka said.

Alex sat next to Ludo on the bench beside the fire and watched him light his pipe. He had strong, calloused hands, and his thick nails were darkened with what looked like clay. There was clay in his beard too. He gave her a slantwise glance as if aware of her scrutiny.

'So,' he said, taking the newly lit pipe out of his mouth. 'You are a writer. Tell me what you have written?'

Alex hated being asked about what she wrote, but

told him – a book on Caravaggio, obscure, well-reviewed biographies of Empress Elizabeth of Austria and the intellectual groupie Lou Andreas Salome; then, before she had stopped writing, two journalistic pot-boilers on Vivien Leigh and Elizabeth Taylor, one of which had become a film for television.

'Ah,' he said as she went self-consciously through the list. 'A proper writer. Well, at least you're an improvement on the last one.'

'Has there been another?'

'Oh, yes. Some American woman came and stayed for six months and didn't write a line. A complete fraud. But of course, Zenia's easily taken advantage of. She's as innocent as a child.'

Alex refused the coffee that Lenka offered, sleep was difficult enough to induce, and stood up to excuse herself, pleading tiredness.

'I'm afraid we keep late hours here,' Freddi said. 'But nobody gets up very early, so don't feel you have to emerge before ten if you don't want to.'

When Alex came back to Casanova Uno, Martin was leaning against the wall, just outside the pool of light around the doorway, smoking a cigarette. She caught the sweet, drowsy scent of cannabis. 'How was it?' he asked.

'Confusing.'

He grinned. 'Just wait until tomorrow. They've invited the Antonelli family to meet you. A real gathering of hyenas.'

Alex looked puzzled.

'Zenia has no children, so every blood relative she's ever had is hoping to inherit the place. Gianfranco's her favourite, very decorative. But he's illegitimate, which pisses the others off no end. They're all terrified she's going to leave it to him. But you'll find out soon enough.'

After he'd gone she stood on the step for a moment in the warm darkness. There were lights in some of the windows, the sounds of doors closing, snatches of conversation, laughter. She wondered how many people lived here and who they were. Across the valley the lights of unidentified villages twinkled through the olive groves and a half moon was just beginning to edge out from behind the ridge of the hill to illuminate the sea. Everything smelled of hot, damp earth. Midnight tolled from a bell tower, echoing across the valley. The air was fresh and clean after the rain and the moon was very bright in a navy blue sky. It looked like paradise.

The mill of suffering grinds very small indeed in that long gap between three o'clock and five in the morning. The body fights sleep because in sleep it can't control the mind. I lie awake in the darkness wondering why I'm still alive. In the beginning, before I'd got used to living with my black twin, I did try to wriggle out of it a couple of times. At Bank station, once, waiting for the tube, listening to it roaring through the tunnel towards the platform, I suddenly thought how wonderful it would be to fall in front of the train as it burst out of the darkness. There would be the shock of the impact and then nothing. Nothing, for ever and ever. But as I stepped forward, caught up in that marvellous thought, a man grasped me by the elbow and yanked me back.

'Wake up,' he said cheerfully. 'Another foot and you'd have been a goner!'

I burst into tears which he interpreted as relief and I don't think he ever knew that they were tears of rage and disappointment.

Next time, I thought I'd be more organised and devious. There would be no rescue. I waited until the world was asleep, locked all the doors, switched off my mobile phone, and prepared my cocktail of codeine and paracetamol, the strongest painkillers I could get at the pharmacy without a prescription. I swallowed them with a glass of milk and then spent the rest of the night vomiting it all into the toilet. I was, it seems, allergic to codeine. My GP, alerted by worried friends, prescribed counselling and Prozac. I met the counsellor once, took the pills and watched the real world of living, functioning people recede even further into the gloomy mists that surrounded me, blotting out the sun, blocking warmth and happiness.

Sometimes I think that if I had a grave to go to, a focus for my grief, a place to remember the person I loved, it would be easier to carry on. But there's nothing. Afterwards they sent me a phial of ash and it goes with me everywhere. Every night before I go to bed I hold it in my hand and close my eyes and try to visualise a face that is gradually becoming more and more remote. The glass is cold and hard to the touch, but it warms in my fingers and I like to think that somewhere in it there is a flake of skin, a fragment of bone, a few remaining atoms of the person I loved. Flesh of my flesh; bone of my bone.

Alex lay awake in the early light and listened to the insistent horns of vehicles negotiating the perilous road. This was presumably how they avoided each other and she wished that she'd known that yesterday. The ceiling above her had terracotta tiles cemented between the stout chestnut beams. Everything, Ludo had told her last night, was made of chestnut wood. It had a dense grain, like oak, but was redder and more opulent, the colour and patina of burnished conkers.

Alex got up and made coffee and went back to bed with her notes. Every biography starts with a chronology: this one had been compiled from the internet and a media pack sent by Zenia's agent. The glossy PR brochure told Alex that Zenia had been born in Trieste in 1923. There was a brother, Bernardo, born in 1926, who had died at the end of the Second World War. The de Braganza family, originally from Spain, had come to Italy in the 19th century, married into Italian commerce and amassed a shipping empire that stretched from Europe to South America. Zenia's father, Ferdinando, was a younger son who worked for the family business. Zenia's mother Natalia was born in Vienna, half Italian, half Russian and had been an opera singer before her marriage. They were part of the map of old Europe before it had been re-drawn, part of Trieste's multicultural heritage.

Zenia's early childhood seemed to have been affluent and secure. She had lived in a huge house above the harbour with servants and an English governess. She could apparently speak Italian, Spanish and English by the time she was six. But then in 1929 the Italian stock market crashed and the family became almost bankrupt. In the thirties they moved to Venice where they lived with distant relatives in a crumbling palazzo and Ferdinando had become an insurance agent. Alex imagined a kind of genteel poverty.

In the nineteen forties Zenia went to art school in Venice where she was taken up by Marco Marconi who brought her to Paris where she painted Picasso and became 'the darling of the post-war art scene'. The brochure skimmed over this period in a single line, but Alex sensed its importance for Zenia's life. The impact of that amazing personality must have been immense and, if the Man Ray photograph was a true representation, her face must have fascinated everyone she met. From Paris Zenia went to England where the PR hand-out stated that she painted the royal family (what had they made of her, Alex wondered?) and a host of celebrities including Peter Sellers, Twiggy, and Winston Churchill. In New York she had lived and worked with the painter Frank Harrison, painting Marilyn Monroe, John F. Kennedy and other icons of American history, before coming to Istria where she bought the Kaštela and established her studio there. Since then, the blurb stated, 'she has divided her time between Istria, London and New York with exhibitions in eleven countries including Canada, Australia, Japan, France, Germany, Spain and Russia'.

There were voices under the window. Martin, from the fluency and tone, answered by more strident female accents Alex didn't recognise. Martin was complaining about someone in colourful, colloquial Italian. 'Queen of the free-loaders. Shagging everything he can find. What does Zenia want with these people?'

'She feels comfortable with them.' The voice was brusque and throaty. 'And at least he is useful.'

'Useful! What does he do for her? She doesn't paint anymore. He just swans around, *con questo e quello*, making money on her name and reputation.'

There was a pause. Then the other voice said, 'You had better be careful. It does not do to say these things with that woman here.'

'I'll say what I like. His pictures are crap. If Zenia's agent didn't take them as a favour to her, no-one would ever have heard of him.'

There was a short laugh, the crunching of feet on the path and then silence. Evidently not everyone was happy in paradise.

Ten minutes later Freddi's voice shouted up to the window. 'Alex? Come on down! We're having breakfast on the terrace.'

She put away her note pad and went down the uneven steps that were still damp and slippery from yesterday's rain. The sun was emerging strongly from wisps of cloud and the valley floor was masked by steam as the moisture evaporated. It looked almost like a Chinese painting.

Freddi, Lenka and Toby were sitting at one of the marble tables spread with coffee cups, brioches and a bowl of fruit.

'Zenia's tired after last night, so Concetta persuaded her to stay in bed late. With everyone coming tonight we want her to be at her best. Do you need to talk to her today?'

Alex shook her head, concealing her disappointment. 'I'll just fit the interviews in when she feels able to talk. There's plenty of other material to be getting on with. I wondered whether I might look at some of the files?' Last night she had noticed a shelf of boxes in the living room marked *Lavori*, arranged in date order.

'Toby did those,' Lenka said.

'Everything was just in boxes and carrier bags when I came.' Toby was really rather pretty when he smiled. Very un-Australian. 'I've tried to put all the letters and invoices in date order, but there's some I can't locate because they're not dated. Zenia's never been very businesslike. I've put all the odd ones in a file at the end.'

Concetta walked past as they sat sipping coffee. The others smiled and said, '*Ciao* Concetta,' and she smiled and waved back. But to Alex she gravely inclined her head as she had done last night. Alex gave a small answering nod and said formally, '*Buon giorno*.'

'I don't think she approves of me being here,' she said to Freddi, after Concetta had disappeared round the corner.

'You mustn't think that. She's just slow to accept strangers. Maybe a little protective. She's been with Zenia for so many years, you see. She knows more about her than anyone.'

'When did she come here?'

'Right at the beginning, back in the nineteen sixties when Zenia bought the place. Concetta had worked for Zenia's family in Trieste as a maid and then she married someone who worked in the docks – not happily – he's a brute! When Zenia saw how miserable she was she brought Concetta here to help her run the Kaštela. Zenia's forbidden the husband to come near her, but he turns up now and then. Concetta can't refuse him; she's a good Catholic.'

'I found her a bit prickly when I first came,' Toby said. 'But now I get on with her really well.'

'As long as you remember who's in charge,' Lenka said, raising her eyebrows expressively.

'She positively hates Kelly and Jolene,' Toby went on. 'You can almost see her spitting fire.'

'How do they come to be here?' Alex asked.

'They came to one of Zenia's exhibitions in London. Or it might have been Paris,' Freddi said. 'I forget which. And then they started dropping into her studio. Zenia's sociable, she likes people, so I don't expect it was hard to strike up an acquaintance and then I expect she just said, "Come and stay with me sometime", the way she does to everybody. So they came and stayed and nobody's ever had the courage to ask them when they're leaving. It's awkward in the summer when we have the tourists. They have to go off somewhere else, some hippy friends of Jolene's in the South of France, I've never enquired where. But they always come back.'

'They do teach the painting courses though,' Toby pointed out.

'The money they hand over to us scarcely covers the cost of their rent, never mind the food,' Freddi complained. 'All those rich Americans Jolene brings in, I bet they pay through the nose. Lord knows what the two of them are earning from it.'

'And what about Ludo?' Alex asked. 'Is he an ex-lover?'

Freddi shook her head. There was a quick, uncomfortable exchange of glances round the table. Freddi's cheeks reddened and Alex felt herself flush with embarrassment. Why had she been so stupid as to misread the situation? She should have guessed. Or Jane should have told her.

'Zenia felt sorry for Ludo after his wife died and invited him to set up a studio here,' Freddi said after a pause. 'She had this idea of a community of artists all living and working together. Ludo's quite old now. He hasn't done any commercial work for years, but he's a good friend. Like Concetta, he's known Zenia almost the whole of her life.' Freddi paused again and then went on, 'We're her protection against the outside world, against exploitation.'

Lenka stood up and brushed the brioche crumbs from her skirt. 'I must go,' she said. 'I have to change all the rooms for the Antonellis. They are so particular.'

'When are they arriving?'

'Tonight in time for dinner. They're driving down from Trento,' Freddi explained. 'There are four of them altogether. Antonio is the eldest. He's Zenia's cousin; his mother was her father's sister. Antonio's been married several times. Caterina is his daughter by the second marriage. There's also an older son, Cesare, who lives in Venice, but he's not coming this time. And then there's Gianfranco, the wild card of the family. Zenia adores him. He won't be coming until later, perhaps tomorrow. He's a musician and I think he said he was playing in Milan.'

'He's very good,' Toby said. 'Last time he came he made a carillon out of prosecco bottles and played it with a glass cocktail stick.'

'You will have to watch him,' Lenka warned. Her dark eyes sparked. 'He is a predator. All the Antonellis are a danger to women.'

Alex went into the big dining room where they had eaten the night before and stood for a moment looking out of the windows towards the sea. There was an amazing atmosphere here, as if the house was a living entity. You could almost hear the stones thinking, the wood breathing. It was like being inside an ark.

She took the first box, marked 1950, and put it on the table, but before she opened it, she went round the walls examining the paintings she had only glimpsed the previous evening. They were a strange mixture. A small Derain hung in one corner, subtle and understated beside the brutal colours of the Matisse placed next to it. An unmistakable black and white Picasso 'Don Quixote' sketch was inscribed 'To Zenia for her Self' in Spanish. There were other drawings and sketches by names that read like a catalogue of European art.

Over the fireplace was a huge Venetian mirror with an ornate frame and candle sconces clogged with wax. It had the type of old glass that is kind to the skin. When Alex looked into it she could see not only her own face, but the reflection of the two people in the painting on the other side of the room. Alex turned and crossed over to have a better look at the portrait, hung above an enormous carved wooden chest, the kind often used in old cathedrals to store vestments.

The painting itself was a mirror image. Two people, a man and a woman standing side by side with linked hands and their heads turned towards each other. Except for their sex they were identical. What made the painting strange was that they were joined together at shoulder and hip like Siamese twins and they shared the same umbilical cord, which coiled around them like a snake, attaching them from navel to navel. The title painted on the edge of the frame, which Alex had to tilt her head to see, told her that this was 'The Divided Self'. The brushwork and the design were bold and confident. There was something about the composition and the symbolic style that reminded Alex a little of the South-American surrealists.

The door from the courtyard opened suddenly. It was Zenia.

'How are you this morning?' she asked. 'Have you everything you want? Are they making you comfortable?'

'I'm being very well looked after, thank you.'

Zenia was dressed as she had been yesterday in tunic and breeches, flourishing a cigar. She pointed to the painting. 'That is me. I am an androgyne. You know what that means? Both male and female. That's what I am. To understand me and to understand my art you must know this. It is what makes my art so special, because art is not usually androgynous.'

'So you think there really is male and female art?'

'Of course. It is silly to argue otherwise. Men and women, they see things differently. That is how it should be and it must be celebrated. How dull the world would be if we all saw things the same. That is what makes me unique, because I can see things from both sides.'

She turned and gestured towards the narrow door in the corner. 'Come up to my studio,' she said.

The door opened into the well of the tower that dominated the whole citadel. Alex had been wondering, ever since she arrived, what was in the tower and how one got into it. Zenia led her up the steep stone staircase that wound its way relentlessly upwards. She moved slowly, and Alex noticed that she had to cling on to the handrail for balance. She stopped on a small landing in front of a heavy chestnut door. Zenia pushed hard and it opened onto a square room with windows on three sides. There was an easel in the middle of the room, half-finished canvasses stacked against the wall, and a clutter of paint and rags on an old table. There was also a wood burning stove in the corner and two comfortable armchairs pulled up close to it. The walls were almost completely covered with paintings and drawings, some just pinned to the wall, all of them crowded between bookshelves that held large volumes in ragged cloth covers that Alex assumed to be art books, well used.

'This is where I have always worked,' Zenia said. 'It was the first place I restored when I came here. At first I slept here too, because the roof leaked, but now I sleep upstairs.' She swept her arm towards the ceiling. 'It has always been enough for me, this small space in the tower.'

'Let me show you something,' she said and went to a shelf in the corner of the room. She took out a large book bound in a loose linen cover. It was a photograph album. As she opened it Alex could see that the brown cardboard pages inside were hanging loose from the spine and the corners were bent and curling.

'This is my family,' Zenia said. She pointed to an opulent woman with coils of shining dark hair wearing an evening dress with a tight black basque and a heavy skirt drawn back into a bustle. She was leaning against a piano, and a sheet of music drooped almost negligently from her right hand. 'My mother,' Zenia said with an expressive lift of the eyebrows and shoulders all at once. 'She was ve…ry beautiful. And this is my father,' turning the page to show a slim, rather dandyish figure, hands propped one on top of the other on the pommel of a polished cane. He had sleek mustachios groomed into identical curves on his upper lip. His eyes were Zenia's eyes, but without the fire, large lugubrious orbs staring beseechingly out of the photograph like a Labrador dog asking to be taken for a walk.

'He was very good to me, my father. He would take me down to the docks with him in the horse and trap, introduce me to all the ships' captains and they used to give me presents and tell me that I reminded them of their daughters back at home. I longed to be the captain of a ship, to sail away across the world. It did not occur to me then that girls did not do such things. I wanted it so much, that once I even ran away from home and went on board one of those ships and hid myself away.'

'And did they find you?'

'Of course! Very quickly. I was only six or seven years old and I did not hide myself very well. There was such an uproar and I was sent home in disgrace. When I got back to the house, my mother was lying on her bed with the curtains drawn and I had to go inside and tell her that I was sorry. And of course I was not sorry at all! She made me rub lavender water onto her forehead and she kept on saying, why couldn't God have given her a good daughter like other mothers had instead of this changeling child. That was what she used to call me. Her changeling child. It made me feel very sad. But I could never be anything other than I was.'

Zenia turned another page. 'Now this is my brother, Bernardo.' There were several snaps of a young boy with a pointed, rather feminine face, taken at different ages between about one year old and ten or eleven. 'He died after the war,' Zenia said. 'Fighting with the partisans in the hills near Trieste. I loved him very much, you know, but we were never close. He was jealous of me because he knew that my father really loved me. And I was jealous of him because he was very spoiled by my mother. Now, of course, it is too late to know whether we could have been friends.'

On the next page was a picture of a small girl in a rumpled white dress with a white ribbon askew in her curls. From the turbulent expression on her face, it couldn't have been anyone but Zenia. 'I used to like to go out and play with the street children, they had a game they called Lussi. You put one stone on another and then balanced some coins on top. Then you had to stand behind a line and throw pebbles at the Lussi to try to dislodge them. If you knocked a coin to the ground you could keep it. I won lots of money that way. I was very good at those boys' games. My mother did not like me to go and play with these common children, but she could not watch me all the time. And my father was very kind to me. "Poor Zenia," he would say, patting me on the head. "One day you will have need of all your friends." He died when I was twelve, of disappointment I think and because he hated the fascists. My mother used to say they had killed him. I used to go into the streets with my friends and shout, "Mussolini *Cacca*! Mussolini *Cacca*!" as the soldiers went past.'

There were more pages of family photographs. Zenia and her brother at different ages, sometimes together, sometimes with other members of the family. Then suddenly, shockingly, a small image that, just for an instant, made Alex's skin prick. It was of a woman standing on a balcony, leaning out over the rail. She had slender arms clasped by bracelets; a young woman's arms. And her dress was the kind that women wore in the thirties and forties; tight at the waist with a wide belt, but full skirted towards the woman's slender ankles and dark, high-heeled shoes. What was shocking about the photograph was that the face had been cut out, completely and cleanly as if with a razor blade. But, almost as soon as Alex had seen it, Zenia turned the page and moved on without saying anything. The way she slapped the pages closed and immediately began to talk about a photograph of herself at college in Venice after the war, made Alex realise that Zenia didn't want her to ask any questions. But she knew it was important, why else would Zenia keep such a mutilated photograph in her album? And Alex wanted very much to know the identity of the woman whose face had been so brutally excised.

Lunchtime. It was drizzling slightly outside. They ate inside the kitchen, just the four of them; Concetta, Zenia, Freddi and Alex. Concetta had marinated anchovies which they ate with chunks of tough local bread and then, fingers still reeking of fish and garlic, spooned up a khaki coloured sludge that Freddi said was made from polenta and spinach and borlotti beans, wiping the bowls out with more bread. It was delicious. Alex said so, licking her fingers to remove the last traces, and got a glance from Concetta which could almost have been approving.

Zenia was still regarding her with intense curiosity,

her eyes constantly searching Alex's face as if trying to see what was behind it. This made her very uncomfortable. So Alex asked, 'Why portraits? Why not landscapes?' She had been wondering why Zenia had opted to become a portraitist during a period when abstraction had been everything. Had it to do with money, earning a living? Most, but not all, of her portraits were of the wealthy and the famous. Alex didn't say any of this, but Zenia answered her thoughts.

'I look at people's eyes and their faces and at once I know them; their base natures, all their secrets. People interest me. Particularly famous people, because their faces tend to be more interesting than others.' Zenia said it dismissively, as if to imply that she didn't find Alex's face interesting. Alex was shocked to find that it mattered. But after a while Zenia peered at her, scowling. 'I like your eyebrows,' she said. 'They are unusual, like little question marks at the top of your face. As if you did not quite believe yourself.' She paused for a moment and then asked, 'But why will you not let me look into your eyes?' making Alex aware how much she avoided that terrible gaze. 'What is it that you hide from me?'

Alex gripped the edge of the table with her fingers thinking, I will not make her a present of my suffering. I am not a sitter for one of her portraits, she is a sitter for mine. But already Alex could feel herself losing the battle for control of their relationship.

After lunch had been cleared away Concetta got up and collected a painted tin from the beam above the stove. The lid was loose, the picture darkened by the smoke, and inside was a pack of cards.

'They always play *Scopa* in the afternoons,' Freddi said.

Concetta sat patiently waiting for Zenia, her hands

folded on the table, plump, lined hands with short, very clean nails. Then, suddenly, Zenia threw the stump of her cigar into the fire and was ready. Concetta shuffled the cards and cut them twice to determine who was to deal. Three cards each, four in the middle. Concetta immediately scooped two with one of hers. Zenia swore in Italian, '*Porca puttana!*' and Concetta laughed. She was very patient when Zenia forgot the rules or laid the wrong card, putting a restraining hand over hers with a mild admonishment as if to a favourite child. It looked remarkably as if Zenia was cheating. But Concetta almost always seemed to win.

Alex sat on the sofa working through the big box files full of invoices and uncatalogued photographs. There were a series of American invoices, a photograph of Zenia at a gallery called Pharos with an address in Greenwich Village. There was a letter about a commission from the Steinberg Institute for a portrait of the humanitarian philosopher Benjamin Aprahamian. She brought it over to the table to ask Zenia if she remembered him but she didn't. Nor did Concetta. Alex began to be aware that much of Zenia's life could well have been lost with the atrophy of her memory, and that others who could have remembered for her were probably already dead. Underneath the letter was a photograph of Marilyn Monroe. Zenia's large hand reached into the file and lifted it out. She sighed as she looked at the image, one of the standard celebrity shots, head back, toothpaste advertisement smile, eyes wide open.

'Poor Marilyn. She was so sad.'

'Did you meet her?'

Zenia shook her head.

There was a pause while everyone looked at Zenia

waiting for her to go on, but she said nothing, temporarily lost in her own memories. Alex looked across at Freddi.

'She was refused permission for formal sittings,' Freddi explained, 'so she sat in the stalls of the theatre while Marilyn did workshops with students. I think it was during the time she was married to Arthur Miller and trying to learn how to act properly. Anyway, Zenia got the theatre manager to let her sit in. She did the drawings on a little sketch pad and then went back to her studio at night to paint from memory. The portrait's in the Metropolitan in New York. It's amazing!'

Zenia listened in silence to Freddi's voice, and then suddenly seemed to come alive again. 'She had skin and hair – *fantastici*! Like an angel, with all the light coming from inside. Then, other days, the light would not be there and she was empty, faded, there was only the spirit, shaded, hidden, but you could see it when she opened her eyes.' Zenia's own eyes were clouded with recollection. 'Maybe that was the second time I went to America. I had to do a big lecture tour because I needed the money. We were travelling, travelling all the time – we would go to one city and I would talk and then paint – they had this programme on television where I had to paint some famous person's head in half an hour – it was crazy! But anyway, somehow I did it. And it was there that I met Paulina.' Zenia stopped.

'Who was Paulina?' Alex prompted.

'She was married to a man who owned shipping companies and oil wells and she was very unhappy with this man because, you know, he was always somewhere else making money. She drove me down to California, along the coast where she had a house, the most beautiful house, and I stayed there for a while and worked and she bought some of my things. Ah, Paulina! She was so good. I was very fond of her you know. I have never been attracted to a man in my life, only women. And especially Paulina. She was my little Mouse. And how she loved me! But then when her husband came back – Boom! It is all over. She came to London the next year and I saw her again and then she came to the Kaštela for the summer and I made a little house for her.'

'Which one is it?'

'The Villa Medici. Every summer she would come there and I would make it beautiful for her. She was very special.'

'What happened to her?' Alex was thinking about the photograph without a face.

Zenia sighed. 'There was some misunderstanding, some arguments. Other people making mischief, perhaps my mother…' She looked very sad, stopped talking and Alex could see that she was listening to things inside her head, watching pictures of past events that she wasn't going to show to anyone. It was time to leave.

'There are letters,' Freddi said as they stood in the courtyard. 'She has a big box of them in her studio. Would you like to go through them?'

Alex would have to, though she didn't relish it. With the long dead, it had seemed acceptable, even exciting, to read their most personal papers, but to read Zenia's private letters seemed revolting and voyeuristic. But if she was going to write the book she needed to do it.

'I'll get Martin to bring them over to you. You know that Paulina left her entire personal estate to Zenia when she died?'

'I didn't. Was it considerable?'

'A house in London, an apartment in New York, as well as investments.'

Freddi looked at Alex very directly, as if challenging her to say something and then went on. 'There are some very malicious people who may tell you that Zenia preyed on lonely, vulnerable women for their money. It is, of course, untrue, but some people believe it.' She sounded almost hostile.

'I haven't formed any opinions yet.'

'Then don't. Women fall in love with her, they want to protect her. She doesn't seek it out, it just happens. But she's been unlucky. She was always looking for a mother-figure I think. But something always went wrong.' Freddi became quiet, standing almost motionless. 'Zenia has secrets. There were very few people she could share them with. Her life has been lonely because of it. I do hope you're going to be discreet.'

Martin arrived with the letters as Alex was switching on the laptop.

'There's almost half of them here,' he said, putting down a carton that had once contained wine. 'Freddi says just shout when you're finished and she'll give you the rest.' He paused and grinned. 'They'll make interesting reading I should think.' Then he went outside again and shut the door behind him.

It was a dull, overcast afternoon, perfect for being indoors. Alex began to unpack the letters straight away, arranging them on the table roughly in date order. Some had envelopes with postmarks to make it easy; others were just folded into bundles held by an elastic band, so that each one had to be opened to find a date. Some weren't dated at all. The postmarks and addresses encompassed America and England, Australia and most of Europe. Some were in Italian, some in English. Not all were from other people, a large number had been written by Zenia herself, presumably returned to her by their recipients. It was a weird quirk of the law, Alex reflected, that copyright in letters remained with the author of them rather than their owner and permission had to be obtained from both.

Quite a lot of the letters were to do with commissions for paintings or sculptures, or the arrangement of lecture tours. It was easy, though boring, work to list these and precis the contents in date order to cross reference later with the files of '*lavori*', so that Alex could establish what Zenia had been working on and when, as well as where she was in the world at the time.

Alex left the personal letters until last. There were several which seemed to refer to a misunderstanding Zenia had had with a third party. 'Frank has asked me to tell you that he could not have put your work into the exhibition, however much he would have liked to… It has pained him very deeply. Why are you so angry with us?' It was signed only with the letter 'T'. The mention of Frank made Alex wonder whether this was the painter Frank Harrison. Hadn't the publicity leaflet said that Zenia had lived with him for a while in New York? Alex would now have to discover why they had fallen out.

Other letters were of little interest out of context, relating gossip, arranging visits, giving thanks for gifts received, enthusing over commissioned work. 'We love your vibrant canvas, Ms Braganza and always think of our little *Comanche* when we look at it.'

But one bundle of creased and torn papers contained love letters written in Zenia's strong hand on an assortment of mediums; hotel notepaper, a sheet torn from a drawing pad, squared pages from a continental exercise book, and several sheets of large blue airmail paper. They were all signed with a big X.

'My dearest Mouse,' the first began. 'Why are you so afraid? The world is not such a big place. I am only a few hours away by plane. You can jump on a jet and be with me any time you choose. All these dangers and difficulties are in your head and YOU MUST NOT LET

THEM STOP YOU. Now is a good time to be here. I have done several new things that you would like. I think of you always – you are wrapped around my heart like a warm blanket.'

There were others, some more passionate and Alex felt very uncomfortable reading these, knowing that Zenia herself was only a few hundred yards away. It was rather like finding your parents' love letters in a drawer and guiltily reading them while they were out.

The last in the bundle was longer than the others and the grammar more confused. 'Mouse, my darling Mouse,' it began. 'I felt very sad reading your letter. It has hurt me very much. But what can I say to you? Everything that bitch has told you is probably true in some way or other – though I know she twists everything to make trouble for me.

You must believe how I love you – but you also have to know that to create art my spirit must be free – I can only work if I can be really free – and it is not possible for me to be what you want. If you want to be with me, you must know this. And I cannot love one person only – it is not possible for a human being – there are many people in my life – but no-one like you. Together we have gone very deep – maybe too deep. I am afraid to be close to people – to tell them what I am. You have made me feel whole – complete.'

There was a brief knock on the door and then it opened and Martin was standing there with the light shining behind him. 'Would you like to come down to the bar for a drink?' he asked. 'You haven't been down to the village yet, have you?'

Alex hesitated. She should really go on working, there were a lot of letters still unread, but she felt suddenly exhausted. She closed the box and stood up. 'A drink sounds a very good idea. Is anyone else going?'

'Sometimes Toby and Lenka come down, even Zenia, though she's not supposed to drink. It doesn't agree with her medication.'

He moved back through the open doorway and Alex caught a whiff of wood-smoke and male pheromones from his clothes. It gave her an odd feeling, not sexual attraction, but a kind of awareness of Martin's masculinity. She grabbed her thermo-fleece from the hook behind the door and stepped outside. The sun had swung across the sky and now hung over the sea so that it glittered like plate glass. The trees and the land were outlined in bold black lines against the fierce glare.

'There's about an hour of daylight left,' Martin said, glancing at his watch.

'Are the Antonellis here?'

'They arrived about four o'clock. Antonio and Caterina. The *Padrone* and the *Principessa*.' His voice was heavy with sarcasm.

'I get the impression you don't care for them?'

'Why should I? They've gained everything they have by oppressing peasants like me.' He flashed Alex a sudden grin. 'Do you know about the Italian share-cropping system?'

She shook her head.

'They used to have a similar system here. In Italy it's called *Mezzadria*. The *padrone* owns the land and he lets out hectares of it, the *poderi*, smallholdings and little farms, to peasants who don't pay any rent, but are bound to give half of everything they produce to the *padrone*. He can sell his share at a massive profit, but they have to use everything they've got left just to live. There's never enough to feed the family and to sell. So he gets rich and they stay just above starvation level. Here, the *padrone* became the communist state, but the result was much the same. There are only a few *mezzadro* left these days, most of them have gone to the cities where they can get a proper wage for a day's work and two days off a week.'

'Is that what your parents did?'

'My grandparents. They used to live in Liguria but they went off to Canada after the war with their children – that's where I was born.'

They were walking now through terraces of olive groves. 'So who owns these?'

'A lot of the *poderi* have gone wild. It's been made worse here by what they call the Homeland War. But people are beginning to come back now.' He pointed up the hill towards the ridge. 'There's a couple of English people up there playing at olive farming. And down there,' he pointed to a big, ochre coloured house surrounded by newly planted fruit trees, 'a German family are doing bed and breakfast for tourists. *Agroturizam.* Most of the abandoned houses will be bought by foreigners. The young people have either gone away or they don't have the money.'

'Is that how Zenia bought the Kaštela?'

'She came here from America or England or wherever in the nineteen fifties or sixties and she found the place in ruins. She traced the families to New York and bought it from them. It wasn't worth anything then.'

'But wasn't Yugoslavia a communist state at the time?'

Martin laughed. 'Supposedly. Zenia says that Tito never did away with private enterprise completely. If you had money and knew the right people...'

They walked down the road Alex had driven the

day before and then branched off to the right onto a gravel track that ended in a wide flight of steps descending towards the village. The stone walls on either side blazed with wild flowers seeded in the cracks. The gardener in Alex, starved by city apartment living, recognised rosettes of pink sedum, smooth leaved valerian, a white daisy-like flower that could have been a marguerite, as well as cactuses and aubretias.

She stopped for a moment just as the path turned a steep corner into the village and looked back up the hill where the falling sun was bathing the terracotta roofs and stone walls of the Kaštela with an intense yellow light.

'I can see why Zenia fell in love with the place. It's so beautiful.'

Martin gave Alex another smile. 'Don't get too attached,' he said. 'People fall in love with the Kaštela, and with Zenia, and then they do crazy things.'

She wondered if he was talking about himself. 'How long have you been here?'

'About eight years.'

'Are you happy here?'

'Happy! What's happy?' The sarcastic note was back in Martin's voice. 'They all seem intent on making my life as difficult as possible. Take today for instance. I couldn't load the olives to take down to the press, because Toby had taken the station wagon down to Pula for his afternoon off. And it's not as if he's a good driver. Every time he takes it out there's another knock, which I have to fix.' He paused and gave a wry laugh. 'Anyway, why should I care. When the oil comes back it'll just be given away to this friend or that friend. To hell with those of us who've spent days picking the olives. It's the same with everything, money squandered on freeloaders who come and stay for weeks on end. And who does the work? I do.'

'But presumably you get paid for it?'

'A pittance, with no security. It's all done on the black side here. The same with Lenka. It's all right saying, "Martin what a great job you do, we are so fond of you, what would we do without you?"' He mimicked Freddi's voice perfectly. 'That gives me nothing! I just want to be paid properly for what I do. Like or dislike, it doesn't matter.'

They were walking down a narrow street, the old stone houses with shuttered windows rising up three or four stories on either side. Below them were terraces of terracotta pantiles, patterned in squares and fans of orange and ochre.

'I love these old roofs,' Alex murmured. 'They're such a glorious colour. But it's a pity some of them have been replaced. The new ones look awful.'

'Now you're talking like a tourist.' The note of grievance was still in Martin's voice.

'What do you mean?'

'They all come here with a "Room with a View" mentality and complain about the houses with new tiles.'

'They don't fit very well though, do they?'

'The Croatian man doesn't think about the aesthetics, he only thinks "I want to repair my roof and keep my family dry as cheaply as possible." Are the tourists going to pay him to keep old, cracked tiles?'

Martin opened a glass door from the street into a narrow, smoky bar with plastic tables. A television was flashing in one corner – large breasted women in pink bikinis dancing around a middle-aged, paunchy presenter. Martin nodded to three or four of the men who were playing cards at a table and led Alex through a fringe of swinging ropes onto a small balcony roofed with reed mats and some kind of green vine. The view was spectacular. In front of her the valley floor dropped away in a dark tide of olive groves towards the church spires and tiled roofs of a distant village, hazy with evening mist and wood smoke. A bell was tolling six o'clock and the Adriatic flamed in the distance.

'Wine or beer?' Martin asked. He seemed in a good humour again after his outburst.

'Wine please.'

It came in a jug, dark and fruity. Alex could taste the whole of the summer in it. For the first time in months she felt truly relaxed.

'So what about you?' Martin asked, watching her face. 'Married?'

She shook her head.

'What happened? You're far too attractive to be on your own.'

The glass rattled on the table as Alex put it down. 'I don't want to talk about me.'

'Fair enough.' He seemed unruffled by the curt refusal. 'I shan't tell you anything about myself either.'

'That's fine. It's Zenia I've come to write about.'

'I'll tell you something before you start. Don't be taken in by her. Under all that child-like charm there's a very sharp operator.'

'But she seems so vulnerable.'

'Don't be fooled. It's an act so she can get what she wants. She's played the innocent child so long she really believes it herself now.'

'What makes you think that?'

'She's spent her life playing parts; her whole identity's just one big act. Watch her with people and you'll notice her change. The only person she's always the same with is Concetta.'

Alex didn't believe him, Martin's viewpoint was prejudiced by his resentment, his politics. Zenia was his *padrona* and he hated that.

'So why do you stay here if you feel exploited? Why don't you move on?'

He smiled disarmingly. 'It suits me here, for the moment. I'll probably stay till Zenia dies. My God there'll be some changes then.'

'What will happen to the Kaštela?'

'No-one knows for sure except Zenia. She could leave it to the family, but Freddi keeps talking about a trust to preserve things as they are. I think she wants Zenia to set up a kind of "*usa frutta*".'

'What's that?'

'Literally it means "the use of the fruit". You leave the property to your relatives but your wife, or husband, or whatever, can live there until they die. The Antonellis would own the Kaštela legally, but Freddi could go on living there. The Kaštela would be a museum for Zenia's art. It would be a tourist attraction in the summer and an artists' retreat in the winter.'

'It sounds ideal.'

Martin grinned. 'Freddi's younger than any of them by a mile, even the children. There's no way the Antonellis are going to let her hold onto the Kaštela while they go toes-up in the ground. They've got good lawyers. Just wait until you meet them.'

The door opened and Lenka came in, rather flushed as though she'd been hurrying. 'Why didn't you call for me?' she asked. There was a petulant note in her voice. 'Concetta told me that you'd gone.' She threw herself into the chair next to Martin and put her head back in a gesture of utter weariness. 'God! I need a drink. What a foul day. The Antonellis are such pigs!'

Martin did what was obviously expected of him and got up to go to the bar. Lenka opened her eyes and looked at Alex, a very challenging glance that clearly said 'stay off my territory'. It was a look that only another woman would recognise. When Martin came back and put a glass of beer down in front of her, she said, 'Thank you,' and leant across to touch the back of his hand with the tip of her finger, a little intimate gesture of possession. But Alex noticed that Martin quickly withdrew his hand, folding it across the table behind his glass and tucking his feet defensively under the chair.

He turned to Alex and smiled, raising his glass. 'Cheers,' he said. 'Here's to your book.'

Afterwards they walked back together in the dusk. Lenka, after a little hesitation, went into the cottage below the main house where she had a room and Martin and Alex walked on down the path to Casanova Uno. Outside the door Martin paused while Alex took her key out of her pocket.

'Perhaps we could do it again?' he asked. There was a definite gleam in his eye that Alex dimly recognised as sexual interest. She had almost forgotten what it felt like to see that flicker in a man's eyes. She thought of Lenka and felt the warning lights flashing, but smiled at him anyway and said, 'Perhaps.' Alex knew that, whatever her personal feelings towards Martin, she needed to be able to talk to him, needed his perspective on the Kaštela. And he was, after all, a very attractive man.

After he'd gone Alex sat outside for a while watching the light fade from the sea and felt almost at peace with herself. Then she heard someone's feet crunching on the gravel path from the car park. She stood up and went to the rail that overlooked the path. A dark figure was coming towards her in the dusk and as it drew closer she could see that it was Concetta. She looked up at Alex, but didn't smile, even when Alex greeted her.

'*Buona sera, Signora.*'

Concetta inclined her head gravely but her lips remained closed.

How, Alex wondered, was she ever going to get her to talk?

Antonio Antonelli was much as Alex had expected. He stood up politely as she entered the room, a slender, silver-haired man who looked in his late sixties or early seventies, although Alex had been told by Freddi that he was roughly the same age as Zenia. Everything about him was beautifully groomed; his skin polished, his hands manicured. He was wearing an exquisitely cut lightweight suit in some glossy fabric with a matching grey silk shirt. When he shook her hand Alex caught the odour of an expensive mixture of vetiver and lemon with undertones of musk. The whole effect should have been effete, but as they exchanged pleasantries Alex noticed that he had very sharp eyes, a banker's eyes, calculating and astute. There was nothing weak or effeminate about Antonio Antonelli.

'Come and meet my daughter Caterina,' he said smoothly and led Alex over to the window seat.

Caterina stood up and held out her hand. She was approaching fifty, tall and angular with big, expressive eyes thickly mascara'ed. Her naturally dark hair had been bleached blonde and hung almost to her shoulders where it brushed the camel-coloured cashmere cardigan she was wearing, loosely buttoned, over a pair of tight leather trousers, which squeaked as she moved and showed rather more of the width of her hips than Alex would have cared to reveal. The hand she offered glittered with diamonds, but the wedding finger was conspicuously bare. The handshake was cool and distant, her fingers barely touched Alex's own.

'So. You are going to write about Aunt Zenia?' she asked.

'I'm being commissioned to write her life story, yes.' Alex sounded more defensive than she'd intended.

'You've got an impressive record,' Antonio said, and Alex realised that he must have taken the time to check her out.

'I hope you're not going to do one of those tales and tattle type of biographies,' Caterina said brusquely. 'She's already caused more than enough embarrassment to this family.'

Antonio clicked his tongue as if to admonish her and then turned to Alex and smiled. 'We must rely on you to be tactful,' he said. 'Zenia has always been controversial. But you must realise that her memory is not always reliable these days. I expect she will tell you she knew Puccini, but it can't be true because he died about eighteen months after she was born. How could she have remembered him? She is also very inventive where her family is concerned. She has spent most of her life in England or America and her contact with us has never been regular. If you want to know the truth, you must talk to my eldest son Cesare.'

'I gather he's not coming this time?'

'He lives in Venice,' Caterina said. 'And his mother is ill. It's very difficult to persuade him to leave.'

'He's a historian,' Antonio explained. 'And he has written the history of our family including the de Braganzas. Zenia's grandparents came from Spain originally. She will tell you that they were brigands and pirates, but they were actually grandees. And her mother's family were Viennese nobles who had fallen on hard times.'

'She told me that her mother was half Russian.'

Antonio made a dismissive gesture with his hands. 'Zenia will also tell you that Natalia was an opera singer.'

'But she did sing, didn't she?'

'In an amateur way, but it would have been very shocking for a girl of good family to have appeared at the Opera. It is all a fantasy of Zenia's, to be descended from brigands and Russian gypsies and women of the street.' Antonio's Italian was as smooth and elegant as his appearance, but underneath Alex could hear something older and coarser. Italy has only had a common language since 1948, and she supposed that, like Zenia, he would have grown up speaking Veneto. Both of them had travelled a long way from their family's origins.

Compared to the previous evening, dinner was a formal affair. Kelly, Jolene and Toby were absent and Alex noticed that no places had been laid for Concetta or Lenka. The atmosphere was a mixture of politeness and hostility. Both Caterina and Antonio were utterly charming towards Zenia, spoke to Freddi hardly at all and were overtly frigid towards Ludo who had been demoted to the bottom end of the table.

Zenia also was unlike herself. She seemed withdrawn and preoccupied. Whenever anyone asked her anything she would assume an air of childlike innocence as if she didn't understand what it was she was being asked. Alex wondered whether she was really senile or only pretending abstraction in order to avoid having to talk to the Antonellis.

Antonio was boasting about his friendship with the Prime Minister of Italy. 'He's a very astute business-man, the kind of man you need to run a modern economy. I can't understand why he attracts so much criticism.'

Zenia gave an abrupt, sarcastic laugh, which both Antonio and his daughter ignored.

Caterina said, 'I've just designed an apartment in Milan for one of his wife's friends. Very minimalist, Cycladic heads and polished limestone. It looked stunning.' She glanced round the cluttered room and said, 'I wish you'd let me do some things for you here, update some of the apartments.'

'I'm afraid Zenia likes it as it is,' Freddi said in a very tightly controlled voice.

About halfway through dinner Alex became aware of a change in Zenia. She had become even more abstracted, playing with the cutlery, marshalling the glasses and condiments into little groups like childhood soldiers. Her eyes, when she looked up and Alex caught her glance, seemed unfocussed, almost opaque.

'What are we doing here?' she asked suddenly in English, with such urgency that it seemed a metaphysical question. But her eyes were full of alarm and confusion as if she had woken from a bad dream to find herself in an unknown place.

'We've just had dinner,' Freddi explained. 'And now we're talking.'

'Oh.' She accepted it like a child. Then she looked across the table and, as if seeing Alex for the first time asked, 'Are you staying here?'

'That's Alessandra. She's come to write your life story.'

Zenia knew that she had forgotten, or simply misremembered and was furious with disbelief. 'How can I be so stupid? How did I not know that?' And then turned to Freddi, suddenly contrite. 'Of course, darling. That is how it is. You are so good to me.'

'You're tired, Zenia,' Freddi said, standing up and going to her. 'Come on, I'll take you upstairs.'

Zenia clutched at Freddi's hand as she stood up, shaking slightly. She looked incredibly fragile. 'And will you stay with me tonight, my darling?' she asked.

'Of course I will Zenia. Don't I always?' Freddi put an affectionate arm around her shoulders and Alex heard a small disgusted noise escape from Catarina's mouth. Freddi ignored it. She helped Zenia out of the room and through the door in the corner that led to the staircase.

'Why do they make such an exhibition of it?' Caterina said, pouring herself another glass of wine. 'Of course we all know. But it shouldn't be pushed in our faces.'

Alex bit the inside of her cheek to prevent an angry retort. There was so much love between those two women, it was palpable. How could anyone be disgusted by it?

'What exactly is wrong with Zenia?' Antonio asked when Freddi came back about fifteen minutes later.

'Well, initially they thought Alzheimer's, but when they did the tests they found that she has a rare form of motor neurone disease. It means she freezes sometimes when she tries to walk, talk, or even paint, that's the worst of it. And she also has arteriosclerosis, too much smoking and drinking. She's had a couple of little mini strokes already and that's caused some deterioration in her brain. You see how disorientated she can become when she's over-tired.'

'Does she still have that old fool of a doctor?'

'Tomas Viviani? I'm afraid so.' Freddi turned towards Alex. 'He's one of the old Istrian Italian families and she insists on seeing him. A friend from her early days in Rovinj.'

'Shouldn't she have a second opinion?' Antonio sounded brusque.

'She was actually diagnosed in London. They did all the scans, ordered the drugs. I telephone her consultant if there's any problem. There's nothing more anyone can do now.'

'Did they tell you how long she might have?'

'Unfortunately the disease is aggressive.' Freddi's knuckles were white as she clasped her hands together on the edge of the table. 'Eventually she'll be bed-bound and unable to do anything for herself at all. We're dreading it.'

'It's not a fate to be wished on anyone. Has she settled her affairs yet?' Antonio's voice was very smooth.

'I don't know. Probably not.'

'She must. We've got to persuade her. Otherwise when she dies there will be chaos and the only people to benefit will be the lawyers.'

'You know Zenia, Antonio.' The defensive note was back in Freddi's voice. 'She won't be told what to do by anyone.'

Outside the courtyard door opened and shut and then there were footsteps across the terrazzo.

'That must be Gianfranco.' Lenka put down the plates that she was clearing and went straight to the door to open it and let him in.

The man who came into the room was one of the most beautiful men Alex had ever seen. He had the kind of profile seen on Roman coins in museums, long dark hair pulled back into a band at the nape of his neck, and tanned skin drawn tight over his cheekbones. But as he came towards the light around the table, he was not as young as he had first seemed. There were deep laughter lines at the corners of his rather muscular mouth and the dark hair was threaded with grey.

Caterina's greeting was very casual. She inclined her cheeks one after the other for a brief encounter with his. Antonio was more formal; standing up for a ritual embrace that had little warmth in it. You could see that they were father and son. Although Gianfranco was taller, he had his father's grace and style. Then Gianfranco turned to Freddi and her face lit up as he kissed her.

'Let me introduce Alessandra – Alex,' she said, beckoning me forward. 'She's the biographer.'

His eyes were Zenia's eyes, probing, masculine, sexually hungry and Alex had to look away in order to avoid their scrutiny. There was a quiver of remembered desire at the pit of her stomach when he took her hand in a warm, firm grip.

'Where's Aunt Zenia?' he asked, scanning the table. 'Gone to bed? Is Concetta with her? I'll just go up and say goodnight.' He went out of the room and his feet could be heard lightly running upstairs and then Zenia's voice, faintly calling out something.

'He's Zenia's favourite,' Lenka whispered in Alex's ear. 'Even if he is *un bastardo*.' Having seen other, legitimate, members of the family Alex thought probably because he was *un bastardo*.

She stood up, feeling all her energy draining away. 'I think if you'll excuse me, I'd better go to bed. It's been a long day.'

The Antonellis murmured politenesses. Freddi got up to come with her to the door.

'Can I take some more letters?' Alex asked. 'I tend to wake up early in the mornings and I can get quite a lot of work done then.'

Freddi took her up to the studio and opened the doors of a big pine cupboard. The shelves were stacked with rolls of canvas, tubes of paint, jars stuffed with brushes as well as boxes of tattered paper with rough sketches scrawled across. Freddi bent to the lowest shelf and remained sitting on her haunches staring at it.

'They've gone,' she said. She put her hand into the empty space on the shelf. 'They were all here in a separate box. I put them in there myself at lunchtime.'

She stood up and began to walk round the studio ransacking the shelves, moving objects, peering into boxes.

'Do you suppose Zenia could have taken them?' Alex asked. 'Maybe she didn't want me to read them.'

Freddi shook her head. 'She wouldn't do that. She's always been reckless about what other people thought of her, and now, well, you've met her. She's quite happy for you to know everything.' She paused. 'I wonder if Concetta could have moved them? Or Toby? He was in here this afternoon.'

'Don't worry about it now, Freddi. I'm sorry I asked. Tomorrow will do.'

'They'll turn up somewhere. It's such chaos here at the moment.'

Outside in the loggia the moon had been partially obscured by cloud and lightning flickered far out to sea.

'There's going to be a storm tonight,' Freddi said. 'It's the Bora. The weather's always like this when it blows.' The sky to the east looked ink black and a cold wind had begun to lift the long seed pods of the wisteria on the pergola. She kissed Alex gently on the cheek. 'Sleep well,' she said. 'Hopefully Zenia will be well enough to talk to you tomorrow. They always upset her, you know. If it was up to me I wouldn't let them cross the threshold.'

Alex's Notebook

Zenia's voice has a presence in the room almost as big as herself.

> *When I look back on my life it is like looking in one of those mirrors that frightened me so much as a child. It is like a dark window onto something else. Images fly past – coming and going like leaves in a strong wind. There's my mother, clutching a bundle swathed in a shawl, holding out her hand to me and saying, "Come Zenia, come and be nice to your little brother Bernardo." But I'm standing with my legs rooted to the floor, my dusty shoes fixed to the spot and I won't go.*
>
> *Then there's Bernardo, eighteen, nineteen, handsome like our father, with good bones and the curved nose of the Branganzas, but with our mother's mouth – thin, rather petulant, and a small chin that unbalances his face. He's arguing with Antonio.*
>
> *"Socialism is the only hope for the human race – co-operation – a just and equal society. That's the future."*
>
> *And Antonio laughs. "It is against human nature, Bernardo. In the end everyone is out for themselves. There*

is no such thing as real altruism. Everyone has their own idea of equality. And who is going to be in charge? To make the laws to enforce this mythical equality? There always has to be someone. At least I am honest enough to admit that I would rather it was me."

Poor Bernardo.

Then there is Rosina. The girl who worked for us. I used to watch her mopping the floor with her skirts hobbled up above her knees. She had plump suntanned arms and sturdy legs with swollen calf muscles. She stood with the mop, her legs braced apart, balancing her weight perfectly over her feet as she swung it to and fro across the tiles as if she stood in a field and wielded a hoe. Her tall, bony face was filmed with sweat and her breasts rippled under her blouse. It gave me a strange feeling to watch her – to see the curve of her thigh against her skirt, her hardened nipples against the fabric of her blouse. Was that when I first knew? Then, or later?

And then another face, fair-skinned, with sleek blonde hair like a golden haze over it. Lucia's face, swimming towards me. A face I haven't looked at in fifty-seven years. The thought of Lucia is like a burn inside me. Even now I ache with it.

I close my eyes. The mirror goes blank. I let it sleep.

'Going to sleep is like entering a museum,' Zenia told me, 'where we revisit all the old, dusty rooms of our lives. There, in dreams, we listen to stories that are more true than anything we have ever lived.' In dreams I wander through my own museum, laying my hand on the smooth surface of one locked door after another. One in particular is double bolted, padlocked, the key turned in a massive mortice that would not look out of place in one of the Doge's dungeons in Venice. I know what's behind it. I know that if I turned the key, if I opened it even the narrowest crack, there would be so much pain, such unimaginable agony, I couldn't survive. So I leave it closed.

When Alex woke at eight the wind was blowing very strongly in the olive trees, rattling the branches along the balcony railings like children with a succession of sticks. Lightning was playing in the clouds over the mountains. She got up and made a cup of coffee and took it out onto the terrace.

Gianfranco was standing at the balustrade, looking out across the valley. Alex hesitated, conscious of her tousled hair and unwashed face, wanting to go back in again, but he turned his head and saw her, so she had to carry on walking towards him.

He was no longer looking at Alex, but at the slim spire of a church rising out of the early mist below the terrace. 'It's so beautiful here,' he said. 'So peaceful.' He turned his head again and smiled. 'Until recently I was living in Rome and it's always noisy.'

'A bit like London then.'

'Which part of London?'

'Ladbroke Grove. It's near Notting Hill.'

He nodded as if he knew where she meant. 'So, tell me, how do you come to speak such good Italian – the Italian of Italy?'

'My grandfather was Italian. He was a prisoner of war in England between 1943 and 45. I've been told that my mother was only one of his illegitimate children, but my grandmother was always very tight-lipped about it. He went back to Italy after the war and disappeared.'

'Have you ever tried to find him?'

'My grandmother never even told us his name. She married someone else a couple of years later and it was never talked about. It was one of my aunts who told my mother. She was very shocked. But I was proud of having Italian blood at school, I suppose because it made me different, and they let me do Italian instead of German as an option. Then I came to Italy in my gap year and did a language course at the University of Perugia.'

'And you went back to England afterwards?' He sounded incredulous.

Alex laughed. 'Unfortunately, yes.' How many years was it now, since she'd been to Italy? Was she afraid of the pull it had? She changed the subject quickly. 'Freddi said you're a musician. What do you play?'

'Tenor sax. Do you like jazz? I mean the real thing, not that recycled trad you get on street corners and at weddings.'

'I don't know. What would you class as real jazz?'

'Modern jazz. Miles Davis, Charlie Parker, that kind of thing.'

'Miles Davis, yes. I've got one of his CDs. I'm not sure about Charlie Parker. But I go to Ronnie Scott's in London occasionally with friends and usually enjoy it.' And she had been to the jazz clubs of New York too when she'd lived there.

Gianfranco grinned. 'I've never had a girlfriend who liked it yet. They all pretend at the beginning and then go back to whichever pop idol is around at the time.'

There was a rumble of thunder and lightning zigzagged down the sky into the sea.

'It's going to be a stormy morning,' he said. 'But these squalls usually burn themselves out by midday. Are you planning to interrogate us all one by one?' He smiled down at her, provocatively.

'I wasn't planning to interview any of you, at least not on this trip. I didn't realise that Freddi had invited you.'

'She didn't. My father heard you were coming and rounded us all up. Curiosity I suppose. So, what do you think of my Aunt Zenia?'

'I think she's one of the most amazing people I've ever met. But also one of the most frightening.'

He laughed. 'That's true. We were terrified of her as children, terrified and fascinated all at the same time. She's a wonderful person, though. I don't know what I would have done without her. I spent quite a lot of my childhood here, particularly the summer holidays. My mother used to go away with Antonio. Then I had a stepfather who found me very inconvenient. It was Zenia who got me into music. She took me to Groznjan, a little hill town somewhere over there,' he waved his hand in a westerly direction, 'for the music festival. I was fascinated by the instruments and kept asking questions and hanging around the band making a nuisance of myself. Afterwards the sax player gave me a few lessons, arranged by Zenia, and she bought me my first saxophone. My mother was furious at the noise, all that practising, but it was too late. I was hooked.'

'It's very sad that she's had no children of her own.'

'A great tragedy. But she couldn't, of course, being as she is.'

There were footsteps behind them.

It was Concetta, carrying an armful of purple and silver artichokes and smiling widely as she came down the path, greeting Gianfranco with a flood of affectionate, teasing Italian.

'*Ciao, caro, il mio bambino grande!*'

Gianfranco bent to kiss her on both cheeks. 'I'm forty-two and she still calls me that,' he said with a rueful smile, looking down at Concetta. '*La mia seconda madre.* I am relying on you to make *fritti* for me. No-one makes them like you do.' He turned to Alex. 'Have you tasted them? She does sage leaves in batter, and aubergine and courgette flowers and it's all absolutely delicious.'

'I'll look forward to it.' Alex smiled at Concetta and got a subdued '*Buon giorno*' and then a grudging, 'Did you sleep well?'

'Very well, until the storm woke me.'

'How's Zenia this morning?' Gianfranco asked.

'So-so. She has been awake most of the night. She is very worried in her mind about Antonio and Freddi and what is to happen after she dies. I tell her she must do just what she wants. But she says that she has to do the right thing and she doesn't know yet what it is.'

'She mustn't let my father put pressure on her.'

'I do not think anyone can tell your father anything,' Concetta shrugged. 'He is a snake.' She began to move off. 'Now, I must make preparations for lunch.'

After she had gone Alex said, 'I wish I could persuade her to talk to me. Those are the first words she's said to me since I arrived.'

'She's suspicious of anyone she thinks is going to rip Zenia off. If she decides you're genuine and trustworthy, then she'll talk to you. It's just a matter of time.'

Alex sighed. Her coffee cup was empty. 'I must go and have a shower and dress. And then there's a stack of files I have to get through.' She smiled at him, feeling shy like a gauche girl. There was something in his eyes, or his manner, a permanent amusement at the human race per-haps, that she found very disconcerting.

'I'll see you at lunch,' he said and wandered non-chalantly off towards the house.

As Alex watched him strolling down the path, his ponytail swinging behind him, she had a sudden, blinding memory of Steve. Alex hadn't expected to be invaded by such memories here, and she wondered whether she had let her guard down for a fraction of a second, or whether there was some small resemblance to Gianfranco that had turned the key to one of the locked doors.

Alex had first met Steve at a party thrown by a friend who was leaving for Kuala Lumpar where she was going to work for Reuters. Steve was an American in London on a year's placement with a city bank. Alex had just got a job as a feature writer on Cosmo and wrote articles on how to have multiple orgasms, infertility, infidelity, in fact anything to do with sex, a job that caused extreme hilarity in mixed company; a job that most single men found rather daunt-ing. When Steve smiled at her across the sparkling char-donnay Alex hadn't had a relationship for nearly a year. Life consisted of work, going to the gym, bar-crawling with girlfriends and attending media junkets.

Within weeks of meeting him, all that had changed. In the beginning, because Steve was already involved with some girl back in the States, they had been just friends, constantly in each other's company. This was a way of re-lating to men that Alex wasn't used to and, at first, it was a relief. Then she began to be afraid that if they ever did get round to going to bed together, it might ruin the com-fortable relationship that had developed. Alex could talk to him about anything, even things she'd never told her girlfriends. It was to Steve she had confessed that, although she wrote about sex a lot, she found the actual thing quite disappointing. Alex hated being seen without her clothes on, hated anyone watching her when she was asleep, never seemed to be able to achieve the level of trust necessary to let go completely and lose herself in animal sensuality. There was always a high level of self-consciousness and reserve. Steve told her, with all the assurance of a man at ease with his own body, that it wouldn't be a problem with him. And it wasn't. Making love with Steve was as natural as breathing. He also told her that all her problems were to do with her mother. But, ironically, so were his, though Alex didn't know that at the time.

Steve was into avant-garde cinema and so she sat through innumerable, incomprehensible French, Czech, Armenian and Japanese movies. Alex liked Kurasawa, was intrigued by Svlansky and Kodescz, but hated the strange visual syntax of the Brothers Quay. Steve spent hours arguing that it was necessary for the human race to have anarchic ways of looking at itself, or explaining the ethics of minimalism and the surrealists. They fought often because Alex, a first class literature graduate, felt patronised by his explanations. And she couldn't see why an evening at the cinema had to turn into a lecture on the human psyche. Did all Americans talk like therapists?

They were very different. Alex's favourite movies that year were *Dangerous Liaisons* and *Rain Man*. Steve liked Glenn Gould playing Bach; she liked Jacqueline du Pre playing Elgar. He was fascinated by mathematical conundrums; she was congenitally innumerate. But, somehow, mesmerised by their differences, they had fallen in love. Not love as Alex had ever experienced it. She remembered once dashing out to get herself a sandwich at lunch-time from the little Jewish deli round the corner from the office and thinking that she saw him in the street, the back of his head, the shoulder of a perma-press suit. The whole of the inside of her stomach was wrenched upside down, leaving her legs trembling and her head giddy, like a stupid, emotional adolescent. That was when she had realised how serious it was.

It seemed odd thinking about Steve at the Kaštela, odd too that she was remembering the beginning of the relationship rather than the end. Alex realised that she had suppressed her memories of Steve for so long she had forgotten there could be good ones as well as bad. Then she realised that the hand holding the cup was quite steady and her eyes were dry. She had thought about Steve and she hadn't fallen apart.

As soon as Alex had showered and had breakfast she went up to the house and let herself into the big room to collect two more box files of *lavori* from the bookshelves. The door to the staircase was ajar and she could hear raised voices from the room above. Zenia was saying angrily, 'But he's my cousin. All right, not a very nice person. But my family, that is important.'

Then Freddi, 'He's a crook Zenia. Corrupt and venial. Someone has to tell you that. God knows where he makes all his money.'

'So. All right. He is a maverick. But then so am I – that is in our family – we have no regard for the law, for rules and regulations – those things are for the bourgeoisie.'

'But he doesn't share your vision, Zenia.' Freddi's voice sounded tired. 'He'll pull it all down and build something else.'

'Why would he do that? He's a businessman. What I have created is a work of art – it has a price – a good price. Why should he meddle with that?'

Alex felt uncomfortable listening to their conversation, so she crept out of the room, leaving the files undisturbed until later. It was time to go exploring.

A steep pathway climbed in a series of steps up through the olive groves above the main house. The steps were made from rough-hewn stone and looked as if they'd been there for a long time. Alex could imagine processions of donkeys with loaded panniers stumbling down them towards the village oil press. On either side, the ground beneath the olive trees was netted in swathes of orange mesh weighed down by stones and a few pockets of fallen fruit, remnants of the olive harvest brought down by last night's wind. Between the trees, just off the path, was a wooden olive-pickers' shack, roofed with corrugated plastic. A lean-to veranda had been built onto it with a rainwater butt in one corner and a table made from a slab of marble on a wooden frame.

Ludo was sitting there with a cup of espresso in front of him and a grappa glass. He rose rather unsteadily to his feet when he saw Alex and bowed. '*Buon giorno, signora.*'

'Do you mind if I come and talk to you?'

'It will be my pleasure.'

'And mine,' a voice said from inside the hut and Gianfranco came out grinning widely, carrying another coffee cup and the bottle of grappa. He set the cup down in front of her. 'Coffee?'

'Don't let me take yours.'

'It's no trouble, I can make some more. I thought you would have been with Zenia this morning.'

'She's upset. There's some kind of argument going on.'

'There's always one when my father's here. His views and hers don't coincide.'

'That is a very subtle way of putting it.' Ludo tossed back his grappa and refilled the glass from the bottle

Gianfranco had set down in front of him. 'Zenia has never been in harmony with her family. They have never understood her.'

'They like her celebrity,' Gianfranco said with a wry twist of his mouth as he turned to go back inside the shack.

Alex turned to Ludo. 'Tell me about the time you were both at college in Venice. What was she like then?'

'A crazy horse. One minute you would be drinking with her in a bar, talking seriously about art or politics and the next she would have dived into a canal daring you to follow. She did that once. It was quite shocking. People did not do things like that in 1946.'

'Was she always exceptional?'

'Ah yes. Always driven. Everyone knew that she would do something sensational. She drew people to her all the time. We were all in love with her at one time or another.' He paused reflecting for a moment with his head lowered and then he looked up again and said, 'You must be very careful what you write about Zenia. It would be too easy to give the wrong impression, to make her life something it was not.'

'So you don't think I should be writing this book? Even if Zenia wants it?'

'It's not that I don't want you to write it, I just think she is not wise to reveal so much of herself. She is, and this will seem strange to you, not very worldly. She hasn't thought about what other people will think, people who don't know her. We all love her and when she does crazy things we make allowances.' He was silent for a moment and then said, 'It is also that Zenia has secrets that are perhaps better left closed.'

Gianfranco re-emerged from the doorway with another cup of coffee in his hand. 'You had better tell her about Lucia, Ludo. It's important. And Zenia won't talk about her.'

'Who was Lucia?'

Ludo sighed. 'A young woman, not much older than Zenia, married to someone in society. She was very beautiful and her family had a huge palazzo on the grand canal near the Guggenheim house. They were an old family, very rich, with a lot of connections. Lucia's husband was a banker from another family that could trace its ancestors back to the Medici. No-one knows when she met Zenia, but suddenly they were always in each other's company, and then after a few months they completely disappeared and everyone knew they had run away together. It was the most terrible scandal. People did not do such things then.'

'Where did they go? Do you know?'

'They took the ferry across to Rovinj. They lived above a bakery in one of the little piazzas. It was a studio belonging to one of the other students at the Academia and it had a little balcony with views across to the sea. They were there about six months, I think, and then Zenia's mother came with the father and the husband of the girl. There was a lot of talking and arguing. Zenia faced it out, she argued and argued with them to be able to do what she had to do, to be free to live as she pleased. She had thought that Lucia would stand with her; that was what they had agreed, but after two days Lucia went back to Venice in the car with her husband. It was a betrayal Zenia could never forgive. It was the hurt that cut deepest in her life. She stayed on. She wouldn't go home with her mother. I went to see her. She was distraught, painting like a madwoman. That was when she did the canvas that hangs in the big room. You have seen it?'

Alex nodded. 'It reminds me of Frida Kahlo.'

'That was a phase she was going through. She was still so very young. But after that time in Rovinj, when she left, she had her own style, her own language.'

'What happened to her afterwards?'

'She wrote to Marco Marconi and became his assistant and he took her to Paris. That was where it all started for her. It was the right place for her to be.'

'Did you go too?'

Ludo shook his head. 'Not then. Later, for a while. For what I needed to do I needed to be here. I am a sculptor – terracotta, marble dust, gesso, cloth, canici – I use all these things – everyday things to make art. We were *communisti*, Zenia and me – but while I stayed with the *arte povera* – the people's art – she began to be a celebrity and more of an autocrat. That too, I think, began in Rovinj. Her whole life changed.'

'It's difficult to explain,' Ludo went on. 'After Lucia her art became more rooted in the personal. She was exploring her own psyche, pursuing her devils. I think she was trying to understand herself.'

'Are you saying it was a kind of therapy?'

Ludo smiled as though Alex had said something crass. 'There is an element in art that is always that. We paint, we sculpt, we make music so that we don't go mad. But with Zenia – look at her paintings – see how many of her portraits contain mirrors – how many twins she painted – all those self-portraits. Reflexive images.'

'Have you ever been to Rovinj?' Gianfranco asked as they walked down the steps to the main house.

'Never. But I ought to go, I need to see all the places that have been important in Zenia's life.'

'Then I must take you one day. It's utterly beautiful, in spite of the war damage.'

As they entered the courtyard Alex could hear someone shouting, it wasn't possible to hear the words, just the sounds of distress coming from an upstairs window.

Gianfranco began to run. Alex followed him through the big room and up the narrow winding staircase at the back that climbed the tower to Zenia's private quarters. The door to her studio was open and Zenia was standing inside wearing a paint-stained hessian smock of the kind that peasants wear in old black and white movies. She had a brush in one hand and a palette knife in the other and was standing transfixed in front of the canvas.

'*Basta! Basta!*' she was shouting. 'Is it not enough to have this terrible thing?'

The muscles of her forearm rippled and she made a guttural, grunting sound as she wrenched her hand towards the canvas with such force that the brush tore through the primed surface. The hand holding the palette knife followed it and she stabbed the painting repeatedly. Gianfranco went up behind her and grasped her arms.

'Zenia, please, the canvas doesn't deserve so violent a death.'

She was still shaking with rage. 'I will never finish a painting again. Do you know what that feels like? No! It is as though I have already died. And then that man comes here. I hate him. Hate him. I could put this knife through his heart.'

'But I'd rather you didn't. I don't want my favourite relative arrested by the police.'

Slowly, as he held her, she began to relax, to slump back against him. For a moment they stood there together, head to head, of equal height and stature, and then he gently turned her and guided her to the armchair nearest the stove.

'Some of Concetta's slivovitz?' he asked, moving towards the chestnut corner cabinet.

Zenia nodded and he produced a bottle with a handwritten label and three tiny shot glasses. 'I don't think Alessandra has tasted this yet, have you?'

Alex shook her head.

'Home-made plum brandy. Concetta's speciality.' He filled the glasses and they raised them together. 'Here's to friendship,' he said.

'Friendship,' Zenia echoed and Alex pledged hers with a clink of glasses before downing the clear liquid in one.

Lunch was a rather uneasy affair. Zenia stayed in her room and Ludo ate in the kitchen with Concetta and Toby. The big dining table seemed vast with only six people grouped at one end. Antonio was preoccupied, picking at his *fritti*, while Caterina carried on an endless conversation about a palazzo whose interior she had just designed for some contessa or other near Verona. Freddi's polite responses had an undertone of desperation. Lenka moved in and out with plates of food, scowling like a thunderstorm.

Gianfranco ate in silence, drinking copious quantities of red wine and filling Alex's glass just as often. Occasionally he would look up and smile at her as if they shared a secret joke. There was a mutual awareness of the comic subtext of Caterina's monologue of gold-plated bath taps and reconstructed Roman mosaics, a white marble staircase lit from beneath like a river of light, and specially commissioned Venetian chandeliers. She could quote the price on every item as if the exorbitant costs increased her own importance. And all the time Caterina talked, she was glancing round Zenia's beautiful room and Alex could see it cheapening under her gaze. The trompe d'oeil painted by Zenia and Ludo, the rustic chestnut beams. She could see Caterina re-decorating it in her head with hand-made French wallpaper and gilded plaster, and when Alex looked at Gianfranco she knew that he could see it too.

Afterwards Alex went back upstairs. Zenia was in the studio, still sitting in the big armchair beside the fire, wrapped in a Burberry rug, staring out of the window towards the mountains. 'I cannot talk to you today,' she said, turning a troubled face towards Alex. Her skin was trammelled by deep lines, her eyes hooded and dark. She looked very old. 'I wish they were gone.'

Then suddenly she asked, 'So what do you think I should do?'

Alex knew what she was asking, but didn't want to be pushed into giving a straight reply. What could she say? Whatever words she chose would affect the outcome and she didn't want that responsibility.

'Antonio is my cousin,' Zenia went on, 'my only blood relative. It is expected that I should leave the Kaštela to him. And then there is Freddi and all the others. They are like my children. What will happen to Lenka? She is a Roma. No-one wants them – her parents died in Zagreb during the Homeland War. And Ludo? He has spent his whole life here – where would he go to spend his last days? Who would look after him? If I leave the Kaštela to Antonio what will happen to them all?'

Alex tried to be neutral and as diplomatic as possible. 'I think you have to ask yourself who's going to look after the Kaštela best. Who do you trust to carry it on as you would like?'

Zenia looked down at her hands, clasping and un-clasping them. 'I worry about Freddi. She is not strong. You have to be strong to make the Kaštela work. And she does not speak Croat at all and Italian only a little. When I am dead they will all take advantage of her. But Antonio is a man. He would take charge of things. If I liked him it would be easy.'

Alex thought that it would be useless to say that she wouldn't trust Antonio to look after a dog. Surely Zenia already knew the kind of person that he was? She probed carefully; 'Why do you hate him so much?'

'It is something that happened when we were children. He was a sneak – always hiding – always watching us and then running to our mothers with tales. And then he behaved in such a cowardly way when they made him go into the army towards the end of the war. Shooting himself in the leg so that he would be sent home to his mother. A coward and a gossip-monger then and now. But I try not to hold it against him… Such things are trivial. Antonio is my closest relation. And I keep thinking – if only Bernardo was still alive!'

She looked at Alex very directly. 'They shot my brother you know. And then they shot all the people in the village where he was hiding. To make an example for everyone else. At the time some people blamed Antonio for it, because he was in the Young Fascists and Bernardo was with the Communist Partisans. But I have never believed them. It was a great injustice. Antonio is a coward, but he could never betray a member of his family. That would make him a monster and you have only to look into his eyes to see that he is not that!' She paused. 'It is a dilemma, is it not?' Her fingers plucked at the material of her jacket.

'But I must decide soon. There is not much time left.'

'What about a compromise? Could you not make some kind of trust?' Alex thought about what Martin had told her. 'A kind of "*usa frutta*", so that Freddi and the others can stay here, but the actual property belongs to Antonio? I don't know much about Croatian law, but apparently you can do it in Italy and in England.'

'I do not know anything about law. It is all a mystery to me. When I bought the Kaštela, Antonio got his lawyers to arrange it for me. I saw it, fell in love with it and then it was mine. All my life I have done just what I wanted to do – it is terrible now that I have to start thinking about the law. Once it was easy. I left everything to Paulina. But she died. Then I left everything to my nephew Salvatore, Bernardo's child. But he died also, very young. Such things should not happen. There are Antonio's children of course but there are three of them and I could not bear to see the Kaštela sold to strangers so that they could divide the money between them.'

'But, Zenia, Antonio is almost as old as you. Surely in a few years, that is exactly what will happen anyway?'

She looked at Alex with a gaze that could only be interpreted as anger. Alex wondered whether she had overstepped the mark. Or had Zenia simply not considered this, perhaps because her reasoning faculties were impaired?

Her expression softened. 'They all want me to leave it to them alone. How do I know who I can trust? They all have their own reasons. I thought that you perhaps could tell me, that you might know…'

Alex felt very sad. 'I don't know anyone well enough, Zenia. But there are people who love you very much and I think you could trust them to do what you want.'

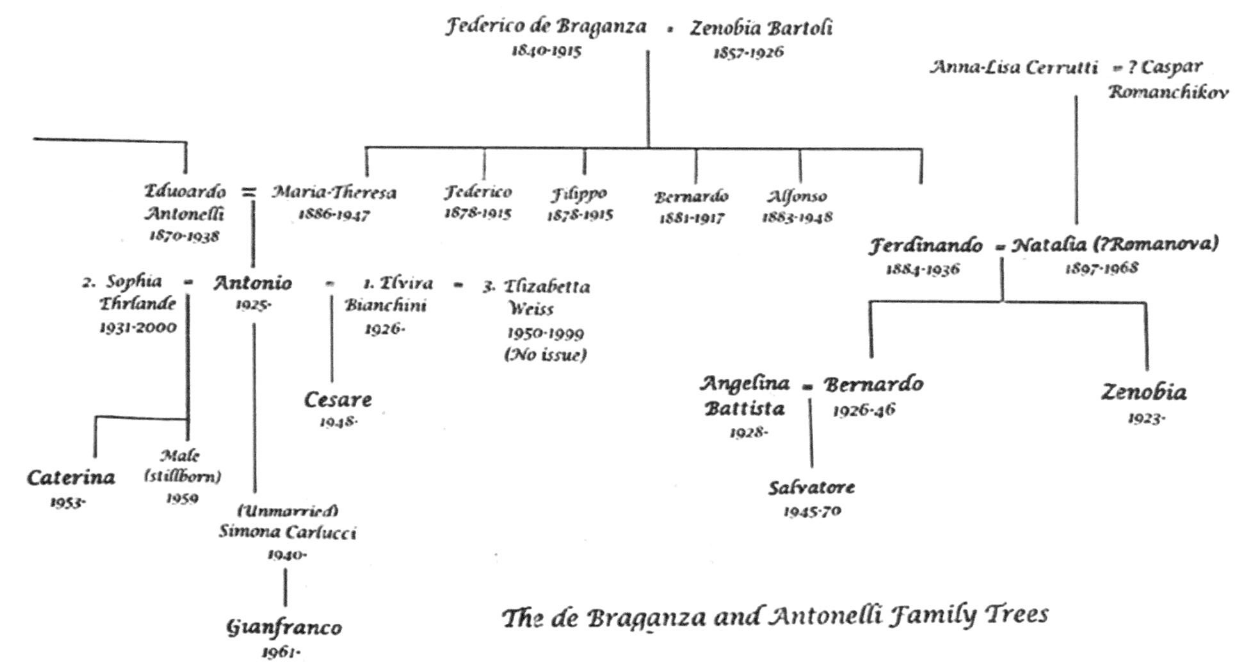

The de Braganza and Antonelli Family Trees

When Alex came down the stairs Gianfranco was waiting for her.

'Let's go out – there's something I'd like to show you.'

She collected her fleece jacket from the room on the way down to the car park.

Gianfranco drove an old, rather battered Audi very fast down the narrow road, but he seemed to have a sixth sense that told him when something was coming round the corner towards him. 'I was driving these roads before I had a licence,' he told her, as if he knew what she was thinking. 'Zenia used to let me drive. She had an ancient Bedford van she brought over from England. It had to be bump-started down the hill from the car park – terrify-ing!'

They were soon on a narrow unfenced road wind-ing uphill. It hadn't been maintained for a long time. There was grass growing through the tarmac and in places the road surface had been washed away. Alex closed her eyes as Gianfranco bumped the Audi across gullies of stone and mud, the wheels rattling pebbles off the edge down through the trees, further down and steeper than she dared allow herself to imagine.

'Only hunters come up here now,' Gianfranco said. 'You really need a four-wheel drive.'

'What do they hunt?'

'Wild boar mainly. Birds, truffles, porcini. This area used to be quite heavily populated but now that most of the people have gone, there's a glut of wild food.'

They turned into a clearing and Gianfranco brought the car to a halt and turned the engine off. Outside, the ground was covered with a soft prickly coat of chestnuts, their green shells splitting open underfoot to reveal the white pith and the polished kernels.

Alex followed Gianfranco along a path through the woodland, faint, but still apparent. She could see that the land on either side of it had once been terraced, though the terraces were now overgrown and the stone walls had been dislodged in places as if animals had scrambled over them. There were olive trees and young oaks, acacia and chestnut trees all growing unchecked and tangled overhead. And the path was littered with fallen olives, shrivelled, like rabbit droppings. Occasionally Alex glimpsed squat stone buildings like small barns, surrendering to the greenery, roofless, doorless, with young saplings peering over the ruined walls. Nearer to the path there were fig trees and pomegranates and a lemon tree with huge misshapen green lemons hanging like lanterns.

Then the path began to open out and started to look more like a narrow country lane. Ahead she could see a group of buildings on either side of what might once have been a street.

'This is rather like the Kaštela when Zenia found it,' Gianfranco said. 'Though that had only been abandoned for about twenty years or so, and hadn't decayed quite so much as this.'

A few houses still had part of a tiled roof, though windows and doors hung from their hinges. Alex peered inside one of them. Two pigeons clapped their way out of the rafters as she put her head through the gap. The floors had gone, oak beams leaned at perpendicular angles, but there was still furniture on the ground floor, rusted bedsteads fallen from the upper storey, crumbling wooden chests, a table with three legs, broken chairs.

The church at the end of the street had been burned out. Only the walls remained, like a fragile scorched crust of stone, and the dissolving stucco had left a white tide-mark on the ground outside.

'What happened here?' Alex asked.

'In 1945, after the war in Europe was over, everyone went on fighting – communists and fascists for control of Yugoslavia. Istria was the main centre for the partisans. The men in this village were pro-Tito, they supported the communists, and one night a unit of Chetniks came into the village while everyone was asleep and massacred them all. Mainly women and children, old men and boys too young to fight. One hundred and two people died including a three week old baby. Zenia told me the story over and over – it made a big impression on her, perhaps because of her brother Bernardo. He was betrayed and shot fighting for the communist partisans just east of Trieste, in what's now Slovenia.'

Alex shuddered. The atmosphere of the place had suddenly become oppressive. As if aware of her change of mood, Gianfranco turned back onto the path. They walked to the car in silence.

'There's something else I'd like you to see,' he said when they reached the clearing and he took another path that climbed upwards, towards the summit of the hill.

They were both breathless when they emerged from the trees into open space. Above them a squat stone tower leaned sideways and chunks of masonry had broken away and lay beside it gaping at the sky, each piece several tons in weight.

'This is amazing. It must be medieval!'

'Possibly even older.'

'What happened to it? An earthquake?'

Gianfranco shook his head. 'It was blown up in the Second World War, maybe around the time the village was wiped out. But come and look at this.' He waved Alex over to what looked like a random pile of fallen stones near the entrance to the path. When she moved one of them with her foot she could see that there were the organic shapes of limbs and folds of drapery. Each fragment had been part of a statue.

'It was an earlier version of the Pieta outside the chapel at Visoko,' he said. 'Have you seen it?'

Alex had looked at it briefly when she first arrived, passing it on the way to Zenia's studio. A mother holding a dead child in her arms, her head bent over it and her breasts dripping milk.

Gianfranco knelt down and cleared the long grass away from the plinth with a piece of stick. The inscription was carved in Italian and Croat. 'In memory of the people of Cec.'

'Zenia put it here as a memorial,' Gianfranco said. 'She even paid for a helicopter to lower it in place. But it was destroyed about ten years ago during the Homeland War. Someone fired a shell at it. Italians weren't exactly popular at the time. This landscape has a long memory.'

'It seems odd, doesn't it?' Alex sat down on the grass beside him. 'The Second World War is old history for us – for our generation, I mean.'

'But not here – the people involved are still alive. Family fought family and the old hatreds never went away. And then, of course, the civil war brought them all back again.'

From where they were sitting Alex could see across the trees all the way to the coast. The sun was glittering on the Adriatic, beginning to dip towards the horizon.

'This is so beautiful and so peaceful. It's hard to imagine such terrible things happening here.'

He took his eyes from the view to look at her. 'I suppose nature has a way of restoring a balance, if you wait long enough. I used to come and practise up here a lot. Zenia said it needed music. I used to play and she used to sing. She had a fantastic voice, probably inherited from her mother.'

'Did you ever meet Zenia's mother?'

He shook his head. 'Natalia died when I was seven and still a shameful secret. But everyone says she was a formidable woman. Angelina, Bernardo's wife, had a lot of trouble with her. Natalia was the kind of woman who should have been controlling a multinational company, not just a household, and of course after Bernardo died, there were fewer people to control. Zenia was in the front line.'

'That's something that's been puzzling me, I thought Bernardo was killed when he was twenty, but then Zenia mentioned a child – I think she said his name was Salvatore and now you say he had a wife?'

'The family's full of black sheep. Bernardo got a local girl pregnant when he was about eighteen and her family made him marry her. The baby was called Salvatore – lots of boys were christened that after the war. Everyone expected Angelina to re-marry, she was only nineteen when Bernardo died, but she never has. There's never even been the hint of a relationship, though I suppose it would have been difficult to meet anyone while she was living with her mother-in-law. Angelina still lives in Trieste near what used to be Natalia's house.'

'Does she ever come here?'

'Zenia and Angelina haven't spoken to each other since her son Salvatore died. Zenia calls her "The Peasant" and Angelina calls Zenia "Il Duce". They hate each other!'

'Do you know why?'

'Not really. Zenia was totally against Bernardo marrying her, but that wasn't the whole of it. Perhaps it was jealousy. Zenia adored their son Salvatore, maybe a little too much. Family gossip has it that there was a disagreement over the way she encouraged him to rebel. Angelina's quite conventional. She thought Zenia led the boy astray. But Salvatore died in a car accident when I was nine or ten, so I've no idea if it's true.'

He paused for a moment as if weighing something up, and then went on, 'In his twenties he became rather wild – drugs, women, fast cars. Angelina was beside herself, but she couldn't stop him. Zenia's mother Natalia had left all her money to him outright, not even in trust.'

'Nothing to Zenia?'

'No. There'd been a big breach between them just before Natalia died. I think she made the will out of spite.'

'Poor Zenia. And poor Angelina with such a mother-in-law!'

'That was said with feeling.' He smiled. 'Are you married?'

'Used to be. And you?'

'Never made it. A couple of near misses.'

'Any particular reason?'

'Musicians aren't a good bet in stable relationships. We move around too much. And I think I was probably put off by the family's record. My father's been married three times, four if you count my mother as a wife. He's had other mistresses too. I wouldn't want to be with a woman if I couldn't make a decent stab at fidelity.'

Alex said nothing and after a brief silence he began talking again.

'I once lived with a woman in Rome for about five years. But it didn't last. She wanted children.'

'And you don't?'

He smiled. 'Zenia's always asking me that question. I do, actually, but not with her. It wouldn't have been right. You have to be sure of a relationship to have children. What about you?'

'I'll soon be too old.'

'What are you? Thirty-six? Seven?'

'Good guess. Thirty-nine.'

'It's not too late.' He looked across at her. 'What happened to your marriage?'

Alex breathed in. Paused the moment. He was so easy to talk to, the afternoon was so peaceful and so beautiful. This would be the time to tell him. But could she trust him enough? He was an Antonelli after all. Alex lost courage and breathed out. What she told him was true, but it was only part of the truth.

'His mother didn't think I was good enough. She was a widow; Steve was an only child. In the end he said he felt like a ping-pong ball being bounced between the two of us. I was furious that he didn't put me first and tell his mother to leave me alone. But he couldn't. He was too nice. I realised in the end that, if I couldn't change him and I couldn't change her, I either had to put up with it or walk away.'

'So you walked.'

She nodded.

Two swallows swooped and twittered conversationally. Wood smoke rose from chimneys in the valley and the bells of a distant campanile tolled four o'clock.

'Are you cold?' he asked suddenly, so perhaps Alex had shivered.

'Not particularly.' It wasn't as cold as October in England, though the trees were beginning to turn red and yellow with autumn colour.

'That's Venice over there.' He pointed out to sea, where a haze was gathering on the horizon. 'You can get a ferry across to Rovinj in the summer. I used to do that sometimes as a child, and Zenia would bring the van down to meet me.'

'The two of you are so close. Why doesn't Zenia leave the Kaštela to you?'

He gave a wry laugh. 'Italians are very strong on family. She may believe that I'm Antonio's child, but she can never be sure. It's always possible that my mother might have had other lovers. So she will leave it to the better accredited members of the family, even though she hates them.'

'Everyone at the Kaštela seems to be hoping that it'll be left to Freddi and stay exactly as it is.'

'I suppose Zenia might, but it's unlikely. Though Freddi deserves it really. She's devoted her life to Zenia. And if they were man and woman, husband and wife, there would be no question.'

'It seems unfair that she should lose out just because they're not.'

'I agree with you. But for Italians blood is stronger than love.'

'Is that why she tolerates your father even though she dislikes him so much?'

'They were brought up together. Although they were only cousins, my father was like a younger brother to her. He and Bernardo never got on well though, always fighting – and then there was some big falling out between the three of them. But after Bernardo died, Zenia began to see my father again occasionally. I sometimes wonder if he's got some kind of hold over her. It wouldn't surprise me. Zenia's life has been full of scandals. She's never cared a toss for what people thought of her. But if you want to know about Zenia and Antonio you must go and ask Concetta. She used to work for Angelina and Natalia – there's not a lot she doesn't know about this family.'

Alex sighed.

'Shall I talk to Concetta for you? You can't write this book without her.'

'If you can. I have a feeling that Concetta isn't easily persuaded to do anything.' Alex pulled up a handful of grass, twisting it in her fingers. 'I've been wondering whether I should give up the idea of the biography. I seem to have walked in on a family crisis and I'm not sure I want to be in the middle of it.'

'The battle over Zenia's will?' Gianfranco pulled a face. 'That's been building up for months.' He stood up and brushed the dust off his jeans. 'It's probably a good job that you're here – at least some of the people involved will feel obliged to behave with a bit of human decency. Otherwise it could get quite nasty.' He held out a hand to Alex. 'Time to get back.'

His fingers were very warm in the cool air.

As they walked back to the car he said, 'Don't worry about whether you should be writing this book. If Zenia isn't afraid of the truth, you needn't be either. I think it would be a pity if she were denied the opportunity to tell her own story.'

When Alex and Gianfranco walked back into the Kaštela, Kelly and Jolene were sitting on the terrace with a big wooden watercolour box open in front of them and identical sketch pads propped on their knees. The scenery below was beginning to arrange itself for a spectacular sunset. Venetian-style bell towers and old stone churches crowning the summits of small hills, ochre rooftops, all protruding through the thick white mist that was pooling in the valley. At the furthest edge, the sea was already pink and gold.

'Halloooo!' Jolene called, waving an imperative hand towards them.

Alex paused reluctantly.

'*O dio!*' she heard Gianfranco murmur, and then, 'Tell them I have to practise.' His feet continued to crunch through the fallen leaves towards the steps. Alex sent an indignant look towards his retreating back.

'Did you have a nice walk?' Kelly asked.

'Beautiful. We went to one of the deserted villages.'

'Aren't they just so sad?' Jolene said. 'But the tourists seem to like them. We sell a lot of pictures of those romantic ruins.' Her hands sketched inverted commas round the word romantic.

'You missed an entertaining afternoon,' Kelly said. 'Martin and Lenka have had a gigantic row – you could hear her shouting all over the Kaštela.'

Alex knew she shouldn't be listening to gossip, but she was curious in spite of herself. 'What were they quarrelling about?'

Kelly and Jolene exchanged a look. Then Jolene spoke. 'About you actually. She accused Martin of having his eye on you. Then he told her to stop flirting with Gianfranco.'

'She's only doing that to make Martin jealous,' Kelly said. 'He's the one she really wants.' She hesitated. 'But sometimes I think she likes Gianfranco too.'

'Lenka wants to stay at the Kaštela.' Jolene's voice was sharp. 'Whichever one it's going to be left to – Martin or Gianfranco, she'll sure as hell want him.'

Alex was baffled. 'I can see that Zenia might leave the Kaštela to Gianfranco, but why would she leave it to Martin?'

Jolene lowered her voice confidentially. 'You know, of course, that he's been like a son to her since he came.'

Alex nodded, because they seemed to expect her to agree.

'He's worked for a pittance all these years to keep it together for her – the Kaštela wouldn't be here like this if it wasn't for Martin. He deserves it.'

'He wouldn't have stayed if he didn't think he'd get something,' Kelly said. 'Maybe not all of it. But some. So now you see why Lenka doesn't like Martin fancying you.'

Alex felt a surge of dislike for both of them. She smiled, a fixed, cold smile. 'I have to go and see Freddi,' she explained, turning to move away.

'She's in the kitchen with Concetta,' Kelly called

after her, already swirling her brush in the water jar. 'See you later.'

Alex went into the kitchen of the main house. It was so small she could hardly believe that Concetta could cook for so many people in such a tiny space. There was barely room around the central table to squeeze to the sink past the gigantic American fridge-freezer that occupied almost the whole of one wall. The left hand corner was squared off by an original wood-fired oven and on the back wall, next to the sink, was a narrow old-fashioned calor-gas cooker. Concetta was stirring something in a battered aluminium pan that occupied three of the four rings. Ludo was sitting at the table with Freddi and a bottle of Concetta's clear plum slivovitz was open between them.

Freddi immediately stood up and fetched another glass from the shelf. '*Ciao* Alex. Did you have a good walk? I'm afraid Zenia's lying down, if you were hoping to talk to her. She's very tired today.' Freddi filled the glass and held it out.

'*Salute!*'

Alex took a sip and felt the liquid beginning to burn all the way down to her stomach. Ludo patted a chair next to him, in front of the wood-fired oven that was already alight, puffing smoke and heat into the kitchen. Alex told them about visiting Cec, the deserted houses, Zenia's broken memorial.

Freddi said. 'I remember once we drove up there for a picnic – it was a favourite place next to the old tower. You can see the hills in one direction and the sea in the other and there's an old olive-pickers' shack, only just holding together against the weather. Did you see it?'

Alex shook her head.

'It's probably fallen down by now,' Ludo said, pouring himself another shot of slivovitz.

'Anyway, that day we had chicken and sausages, cheese and bread – a typical Zenia feast with bottles of wine and beer. And suddenly this huge dog came up out of nowhere. A hunting dog with a shaggy coat. He looked hungry and thoroughly uncared for – briars caught in his hair and there was a wound on his back leg as if he'd been in a fight. Zenia gave him all the food that was left. She decided he must be a stray dog and she wanted to adopt him.'

'She is always doing things like that,' Ludo said, waving his arm round the room. 'Look at us! We are all Zenia's adopted children.'

'*Basta*, Ludo,' Concetta said, tapping the side of the pan with the spoon. 'Let Freddi tell the story.'

Freddi smiled. 'I looked at this awful dog and I said, "Zenia, you're just about to go off to Japan. What are you going to do with him? Who's going to look after him?" It was high season here, and he looked wild, not the sort of dog to have around tourists and children. She listened to me and then agreed and we packed up the van and set off back down the hill. Then suddenly she stopped. "I have to go back for the dog," she said, and turned the van round somehow on that narrow road – the back wheels hanging over the edge. When we got to the shack the dog came running out and she managed to get him into the back of the van, though she got bitten in the struggle.

'When we got to the Kaštela, she bathed him and brushed him and treated his wounds with medicated powder. She had to shut him out in the loggia when she went to bed because he didn't seem to like being inside, and howled all night keeping everyone awake. Then the following day a man, looking like a tramp, turned up on a bicycle and started shouting at Zenia for stealing his dog. Apparently he was living in the shack. Zenia started shouting at him for not looking after the dog properly and Concetta had to step in between them to stop them fighting.' Freddi waved a hand towards the cooker. 'She was magnificent. And then she gave the man a few glasses of slivovitz and some lunch in the kitchen and he wobbled off down the road on his bicycle with the dog running behind. We all breathed a sigh of relief.'

'Apparently he was living up there wild,' Ludo said, 'both man and dog. Concetta knew about him.'

Concetta nodded. She put down her spoon for a moment. 'He was the only survivor of the massacre – a small child lying underneath his mother, shot in the leg but still alive among all those dead people. They say he lay there for three days before he was found. God knows what that does to someone.' She crossed herself. There was silence in the room as if everyone was remembering something uncomfortable. Concetta turned back to the stove, picked up her spoon and resumed stirring. Alex finished her drink and stood up.

'I was wondering if the letters had been found yet?'

No-one asked, 'What letters?' Concetta carried on stirring the pan; Ludo's eyes were on his drink.

Freddi suddenly looked weary. All the humour faded out of her face. 'I don't know. Why don't you go up to the studio and have a look? Toby's in there working – he'll show you.'

It seemed a good opportunity to talk to Toby about Zenia, if he was in the mood. Alex hoped he might be able to tell her something that would illuminate Zenia's life as an artist – the way she worked, her rhythms, her idiosyncrasies.

He was standing at the easel, just as Zenia had been standing earlier in the day. Under the harsh daylight bulb that hung from the ceiling Toby looked different, but it wasn't just the unflattering quality of the light. When Alex had encountered him around the Kaštela, he'd seemed slight, effeminate, self-effacing. But in front of the canvas, the sleeves of an old plaid shirt rolled up, brush in hand, he looked taller and more imposing – more at ease with himself, she decided. He looked round as she came in, saying nothing, just giving her a nod and turning his attention back to the painting.

Alex wandered round, searching the shelves, but it was obvious from the first glance that the box of letters wasn't there. As she moved behind Toby, Alex had a very clear view of the canvas he was working on. She was surprised to see what a unique style he had, dotted lines and flowing islands of colour, ochre, yellow, white and blue with a spot of red almost like an angry eye in one corner. He noticed her watching and stood to one side so that she could see clearly.

Alex said, 'It looks rather aboriginal. Does that offend you?'

'No, not at all. And yeah, that's where I started out. I love the way their lines flow – time lines, story lines, song lines – whatever you like to call them. There's an artist in Perth called Yamaroodo – I used to love to watch him paint. They stipple it on with a stick – but it's a ritual rather than a method of painting.'

Alex nodded towards a group of canvases stacked against the wall. 'Are these yours or Zenia's?'

'Mine. Zenia's sponsoring an exhibition for me in London in March. There isn't much time left.'

'For you to finish these, or for Zenia?'

'For her. It's almost unbearable. She's getting worse every day.' He put down the brush he was holding. 'It means there's a lot of time for me to do my own work. When I first came it was really busy. I used to prime her canvases, wash her brushes, prepare the paint, make sure there was enough of everything – but she doesn't paint much anymore.'

Alex remembered the scene she'd witnessed that morning.

'Freddi says it's the motor neurone disease. Her brain won't transmit the messages – it's the same when she's walking. Some days she can barely shuffle. It's painful to watch – when you've seen her striding around with such fantastic energy and you see her now…

'She used to go to London or New York in the summer months, when it's hot here and full of tourists – but she came back after a couple of weeks last year and this year she didn't go at all. She's always loved travelling and meeting new people, but now the stress of it only makes her worse. She gets confused and then frightened and miserable.'

'So you're here all the time?'

'I come and go a bit – packing up stuff for her exhibitions and then making sure they hang it properly. Zenia's also agreed to some limited edition prints, so I've organised those. The first year I was here I catalogued her work – that was awesome! She had things everywhere and there were no lists or proper records of who had what. She'd lent some pictures to a stately home in England, years ago, and then forgotten them. They were just hanging on to them – really spat the dummy when Freddi wrote asking for them back! I guess that's how the rich get rich.'

'Do you manage to sell much yourself?'

'Yeah – one or two. It's pretty tough at the moment. But I sell a lot of stuff down in Pula and Rovinj during the summer – commercial tourist pics and that buys the canvases and the paint.'

Toby was obviously paying his way here, whatever Martin thought of him.

'How did you meet Zenia?'

'I went to an art college in Perth, just about the time Zenia's agent Andrew Kir – have you met him? – he was there sorting out a travelling exhibition that'd just arrived from Sydney. I was mad to get to Europe, but I didn't have the money. Anyway, I happened to be in the gallery when he was there and he talked to me and I asked him about scholarships and things like that and he told me that Zenia needed an assistant – bed and board and pocket money. He warned me Zenia wasn't easy to work with, but I jumped at it and the next month I was here.'

'Do you ever go back home?'

'My parents haven't spoken to me since I told them I was gay. My grandparents were Swedish immigrants – Lutheran, pretty traditional. There are a lot of places in Australia that put up invisible notices – no gays, no blacks, no cripples. That's just how it is. Where I come from it's hicksville – a bit like where Jolene was brought up.'

'Where does Jolene come from?'

'Somewhere in Canada I think, from her accent anyway. She doesn't talk about it much but I gather it was pretty tough. Living in the back of beyond and a lot of religion. She's not in touch with her folks either.' He paused to wipe his hands on a rag that wafted turpentine across the room and then he gave Alex a very deliberate look. 'Don't go assuming that just because I'm gay, and Zenia is, the rest of them are too. It's complicated. Kelly and Jolene aren't what they seem at all.'

'Oh?'

But he didn't offer to tell her, and Alex liked him for that. What was private could stay private with Toby. Instead he said, 'Would you like to see what I think is Zenia's best work?'

Alex nodded and followed him out onto the staircase and up onto the next landing. The painting was full length on the wall, lit obliquely by an oblong window cut into the stonework. The background was of forests and hills with churches and houses, recognisably Istrian, in the style of the medieval and renaissance periods. Against this intricate landscape a figure was painted, the paint applied so thickly it was almost sculpted onto the canvas. Alex could sense the muscular arm dragging the paintbrush here and there, with occasional violent movements that ploughed the paint into deep furrows. The figure was half human, half four-legged beast. The human part had breasts and long hair and carried a bow and arrow, strung ready to shoot something just out of the frame. The animal part was rearing up on its hind legs as if to wheel around and gallop off as soon as the arrow had been shot. The pose seemed deliberately staged to reveal the male genitalia painted in full view of anyone who stood in front of the canvas. The face of this androgynous beast was drawn in an expression somewhere between grief, savagery and anger. There was a real tension in it and an energy that pricked the hairs on the back of Alex's neck.

'It's called The Centauress,' Toby said.

Alex couldn't think of anything to say, except to

stand in front of it and look. Then, as she turned to go back down the stairs Toby said, 'You wrote about Caravaggio, didn't you? I read your book when I was a student. You really made the connection between the man and the painting. That's why I told Freddi you'd be OK.'

13

Alex had first become interested in art during those long hot days of July and August when New York's concrete canyons become stifling voids choked with exhaust fumes and the air is too heavy to breathe. After her marriage to Steve they had lived in an old brownstone apartment block that had a wonderful location but no air conditioning. The heat made Alex feel dizzy and sick.

As that first summer advanced she found herself escaping more and more into the cool spaces of the Metropolitan or the Guggenheim, reading narratives in paint; the ravishing excesses of Raphael, the inexplicable colour symphonies of Rothko. But it was faces that Alex was drawn to most, portraits of unknown people staring out of the canvases, daring her to imagine their lives. When she began to write again, after the transatlantic shift, it wasn't women's magazine features, it was articles on art, edgy reviews of new shows, cameos of painters' lives, that she produced.

'It isn't the life that's important,' Steve would say, scathingly. 'It's the work.' It was something they disagreed on strongly. In New York they disagreed a lot.

Many of their arguments were caused by Alex's mother-in-law. Steve adored her with the uncritical affection of the only child. Alex found her possessive, neurotic, and endlessly controlling. Even though she lived a two hour train ride out of New York, she seemed to be able to control their relationship from a distance. She insisted that Alex and Steve had her car, although they didn't want an old-style Cadillac that cornered like a tank and had a boot big enough to live in, gas guzzling, impossible to park. It was the same with the furniture. Alex wanted to choose her own, but how could she defeat the argument that it was stupid to spend money they didn't have on things that could be given for free. The final insult was the new kitchen in the apartment. It was to be a wedding present. Alex spent hours in showrooms looking at stainless steel and marble work-surfaces and cupboards that slid noiselessly shut on their own. After weeks of poring over catalogues she finally chose what she wanted. But when her mother-in-law went to the showroom with Steve to pay for it, deliberately, so Alex thought, at a time when she had to be somewhere else, Steve's mother replaced some of the units that Alex had chosen with others she thought would be more suitable.

'You wouldn't have liked it. It would have looked all wrong in here. Much better to have the other model,' she told her by way of explanation.

Alex was incandescent with rage she couldn't express. She went to bed and cried for hours. Gradually, over the months, the apartment filled up with old family furniture that had come from Belgium with Steve's grandparents – ugly continental gothic that wouldn't have been out of place in Dracula's hunting lodge. Alex hated it, but was made to feel an ungrateful bitch who'd rather spend her son's hard-gotten money than accept a gift. 'Look what I'm doing for you,' was the subtext of every conversation.

'Look, just say yes,' Steve would plead. 'It isn't

worth the hassle.' Anything for a quiet life. But peace was never achievable. There was always some other point of discord. Steve's mother disapproved of Alex having a career, which was illogical, since she also seemed to resent every penny he might spend supporting her. It was no secret that she would have preferred Steve to marry the girl he'd been engaged to before he left for England, and she always seemed to know exactly what Maggie would have thought or felt on any given occasion. 'Maggie would never have done that' was a phrase Alex came to know well.

By the time Alex had showered and changed for dinner she felt tired. The day had been emotionally draining and she was not looking forward to having to socialise with the Antonellis at dinner. As she dried her hair in front of the mirror, there was a discreet knock on the door.

It was Antonio Antonelli. 'I do hope I'm not inconveniencing you. May I come in?'

In the room he looked taller and broader, filling the small space with the scent of his cologne. Alex wondered what he was here for – men like Antonelli didn't pay casual visits. To fill the silence she said, 'I'm sorry I don't have anything to offer you to drink.'

'Please don't disturb yourself.'

He wandered around looking at things, picking objects up, putting them down, examining the shelf above the fireplace, the trompe d'oeil on the ceiling. 'Of course it is all very shoddy,' he said. 'Well meant, but not quite up to standard. These days the finish has to be very good to attract the tourists with money. They are no longer content with "quaint". But of course Zenia won't listen. If I had this place – what could I not do with it!'

'And do you think you'll get it?' Alex's boldness surprised even herself. Antonio's eyebrows rose sharply.

'I am the most senior member of the family apart from my cousin Angelina, who is only a relative by marriage. Why should I not inherit?' He waved away her question. 'Oh I know there is talk of a trust. Signora Thompson would love to get her hands on the Kaštela. She sickens me. Zenia is surrounded by dependents.' He paused in the middle of the floor and pressed his fingertips delicately onto the table, making a kind of pyramid. 'Of course her judgement is not good – she has often been ill-advised – and now that she has this illness…'

He gave Alex a very direct look. 'Pardon my asking so frank a question, but how much are they paying you as an advance?'

She was startled. 'I don't know. Nothing's settled yet…'

'Then let me make you a proposition. Whatever they offer you, I will double it – on one condition.'

'And what is that?'

'That the book is never written.'

There was absolute silence for moment. Alex could hear someone, possibly Martin, whistling in the distance and a bell chimed the hour down in the valley.

'I can't do that.' Alex tried not to let her voice betray the anger she felt.

The eyebrows went up again.

'It is not many people who would turn down a substantial sum of money for doing nothing,' he said. He took a small square of card out of his inside pocket. 'Here's my number. If you think better of it, let me know. There would be a lot of people who would be glad to have the project dropped.'

Alex thought about the American author Ludo had talked about and wondered if Antonio had made her a similar proposition. She made herself smile at him and slipped the card into her pocket. His hand was soft and papery to the touch as she shook it. He leaned over to kiss her first on one cheek and then on the other and Alex caught the acrid smell of alcohol on his breath.

'I hope you will contact me,' he said on the doorstep and he gave a little bow of the head before turning and making his way back to the house. Was he serious, Alex wondered? Did he really mean to offer her a large amount of money? No-one had ever tried to bribe her not to write a book before. More than anything she wondered why?

Dinner was a rather strained affair. Zenia was quiet. She insisted on having Gianfranco next to her and occasionally she said something to him in a low voice. On the other side of the table, halfway down and caught in the crossfire of Antonio and Caterina's conversation, Alex couldn't hear anything that they were saying and was ashamed of herself for trying. Suddenly writing the biography of a living subject seemed like eavesdropping on someone's life.

Something had happened to upset Freddi. Her cheeks were patched with colour and her eyes were unusually bright, but she kept up a facade of lively, inconsequential chatter. Antonio had bloodshot eyes and the relaxed, expansive air that comes from having drunk too much. He'd brought a bottle of grappa with him when he arrived, the kind that has a whole pear in the body of the bottle and Alex noticed that, although he was now drinking wine, the level of the grappa on the sideboard had already dipped below the plump belly of the pear.

He was asking Freddi what kind of summer season they'd just had.

'Only so-so. The Americans still haven't come back. It's all the fault of the Homeland War.' She sighed. 'This place was wonderful before – now it's altered beyond recognition. There are empty houses everywhere. All those beautiful hotels on the seafront in Pula – full of refugees just squatting in them because there's nowhere else to go. It'll take years before the tourists come back.'

'I don't understand it,' Caterina said. 'Everything was fine under Tito. Why did it become so violent after he died?'

'It's all because of what happened in 1945,' Ludo said. 'History begets history. Do people not remember?'

'Some of us,' Antonio said, 'have very long memories. Istria should have stayed with Italy. It belonged to Venice – they should never have put it into Yugoslavia.'

'Ah. But you vote for the Lega Nord,' Ludo responded. 'We are Croats here – not Italians. Actually it is all the fault of the British and the Americans – dividing countries after the war like slicing a cake – and afterwards putting their hands behind their backs and refusing to clean up their own shit.'

Everyone laughed.

'*Inculare tutti gli Americani!*' Ludo said, holding up his glass at the bottom of the table. His arm wavered uncertainly in the air and Alex wondered how much more plum slivovitz had been consumed in the kitchen after she had left.

Gianfranco broke off his conversation with Zenia and raised his glass in the toast.

'I'm afraid you won't get the American tourists back until they've eliminated the terrorist threat,' Caterina said. 'They're all so totally paranoid.'

'Well, wouldn't you be?' Freddi asked with some spirit. 'If 9/11 had happened in Rome, or Milan?'

'But it wouldn't,' Gianfranco insisted. 'It could only have happened in America, except that the Americans were so self-satisfied they couldn't see that. All those years of economic colonialism, the whole world revolving round their greed. They had it coming to them.'

'Are you saying those people deserved to die?' The words had leapt out of Alex's mouth before she realised she'd spoken.

Gianfranco turned to look at her. He seemed to be opening his mouth to carry on arguing.

'And what about my daughter? Ten years old – did she deserve to die? My husband. And all those other innocent people?' Alex found herself standing up, one hand on the back of her chair staring at him.

There was an appalled silence. And suddenly Alex realised what she'd done. She had tossed her own personal tragedy into their dinner party like an explosive device, shattering all their tranquillity. It was unforgivable. Alex could see them looking at her. They were shocked, at this moment, but soon they would all be feasting on her grief at second hand, saying to friends, 'I know a woman who…' or, 'I met a woman last night whose daughter…'

It was unbearable. Alex turned and rushed out of the door, through the loggia and out onto the terrace in the darkness, misjudging the distance and colliding with the wall. For a moment she stood paralysed in the shadow just outside the chapel with her face against the stone. Then she heard shuffling footsteps in the darkness behind her.

'Alessandra?' It was Zenia.

'I shouldn't have said anything. I'm really sorry. It's

not something I usually talk about.'

'Why not?' She put her hand on Alex's arm. 'You must talk about it. How else is your daughter to be remembered? If you do not, no-one will ever mention her name and it will be as if she never existed. She is part of your life and you must not deny her.'

'It hurts so much I'm not sure I can go on living.'

'Come here,' she said. 'Come here.'

She held Alex in her arms like a mother, except that it was something Alex's own mother hadn't done since she was a child. Alex could feel the rough linen of Zenia's tunic against her bare arm, her belt buckle digging into her hip.

'Darling,' Zenia said, touching Alex's cheek, 'nothing is as bad as that. Nothing. Everything fades and there are only memories in the end like dried flowers. Painful memories at first, then not so painful, until at last there is only the memory of pain.' Alex could feel her pause, draw a breath and then another and then she began to speak again in a softer more intimate tone.

'Sit down here with me.' Zenia drew her towards the marble bench overlooking the valley where the lights of the villages below were twinkling in and out of the trees. Zenia pulled Alex down beside her, still cradling her tightly. 'I am going to tell you something about myself, something you must know if you are to write my book. I have been waiting for the right moment, to know if I can trust you. But I know now that I can.' She pushed Alex slightly away from her so that she could look into her face. 'I am not going to tell you tonight, because you are too upset and I am too tired. But tomorrow – if you come and see me tomorrow, we can talk.'

Alex put her head down on Zenia's chest again and

could feel her rough bony hand stroking her hair.

'You have lost your child. Nothing can ever take away the tragedy of that, but you mustn't let the bad things make you feel it is not worth living.'

A wind got up in the night, rattling the leaves of the lemon tree together like someone flicking through the pages of a book. The cypress was having a violent conversation with itself outside Alex's window. Then the rain came, heavy drops she could almost count, faster and faster until they all merged into a waterfall of sound, sluicing from the roof to the ground below, gurgling and rushing in the open gutters. Behind the wind came the thunder and then flashes of neon strobing the room. Alex gave up trying to sleep and leant her elbows on the windowsill to watch the storm cross towards the sea.

Gianfranco had come to her door last night after she'd gone back to her room, and when Alex wouldn't open the door to him, he had stood outside and apologised and explained and pleaded. 'Why didn't you tell me?' His voice had cracked. 'If I didn't know, how could I know not to say anything that would hurt you?' Finally he had become angry. 'If you don't tell people, you can't blame them for putting their feet in their mouths.' Alex heard his footsteps walking away and in the distance, a door slammed.

Why hadn't she told him when she had the chance? That moment sitting in the woods. She should have trusted him. There was regret, like heartburn under her ribcage.

He had seemed to be a good man, *molto simpatico*, and she had rejected him spectacularly. There was no way back from that. Alex' fingernails bit into the heel of her thumb.

And then she could see the other side of the page, *verso*, he was insensitive, prejudiced, he had only been nice to her because he was an Italian man. They couldn't help themselves. What was it Lenka had said? 'All the Antonellis are a danger to women.' Had he charmed her too? Alex remembered the way Lenka's face had lit up when she had heard his footsteps in the loggia. Remembered Jolene's snide remark.

Soon, what bit deepest and hurt most, was that she had almost trusted him.

The next morning it was cold, really cold. Alex shivered out of bed and her toes curled automatically as they made contact with the icy terracotta floor. Almost as if he could hear what she was thinking, Martin arrived with a portable gas heater just as Alex was filling the kettle.

'You need a *bombola* on days like this.' He made a great show of linking up the cylinder and lighting the heater with a bang and a pungent smell of gas. Then he hesitated, shuffling his feet. Eventually he said, 'I'm sorry,' very softly. 'Freddi told me.'

Alex wasn't sure what she replied, but after he'd gone she went back to bed and cried. How was she to get up and face everyone? Seeing that in their eyes – that mixture of pity and relief. Pity for the person in front of them and relief that the burden wasn't theirs; that rather doleful expression people put on when confronted with grief – the special tone of voice adopted by commentators at the scene of disasters.

After about an hour, Alex made herself get up. She showered, dressed, opened the lap top and arranged her face into what she hoped was a suitable expression to look at the world. There was knock on the door, more tentative than Martin's, and Alex froze. But then Freddi's brisk voice called out, 'Alex? Are you there? I've got something for you.'

Alex opened the door and Freddi was standing outside with a cardboard box.

'Martin found these in Antonio's room, apparently. So I thought I'd bring them over to you straight away.'

She came in and put the box on the table. 'The Antonellis have all gone, you'll be glad to know. But Gianfranco was in quite a state when he left.' Her eyes had an element of accusation in them.

Alex shrugged. 'Did you know Antonio tried to bribe me not to write the book?'

'No. But it doesn't surprise me. God knows why though. Something to do with his complicated business affairs probably, not wanting the family name in the public eye.'

'I turned him down. He was a bit shocked.'

Freddi laughed. She looked very young. Today her dark hair was drawn back from her face by a velvet hair band and she didn't look a day older than eighteen. 'I came to tell you that Zenia wants to see you when you've got time. She's in bed and I hope she's going to stay there today. She's been overdoing it while everyone's been here.'

There was a pause.

'I'm sorry about last night,' Alex said.

Freddi shook her head. 'They were all out of order.' She looked directly into Alex's face. 'It must have been hard for you. Very hard. Was she your only child?'

'Yes.'

'And your husband?'

'We were divorced, but we were still friends. I think maybe I hoped…'

Freddi put a hand on Alex's arm and squeezed. 'I'm sorry,' she said.

When she'd gone, Alex opened the box. It contained the missing letters, but there was something not quite right. The first box had been full of haphazard layers of paper and envelopes, just as they must have been slung casually in the box over time; this one was carefully ordered in tidy rows. She took one of the letters out and looked at it. The paper had been folded neatly, edge to edge, to fit the envelope exactly. But as she opened it the brown lines made by age and dust across the handwriting, lines that marked the original folds, became visible. And these fold lines were not neat at all, but random, as if the letter had been stuffed back in its envelope with little regard for its condition. These letters had recently been read by someone. Antonio and Caterina? It was possible. But Alex felt that Antonio was too clever to have left them so conveniently where they would incriminate him. But if not him, who else would have an interest in censoring the information the box might hold? There was no way of telling whether any of the letters had been taken out, but Alex felt quite certain that the box no longer contained whatever it was the searcher hadn't wanted her to know.

Zenia's bedroom was like a cave. The shutters had been partially closed against the stormy wind, plunging the room into twilight. The stone walls were almost obliterated by kilim rugs that twitched in the draughts and nails had been recklessly hammered through the rugs to hang pictures, wood carvings and other objects. A pair of wooden puppets from eastern Europe, a Japanese kimono painted with storks against a setting sun, an African mask – these were only some of the things Alex could see as she glanced round. A wood-burning stove in the corner radiated heat. The air smelled of hot metal, musty fabric and stale body odour. Zenia's bed was against the wall, a big four poster with faded hangings looped back and an enormous wooden chest at the foot piled with cushions and books. She was propped up at the head of the bed, hair tousled, a woollen shawl around her shoulders, and she patted the bed beside her to invite Alex to sit down.

'How are you today?' she asked, and added, 'I'm not being polite – you must tell me how you really are.'

'I'm OK. Not good, but alive.'

Zenia looked into Alex's eyes, staring inside her head in that disconcerting way. 'Yes,' she nodded. 'I can see that you are.'

Alex waited, not wanting to prompt her. It was Zenia's story she had come for, not her own.

'So,' Zenia said at last. 'I am going to tell you about me.' There was a fractional pause and then she began abruptly. 'I was born a hermaphrodite – do you know what that is?'

Alex stared at her, momentarily shocked. When Zenia had talked about being an androgyne, Alex had thought she meant simply being bi-sexual. Hermaphrodite wasn't a word she associated with the human animal. Zenia was waiting for an answer. 'Someone who is both sexes?'

'The conjunction of Hermes and Aphrodite. When I am a baby, my parents think – a little imperfection – it will go away – she will grow out of it. But it did not go away. Then when I reach puberty and I should become a woman this thing between my legs begins to grow and suddenly I do not know what I am – a man or a woman.'

Alex had heard of children who were born of indeterminate gender, but knew nothing about the subject and she'd certainly never met anyone who confessed to being between genders. 'It must have been difficult for you,' was all she could think of to say.

Zenia closed her eyes, still in some private space inside her head, and went on talking.

'It was my secret and it explained a lot to me about how I felt inside. But it was also confusing and there was no-one I could talk to about it. I would have been all right like that, I think. I was getting used to my own strange body, but then someone told my mother that I was not the same as other girls. I have always thought that it was my cousin Antonio. I can imagine him saying the words that betrayed me; "Aunt Natalia, why does Zenia do pee-pee like a boy." We used to swim together – Bernardo, Antonio and I – and I think he spied on me. One day my mother came to my bedroom when I was still in bed and she pulled down the bedclothes and wrenched my nightdress up even though I tried to stop her. Her face was like fury. She looked at me as if I was something shameful and dirty.'

Zenia stopped, clamping her lips firmly together. When Alex looked at her she could see that her eyes were flickering as if the story was still going on in her head, even though she had stopped speaking. Her face was distorted with pain.

'Are you all right, Zenia? Can I get something for you?'

Zenia took a gasping breath. 'What happened was

terrible. Terrible. Even remembering…' She shook her head. The whole of her body seemed to heave and tremble. She closed her eyes.

Alex was alarmed. She stood up to leave. Should she get Freddi?

Zenia's eyes fluttered open again. 'I'm sorry. I can't tell you any more now. Perhaps… This afternoon?'

Alex picked up her notebook and MP3 recorder. 'Yes, of course. I've tired you out. Freddi will be so cross with me!'

'Listen,' Zenia said, reaching across the bed to grasp Alex's hand. Her eyes bored into Alex's. 'Before you go, there is something I need to say to you that is important. One thing I have learned through all this pain and muddle that has been my life. You must go back; to the place where your daughter died – you must look your fear in the face, so that it can no longer control your life. It is only by going back that we can make sense of things, however painful it is. If you do not allow yourself to remember, how are you ever going to understand?'

Alex's Notebook, October 2003

At the time I watched it for hours and hours, watching the towers miraculously restored only to be pierced again and again by the flying bombs. Watching their descent into a billion trillion airborne fragments. At first I tried to believe that Katy wasn't answering her mobile because the networks were jammed. And then, in desperation, I rang Steve's mother. A stranger answered the phone, but I could hear my mother-in-law sobbing in the background. And that was how I knew. The policeman who had come to tell her, also told me.

In every tragedy there is the accidental moment – choosing a particular seat on a train, turning down the wrong road, deciding to take a lift from the 89th floor – the arbitrary, pivotal moment that means destruction or survival.

Steve had been over in London on a business trip and he'd asked if he could take Katy back with him to New York for a week. Katy was really keen to go, since it meant time off school, which she currently hated. Steve wanted her to see his mother, playing the guilt card – "Katy's her only grandkid. She doesn't see enough of her." So I had waved my daughter off at Heathrow and we'd made arrangements for me to pick her up a week later. For three days I'd had ecstatic phone calls, as I moped around the empty flat. She'd been taken on the Amtrak train to her grandmother's house in New Jersey. Then they'd visited the Empire State building and gone shopping for presents on Fifth Avenue. Steve had even taken her to a show on Broadway – *Annie*. Katy's voice on the phone was almost incoherent with jet-lag and excitement. On the day of the hi-jackings she had gone with her father to the office to see where he worked. It was to be a special treat. He was going to take her up to the restaurant on the top floor and then afterwards they were going to go on the Staten Island ferry to look at the Statue of Liberty. He was showing her New York.

Lunch was something of an ordeal. Zenia remained in her room. She was sleeping, Freddi said. With the Antonellis gone, Kelly and Jolene were back at the foot of the table, next to a rather silent Toby, and Alex found herself opposite Lenka, who was frowning down at her plate and not speaking to anyone. Ludo and Freddi talked briskly about the olive oil which Martin had just picked up from the *Frantoio*, and although Kelly and Jolene were whispering to each other across the table, Alex could sense them straining their ears to listen to the conversation, presumably to pick up whatever gossip they could. Concetta sat at the bottom of the table, convenient for the kitchen. Sometimes when Alex glanced around, she caught Concetta looking at her, but as soon their eyes met, she looked away.

Afterwards, as Alex walked back to her room, Martin came towards her. 'You need to come to the office. There's someone on the phone who wants to speak to you.'

The office was a low, dark room that had probably once been a *cantina*. There were racks on the wall that had been converted into shelves to hold bedlinen, bath towels and boxes of toilet rolls, and in the middle there was a desk with a computer where Lenka sat peering at the screen. The telephone receiver was resting on the desk and Lenka made a point of going out of the door as Alex picked it up, though she was aware of her just outside, murmuring to Martin.

'Hello,' she said. 'This is Alessandra Forbes.'

A thin, reedy, but still autocratic voice said, 'My name is Angelina Battista de Branganza. I am the widow of Zenia's brother Bernardo. I have heard about you from Cesare Antonelli.' The voice was old, with a slight tremor, but very precise. 'I would very much like to meet you,' she said. 'There are things we should talk about if you are going to write this book.'

Freddi came into the bedroom while Alex was packing and hovered nervously just inside the door. 'I'm afraid I've had second thoughts about the biography,' she said. 'I think Zenia's making a big mistake.'

Alex faced her across the room. The suitcase lay open, half-packed on the chair beside the bed. 'What's happened to change your mind? Is this something to do with Antonio?'

Freddi shook her head.

'Then why, Freddi?'

'It's going to cause so much trouble. I realised when there was that muddle over the letters. You have to stop, Alex. This biography should never have been agreed on. It's all Jane's fault. Putting Zenia's life out there to be trampled on by people who don't understand. You shouldn't be writing it.'

'But I've promised Zenia – it seems to be very important to her. Besides, if I refuse to write the book, Jane would never forgive me.' Having already broken one contract, it would be end of Alex's career if she walked away from this now. Word would get round the publishing world that she was unreliable. 'I'd never be allowed to write a book ever again.'

Freddi nodded reluctantly. 'I can see that. And I know how much this means for Zenia. But she hasn't considered what it will mean for the other people in her life. She's always been like that – single-minded, I suppose you'd call it. It just hasn't occurred to her that her biography, if it's published, will affect the people around her.'

Alex felt troubled. So many people who'd been important in Zenia's life were still alive. She had Zenia's permission to be frank about her own life, but Freddi had a valid point. What right had Zenia to expose the lives of others to public scrutiny? Freddi was leaning against the wall watching her.

'I've committed myself to writing it now, Freddi, and I don't think I can go back on it. But I will be very, very careful about what I write. Trust me.'

'You promised Zenia you'd tell the truth.'

'Yes, and I will. But if that truth is going to cause problems for others, then I'll think very carefully before including it.' Even as she said it, Alex was thinking about Antonio. How much of his story was she going to include? If he was prepared to bribe her not to write it, then there were obviously details she hadn't uncovered yet that he didn't want her, or anyone else, to know.

Freddi ran her hand through her hair. 'I suppose I'm going to have to trust your discretion. But I know I'm going to hate the book. I'm afraid it's going to destroy my own view of Zenia – my memories of her. You'll put some other person in front of me that isn't her – or at least not the Zenia I know.'

Alex remembered Martin's comments about Zenia being different to everyone. Her biography wasn't going to please them all. 'I'm sorry Freddi. I'll do my best to be as honest and discreet as I can be. That's all I can promise.'

Freddi didn't reply. She turned and went out of the door without looking back.

'The only way to arrive in Venice is by boat,' Gianfranco had said, and Alex, standing on the deck, could see that he was right.

The ferry was late, edging into the lagoon just as the evening mists were beginning to gather. Stucco palazzos, terracotta towers and marble domes rose out of the water like mirages, as if they had grown from the sea bed. The whole of Venice was a miracle, veiled in shifting fog, lit first here and now there by the orange sun settling towards a dark bar of cloud near the horizon.

Alex took a Vaporetto 41 to Madonna del Orto and walked along the canal towards the hotel, trailing her weekend case behind her. At the junction of the Corte Cavallo, just before the bridge, her path was blocked by a pile of furniture stacked on the footpath. Two men, in the orange overalls of the commune were loading it into a flat-bottomed boat. Alex paused while they manipulated a table up the ramp, its legs towards the sky. Through the open rectangle of the door on her left Alex could see into the apartment. The shutters were closed over the windows, but one of them must have been slightly ajar allowing a shaft of winter light to slant across the marble tiles.

A white-haired woman was sitting on a wooden

chair in the middle of the empty space. She sat with her legs apart, the skirt folded up over her knees and a shawl around her shoulders, with a look of total resignation on her face. A brown tidemark on the wall of the room about a foot from the floor registered the repeated level of '*Acqua Alta*'. The legs of the carved dining chairs stacked up beside the canal were similarly stained.

Alex found the Calle Loredana easily and the small hotel, the Fiore del Mare, which Freddi had recommended. It too had its feet in the water and a plaque halfway up the wall to mark the level of the *Acqua Alta* of 1966. A young, blonde woman who spoke bad Italian and had the cheekbones of Eastern Europe wrote Alex's name in the book, swiped her credit card through the machine and gave her the key to room 231. There was a small lift with an ancient metal grille. The way it wheezed its way down into the lobby convinced Alex that it might be safer to walk up the stairs. The landings and corridors were lined with old Venetian furniture, hung with Murano glass chandeliers, all dusty and some broken. It smelled of mildew. But the room, with its view out over the canal, was large and there was a desk under the window and a gigantic bed carved and gilded, resting on lions' paw feet. Against the walls were carved chests and wardrobes big enough to sleep in. The bathroom was smaller, with antique fittings and black and white tiles. The taps coughed like elderly asthmatics. There was no shower.

Alex ate in a tourist café near Ospedale, went to look at Vivaldi's house, the nunnery where inconvenient babies were posted through a hole in the wall, and then returned to the hotel to while away what was left of the evening. She read through all her notes about the complicated relationships of the de Braganza and Antonelli families and then lay on the bed listening to the recording Zenia had made for her the night before.

You ask about my cousin Cesare? The eldest son of my cousin Antonio from his first marriage, so a second cousin I suppose, but he has always seemed more like a nephew, and not one of my favourites. He is a pedant. Bookish. Rather sly. Going with women without his mother knowing. Elvira was a fool of course and probably still is. She was the kind of woman men make into what they want – the daughter of a Venetian politician. Antonio thought he could use his connections by the marriage, but after the war things were very turbulent and Elvira's father didn't last long and then Antonio lost interest in the girl. She bored him. After Antonio divorced Elvira, she put everything into her child. Italian mothers are the worst – they turn their sons into little gods. Always the women take second place. In my family there were three women on their own – my own mother with Bernardo, his wife Angelina with Salvatore, and then Elvira and her son Cesare. What chance did those boys have?

When they are grown up Cesare becomes the model son, but still he has a secret life. And there is no hope for Salvatore, brought up by Angelina and my mother. He runs wild until he kills himself with drink and drugs and fast cars and too many women. There is somewhere out there a child of his – I think. There was talk of an abortion – but I would not give him the money. I have tried to find out what happened to the girl and the child, but I can find nothing. And Cesare – who knows what things he keeps hidden from his mother? A mistress at the very least! He deals in books – fine art and military history – but there are people who tell me that you can get books of another kind from him if you know how to ask. He once showed me a volume of 17th century etchings of an erotic nature – and he told me that it would fetch more than a hundred million lire. He showed it to me because there was a drawing in it of a man-woman – both sexes in one. It was the first time I had ever seen anyone like myself. But in the book she was placed with the freaks – women with three breasts, men with big penises like donkeys.

He used to paint, you know – oil paintings so small and fine you needed a microscope to see the detail. In the Middle Ages he would have earned a fortune painting miniatures. But he will never paint people – always landscapes. I think he is not comfortable with people. Venice is very corrupt. Cesare lives in its shadows. And he has two mothers now – Elvira and Angelina. I think that Angelina will leave him all her money – my mother's money – when she dies. That is one reason why I won't leave him anything of mine. If there was a child – that might be different. There is a great lack of children in my family. Caterina for instance – she has none – whether it is because she won't or can't have them, no-one knows – but that is why her husbands keep divorcing her. An Italian man wants children. I feel sorry for her because of this.

The following morning at eleven found Alex outside Cesare's house on the corner of Calle D. Locande. It was a big, brown palazzo with its door sills in the canal water. There was a tidemark halfway up the wall and the bottom panel of the door was already rotting through. On the right-hand frame there was a row of brass bell pushes with circular microphones beside them. The one at the top had a label behind the glass which read 'Antonelli'. When

Alex pressed it, a disembodied voice enquired about her identity, and then the massive door clicked open to reveal a dark, cavernous hallway that smelled of the lagoon, mud and rotting shellfish, mixed with cooking smells and the pungent odour of an un-neutered tom cat. The marble mosaic tiles of the floor rattled underfoot. Alex pushed a plastic switch and a dim bulb somewhere overhead illuminated peeling walls, two bicycles leaning against the tide-marked panelling, some wooden boxes stacked on top of each other, and a child's pushchair. In the centre a gigantic oak staircase spiralled upwards out of sight. Alex followed it up to the fourth floor, where a door on the landing was open and a man was waiting for her.

Cesare Antonelli was of medium height, a grey man who looked almost as old as his father. As Alex shook hands with him she noticed that he was well-groomed, with neat fingernails and eyebrows, clothes not new but beautifully kept. A slight tear at the edge of the breast pocket of his jacket had been finely feather-stitched.

Alex followed Cesare across another echoing, chilly, marble-floored hallway, through double doors into a long room with three windows facing out over the rooftops of Venice. There were marble fireplaces at either end, topped by ornate gilt mirrors, but the silvering had blistered on the mirrors and the furniture that cluttered the room was shabby. At the left-hand end of the room a portable gas heater burned in the fireplace and three chairs were drawn up in front of it. A woman, who had been sitting in one of them, stood up as Alex and Cesare came in.

'My Aunt Angelina,' Cesare said, extending an arm towards her.

Alex wasn't sure what she'd expected Angelina to be like; voices don't always sound like their owners. Angelina was short; her head only came up to Alex's shoulder. She had strong white hair that sprung from her temples and the coarse, sallow skin of her cheeks was deeply grooved. As she came towards Alex, holding out her hand, her expression was also a surprise. So many older Italian women exuded resignation, an air of being beaten down by fate. Angelina's eyes were bold and direct as she held Alex's gaze, and her facial expression signalled that this was someone to be wary of, not someone easily intimidated.

'I am Signora de Braganza,' she said, as she took Alex's hand in a solid grip. Angelina was expensively dressed in a tweed suit with velvet lapels and she wore a great deal of heavy gold jewellery, but she lacked elegance. She was what Alex's Yorkshire-born mother would have called 'stout', with broad shoulders and a thick, muscular neck. Alex's lips twitched as she remembered what Zenia had said about her. 'She has the legs of a mule – and she is as strong as one. *Contadina!* It is her peasant blood – she will live for ever.'

There was a moment of awkward silence as Alex sat down in the chair that Cesare pulled forward for her, on the other side of the fireplace, opposite Angelina.

'You would like coffee?' he asked.

'Please.' Alex didn't really want another coffee, but felt it would be impolite to refuse.

Cesare went out of the room, presumably towards the kitchen.

Angelina's eyes were on Alex. Sharp, dark eyes, not particularly friendly.

'So,' she said, as soon as the door had shut on Cesare. 'How did you find my sister-in-law?'

'Signora de Braganza's in poor health,' Alex began, but was interrupted by Angelina raising an imperious hand

and saying, 'Signorina de Braganza,' with considerable emphasis on the 'signorina'. Apparently there could be only one Signora.

'Signorina de Braganza,' Alex began again to an approving nod, 'is often ill, but she seems quite lucid.'

'I have heard from Concetta Tonone that she is much worse lately.'

'You are in touch with Concetta?'

'Of course. She was my maid – she worked for Zenia's mother too before she was stolen by Zenia and taken off to Istria. I talk to her from time to time.'

A spy in the camp, Alex thought.

'Zenia has caused a lot of trouble for her family you know. She is very mischievous and very indiscreet. Her poor mother! One scandal after another.' Angelina paused and then went on. 'You know about her deformity?'

'Yes,' Alex said through gritted teeth. 'It has been a great tragedy for her.'

Angelina shrugged. 'Zenia loves it – if she did not have something exceptional about herself she would have had to invent something. She has always been so dramatic!' She leaned towards Alex as if to suggest that she was going to tell her something very important. 'Did you know that she went to Vienna during the war, to see a doctor in a Nazi clinic? Her mother wanted her to have treatment that would have helped her, you know. But she escaped and ran away.'

The shock that Alex felt must have been obvious. Angelina sat back abruptly.

'You see, there are things that she will not tell you – that is why you have to come to me. It is this business that has split the family, you know, because Zenia could not forgive the person who betrayed her condition to her mother.'

'Zenia told me that it was Antonio Antonelli.'

'Ha!' Angelina gave a snort of indignation. 'That is Zenia's own lie, because she doesn't want to tell you the truth. It was Bernardo who told her mother.'

'That's not what Zenia believes!'

'She knows the truth. Her mother Natalia told me that was the reason why Zenia caused the death of her brother – for revenge. Her mother did not speak to her for many years. It is why I do not speak to her. If Zenia caused Bernardo's death it was not something I could forgive.'

Alex' senses were reeling. She had understood that Bernardo had been killed by rival partisans, fascists, and a whole village had been massacred. How had Zenia been involved with that? As far as Alex was aware, she had shared his communist sentiments. Zenia loved Bernardo. She would never have done such a thing. But Angelina obviously believed otherwise.

'How did Zenia cause her brother's death?' Alex asked.

'It was Zenia's own mistake that betrayed Bernardo. They followed her. All her stupid ideas of heroism, of being a *communista* fighting against the *fascisti* as if she was a boy! She took messages to him, food he didn't need, wanted to join him, and they followed her. That was why Natalia hated her. Because she was responsible for Bernardo's death. Natalia thought it was revenge because he had betrayed her as a child.'

So this was the heart of the family feud. Zenia's mother believed that Zenia had caused her son's death in revenge for his betrayal and the events that followed, and Angelina also believed Zenia had been responsible for Bernardo's death. Yet Alex would have sworn any kind of oath that Zenia had been telling her the truth when she said that it was Antonio who had been responsible for telling her mother about her strange anatomy. Although when she thought hard, Alex realised that Zenia had said little about Bernardo's death and the circumstances of it.

Alex abruptly changed the subject. 'Do you live in Venice now?'

'In Trieste, but I stay here often. Cesare's mother Elvira and I have always been good friends. We have a common enemy in Cesare's father.'

'You don't get on with Signor Antonelli?'

'He was against my marriage to Bernardo and, when Bernardo died, he would not lift a finger to help us even though he was in a position to do so. He treated Elvira very badly too – first the women, then some strange business dealings, problems with money. Afterwards he left her to bring up a child on her own. So, we used to help each other.'

The door opened and a trolley clattered through, pushed by a young girl in black overalls. Cesare closed the door behind them. There was a coffee pot and a plate of small almond cakes.

The girl served them all rather clumsily, slopping coffee into the saucer of Alex's cup, banging the plate of cakes down onto the trolley. Eventually Cesare said, in very careful Italian, 'You can go now, Katya. Lunch in about an hour?'

There was another awkward silence until the girl had closed the door.

'I wanted to ask about Zenia's mother, Natalia,' Alex began carefully. 'You all knew her well. What was she like?'

Angelina shuddered. 'A terrible woman. Selfish and

not kind. She always had to be in charge of everything and everyone had to do what she wanted. Natalia treated me like a servant and she ruined my son. Whatever I said, she would say the opposite. Salvatore must not be disciplined – his spirit must be free – he must be indulged. He was all she had left of her Bernardo and, of course, of Bernardo's father. Whatever he wanted he must have. My Salvatore grew up to be just as selfish and wilful as his grandmother. And then, as you must know, when she died she left him all her money. He was nineteen. There was nothing we could do but to watch him destroy himself.' Her face had darkened. Alex noticed that her hands were clenched in her lap.

Cesare spoke. 'She was a formidable woman, my grandmother. Zenia takes after her in many ways. Two strong women.'

Alex smiled. 'Your father told me that you'd written a family history?'

'Ah.' Cesare rose from his chair. 'Yes. So now, if Aunt Angelina will excuse us, you must come to my study and I will show you the family tree.'

In the hallway, Cesare said, 'First, I would like to introduce you to my mother. She is very ill – a heart condition – so she is not well enough to talk, but she would like to meet you.'

He opened one of the big, cream and gilt-painted doors at the other side of the hall. The shutters on the window were almost closed, making the bedroom dark. A heavy wooden bed piled with blankets and quilts almost filled the room, leaving a narrow gap between the bed and the big carved wardrobe.

'This is my mother, Elvira Antonelli,' Cesare said, gesturing towards the frail grey figure propped up on the pillows.

Alex went towards the bed and took the bony hand that was held out to her. Plastic oxygen tubes were taped to Elvira's face and a black tank hissed quietly in the corner. There was an expression of endurance in the faded, almost opaque eyes. 'I am very pleased to meet you,' Alex said, as the hand was withdrawn from her own. Elvira murmured something inaudible, puffing her slack cheeks out with the effort.

'You must not disturb yourself, Mamma,' Cesare said. He adjusted the shawl around her shoulders and moved the water glass on the bedside table a fraction closer. 'Has Katya been in?' The old woman nodded and he seemed satisfied, turning to leave. 'I am going to show Signora Forbes the family history, Mamma. Then we will have lunch. We will leave you to rest.'

Cesare's office was a small room that might once have been a dressing room, positioned between Elvira's room and another. The connecting doors were obscured by bookcases on one side, but still visible on the other, behind Cesare's ornate mahogany desk, which was the size of a dining table. Cesare had spread out a selection of papers across it in anticipation of Alex's visit.

The de Braganza and Antonelli family tree was written in careful calligraphy on a roll of parchment, weighted down with books at either end to keep it open. The de Braganza's were on the right and the Antonellis on the left. The two family trees met in 1922 when Maria-Theresa de Braganza married Eduardo Antonelli. In the same year her brother Ferdinando married Natalia Romanova whose surname was enclosed in brackets with a question mark.

Alex put her finger on it. 'Why the brackets?'

'Because we're not certain who she was. On her marriage certificate she writes her name as Romanova, and she always told us that she was the child of an Italian opera singer and a Russian prince. There was a Russian in Vienna at the time called Caspar Romanchikov but there is no trace of a marriage, or of the birth of a Natalia Romanova or Romanchikova in 1897 in Vienna.' He paused. 'However... there is the birth of a Natalia Cerrutti, though the mother, Anna-Lisa Cerrutti, is an actress and there is no father listed on the birth certificate at all, but I think this may be closer to the truth.'

'Your father Antonio told me that Natalia's birth was utterly respectable, and the rumours about Russians and opera singers were only Zenia's inventions.'

'Ah, my father does not like to think of himself as related to such disreputable people. The Antonellis were solid merchant stock, and Maria-Theresa and Ferdinando de Braganza were the children of a Spanish aristocrat, their father, Zenia's grandfather,' Cesare tapped the parchment, 'had been an officer in the Austro-Hungarian army. He married a wealthy Italian shipowner's daughter from Genoa and eventually settled in Italy. My father chooses to make his connections with the male side of his mother's family, Zenia from the female.'

Cesare handed Alex a smaller roll of paper. 'I've made a copy for you, not all of it, but the parts that are important for you.'

'Thank you. I'm very grateful. The relationships are so complicated!'

There was a knock on the door and a voice in the hallway said, '*Pranzo*'. Cesare began to roll up the family tree. Alex looked around the cluttered room at the piles of books, the crowded shelves. Was there anything she should ask? Her brain was reeling with names and relationships. It made sense that Zenia's mother had been illegitimate, a woman with something to hide, someone Zenia could build legends around.

'Who was Caspar Romanchikov?'

'He was an attaché at the court in Vienna, a diplomat with a wife in St Petersburg.'

'So it is possible that he is Zenia's grandfather?'

'Possible.' Cesare's voice was dismissive. 'But there is not a strand of evidence to connect them.'

'The name? Romanova?'

'The correct female form would be Romanchikova. But it seems that Natalia used Romanova as a stage name.' He looked at his watch. 'Come, we must have lunch.'

The meal was served in the dining room at a round table with a white cloth and lots of rather tarnished silver and chipped Murano glass. Cesare ate delicately, Angelina heartily, mopping her plate with the bread. First Katya brought clear soup with the tiny pasta they called *tempestino*. The second course was a *bollito misto*, a bowl of vegetables cooked whole with the meat, courgettes, fennel, carrots, potatoes, and then the platter of boiled meat, small portions of pork, chicken and veal. Cesare carved the meat apart and Katya plonked the plates down vigorously in front of Alex and Angelina. Afterwards there was salad and a pecorino cheese. The dining room had the musty smell of a room rarely lived in and Alex wondered if they ate in the kitchen when they were alone. Katya was clumsy with the dishes, slopping food over the edges of the plates, and seemed unused to serving at table. Cesare frowned at her and Angelina made sharp comments whenever she left the room.

As they were drinking their coffee Angelina said, 'She is Slovakian, you know. There are no young Italian people in Venice any more. They have all left. They can't afford the prices for property here.'

'The Venetian population is just about to drop below sixty thousand for the first time,' Cesare said.

Alex raised an enquiring eyebrow.

'Sixty thousand is the figure usually regarded as a sustainable population.'

The doorbell rang. Cesare wiped his mouth with his napkin and stood up. 'If you will excuse me *signore*, but I think that is one of my clients.'

'He is such a good man,' Angelina said after he had left the room. 'He has been so good to his mother. All his life he has put her first. But perhaps now…' She gave a furtive glance towards the hallway and the bedroom where Elvira struggled for breath.

'I am going to leave him some of my money, you know. I had always thought I would leave it to the next baby in the family, but there are none. Perhaps once his mother has gone and he has some money, Cesare will marry. It is not too late. Many men have children in their fifties and sixties.'

Alex decided to take a risk and ask the question that had been burning in her mind since she left the Kaštela. 'Zenia seemed to think there might have been a child, that one of Salvatore's girlfriends had been pregnant…'

Angelina grunted. 'I gave her the money to go a clinic in Milan. She was not the kind of girl to make him happy. And I did not want her to be trapped, as I was.' She paused, her face altered by the memories she had called up. 'Of course, if I had known what was going to happen, I would have made a different decision. I have often thought about it. But you cannot change the past. It's useless to dwell on it.'

Alex wondered whether Angelina had ever checked

whether the girl really had gone to Milan.

'Is there anything else you would like to know?' Angelina asked as she poured herself another cup of coffee.

'Can you tell me anything about a woman called Lucia? All I have is the first name and the sketch of a story.'

Angelina gave a barking laugh. 'My God, that was a scandal. Natalia, her hair turned grey overnight!

'Lucia Pardini.' Angelina went on. 'Her father was Giuseppe Martinelli, a banker, and she married Enrico Pardini, another banker, two of the most wealthy men in Venice. And then Lucia ran off with a woman, Zenia, to Istria, abandoning her husband, her family and her child. There was a son, Enzo. It was so unnatural, to leave her child. Natalia told me that when they went to Rovinj to fetch her back, they had to drag her into the car.' Angelina paused and tugged at her skirt. 'Of course, she was not well. Afterwards they sent her to a clinic in Verona, on Lake Como – very beautiful. They had the money to buy the best. When they brought her home, apparently she was much changed, a walking shell, Natalia said, like a doll. And then later she had to be sent away again and that time she never came back.'

'What happened to her?'

'One day she went out for a walk and, because they thought that she was getting better, they let her go alone. Then she was found floating in the lake.'

'Poor woman.'

Angelina looked at Alex scornfully. 'Everyone knew of course, you can't keep anything quiet in Venice. When she came back from Rovinj, it was only her father's money and her social position that meant people went on receiving her. But even then, some of the older families refused to invite her to their homes. It was very embarrassing for the Pardinis. She brought shame on the whole family. So perhaps it was better ended that way.'

What Alex was thinking must have showed on her face because Angelina reached across the table and put her hand on Alex's arm. Her skin felt dry and cool.

'*Senta!*' she said. 'Listen! I wanted to talk to you because there are certain things you must get right in this book. If you listen to Zenia it will be all wrong, like a novella, a work of fiction. I can see that you admire her. She always has this strange effect on people and they think she is some kind of wonderful person, a heroine in a fairy tale perhaps. But she has done some very bad things in her life. Did you know that she held a knife to her mother's throat?'

'No! When did that happen?'

'In New York. Natalia went to live with her there for a while. Zenia was mixed up with some other woman, I don't know exactly who, but I do know that she was married to a painter that Zenia was sharing an apartment with. Natalia was very shocked. It was going to be the same scandal all over again. So there was a *boom!* Sooner or later there was always a *boom* with Zenia. And then she attacked her mother with a knife. What kind of woman does that?' Angelina's mouth twisted as if she had suddenly tasted something sour. 'But what she did to my husband, to my Bernardo, was the worst. I have lived for more than forty years a widow because of her stupidity. And it has been hard, so very hard. Twice, you know, I could have married again. But Natalia made sure that it couldn't happen. She wanted everyone under her control.'

'I've been told that Zenia was very fond of Salvatore.'

'They adored each other and he was blinded by the romantic life she led – he wanted to be like her. It was always "Aunt Zenia says this" and "Aunt Zenia says that". Between Natalia's spoiling and Zenia's example he was ruined. She could have had such influence for the good – she had only to lift her hand. But she didn't. And I lost both my husband and my son.' Angelina beat her fist against her breastbone.

Alex sat silently, unable to think of anything constructive to say. Angelina's words had cut into her like a sharp blade – a physical pain under her ribs. The woman sitting in front of her had also lost a child and a husband and her whole life had been shattered. The parallel was inescapable. But did it have to be the same for herself?

Angelina's fingers were compulsively sweeping together a little pile of crumbs on the tablecloth, and when she spoke again it was almost as if she was following the path of Alex's thoughts. 'Recently I have begun to think that perhaps I should try to forgive her. Forty years is a long time to hate anyone and my priest tells me that it is not good to approach the Kingdom of Heaven with things unforgiven. Concetta tells me she is dying.'

'Apparently the doctors have said that there isn't a lot of time left.'

'Would she see me, do you think?' Angelina raised her head but her eyes were averted as if to conceal the intensity of the need behind the question.

'I don't know her well enough to say yes or no, but I think it's worth asking.'

Alex left the house exhausted. It was a relief to walk through the cool dusk along the canal to her hotel. She almost stopped for a drink at one of the small cafés, then decided that she really needed to have a bath and leave her bag behind in the room before she went out. But when Alex got to the top of the stairs at the hotel, she saw that someone was sitting on the floor outside her door. He looked up as she turned the corner, a serious face, the face of a supplicant. It was Gianfranco.

He unfolded himself and stood upright as she walked down the corridor towards him. There was an urgent appeal in his eyes.

'Can we talk? Please?' he asked, and Alex nodded.

In the room she put her bag down on the bed and turned to face him, but before she could say anything he said, 'I hate to fail at anything, so I thought I'd come and have another try at an apology. Freddi told me where to find you.'

Alex dropped her eyes. She felt shamed by his humility and persistence. 'I over-reacted. I'm sorry. I've spent so long shutting it all out, keeping the door closed, I just couldn't handle it.'

'Will you have dinner with me? Or have you been

invited to Cesare's?'

Alex shook her head. 'I would like to have dinner with you. Where are you staying?'

'I'm not. I'm living in Vicenza now, in my mother's old apartment, only a forty minute drive away. Do you know the town?'

Fragments of her research for the book on Caravaggio surfaced in her memory. 'Isn't that where Palladio was born?'

'Yes, it's got the most beautiful buildings, but very few tourists. I think that's why I like it. And it's close to Venice, which is perfect.' He was smiling now. 'Shall I pick you up in an hour? I've got a favourite restaurant on the Fondamente Nuove.'

'I'll be ready.'

'I'll be downstairs in the bar.'

The restaurant was small – a narrow door and a steamy window with looped lace curtains – it would have been easy to walk past without noticing. Inside, the warmth met Alex like a breath – an exhalation of fish, garlic and the smoky undertow of a chargrill. The room was narrow with tables on either side, stretching back into the building. Every table seemed to be occupied. A waiter came towards Gianfranco and said, '*Salve!*' turning to Alex with a little bow and the more formal '*Sera, signora*'. He led them past the bar and the cash till where an ample figure, wearing one of the dark flowered dresses favoured by older Italian women, sat writing out receipts. She smiled at them, nodding her head to Gianfranco.

Finally they were taken to a small room at the back, also full, except for one table in the corner set for two.

'They obviously know you here,' Alex said as they sat down.

He grinned. 'I've been coming here for years – Zenia brought me the first time. The same family still run it. And they don't serve tourists. If any "*stranieri*" are bold enough to put their heads round the door, it's always fully booked.'

'Why's that? It seems a bit unfair.'

'There has to be somewhere for the Venetians to go, a quiet refuge from the a…verage tourist.'

Alex noticed the hesitation. 'You were going to say American!'

He looked unrepentant, saying cheerfully, 'I keep putting my foot in it, don't I?'

'Just a bit.'

The waiter put two glasses of prosecco in front of them and a small basket of focaccia. It was still hot when Alex helped herself to a crisp, salty fragment. 'What have you got against them?'

He thought for a moment. 'Nothing, against individual Americans anyway. I spend a lot of time in New York. Zenia still has an apartment in the Village and she lets me use it when I'm over there playing. I have a lot of American friends, most of them jazz musicians, none of them rich. I suppose I'm just prejudiced against the rich right wing, the "I'm all right so fuck the rest of you" type of American. We get a lot of them over here behaving as if they're the kings of the world. And just now they seem to be running America as well.'

'The Bush administration?'

'Yes. It just epitomises everything that's wrong. I've got a friend who was a war photographer in Vietnam and Cambodia. He'll tell you stories of what Kissinger and

Nixon did there that will make your blood curdle. And closer to home, here in Yugoslavia, they stood by and let people massacre each other. It was just a sideshow, a small affair in the Balkans. Ask Ludo. He was there. He really is anti-American.'

'I lived in America for seven years when I was married. I made a lot of friends.'

'But you left. Has what happened put you off going back?'

Alex nodded. 'I haven't been able to face it. But Zenia says I must.'

'She's right. And if you do come to New York, let me know. I've got several gigs lined up over there in the next few months.'

The arrival of the platters of antipasto put an end to conversation for a while. The smoked swordfish, deep fried langoustines, bruschetta and prosciutto required total attention. But after the plates had been replaced by a creamy asparagus risotto, Alex asked Gianfranco about Zenia's dual sexuality.

'Have you always known about it?'

'I can't say exactly when I first found out. As a kid I was always aware that she was different – when I was old enough to think about it I probably just assumed she was a lesbian. Some people, particularly in America, thought she was a transexual. The truth was a big family secret, though Zenia's always been very frank about it with her friends. I suppose it should have inspired a bit of prurient curiosity when I was younger, but I don't remember any.'

'Would you say she was more masculine than feminine? I'm hampered by the fact that I didn't know her before she was ill. How do other people see her?'

'That's a difficult question. You're aware of shifting

personalities, a subtle change from feminine to masculine and back, if that makes sense to you.'

Alex nodded. She had an image in her mind of an octopus assuming camouflage, now dark, now light, now mottled. Zenia's survival mechanism. 'I'm also interested in the Homeland War period. How did she manage? I've been told that Italians weren't exactly welcome in Istria.'

'She spent most of it in London and New York. She knew she'd be a target because of her links to the old regime. Did you know that she was once commissioned to make a bust of Marshal Tito? It used to stand in a square in Belgrade.'

'What happened?'

'That got blown up too. Luckily the Kaštela survived – a bit of looting and damage but nothing major. Knowing Zenia she'd probably done a deal with someone.'

'How much do you think I can trust her?'

Gianfranco inclined his head. 'In what way?'

'The story of her life.'

Gianfranco began to laugh. 'She's a storyteller. She tells her own life the way she sees it. If it's facts you're after… What made you suddenly ask that?'

'It seems to me that one of the most important events in Zenia's life is the death of her brother Bernardo. I have one version from Angelina, who says that it was Zenia who betrayed her brother to the fascists.'

'Impossible! Zenia loved Bernardo.'

'I know, that's what I thought. Angelina implies that it could have been accidental, but says that Natalia thought she did it deliberately in revenge because Bernardo had told Zenia's mother the extent of what Angelina calls "her bodily deformity". Angelina said that afterwards Natalia put Zenia in a Nazi clinic in Vienna.'

'That has a rather gruesome ring to it. The Nazi attitude to any kind of human difference was hardly compassionate.'

'According to Angelina, Zenia escaped before she could have the treatment. But Zenia hasn't told me anything about it at all. She was too unwell to talk before I left. All Zenia has said is that she thinks it was your father, Antonio, who told Natalia that she wasn't quite the normal developing teenage girl her parents thought she was. And she went on to say that apparently many people believed it was Antonio and his links with the fascists who were to blame for Bernardo's death and the massacre.'

'*Porco cane!*' Gianfranco shook his head. 'I knew my father had done some very shady things, but I would never have suspected him of betraying members of his own family.'

Alex wondered privately whether this was why Antonio had tried to bribe her to abandon the biography. But reason also told her that if Zenia really believed that Antonio was guilty of either of those actions, she probably wouldn't have anything to do with him at all. It was a muddle. 'How can I ever find the truth?'

'I'll bet that Concetta knows.'

'I think you're right. But how am I to get her to talk to me?'

'Perhaps I can persuade her.' Gianfranco leaned over and filled Alex's glass with the dark red wine that had just been put in front of them.

Alex sighed. 'I've begun to wonder whether I've been wise to agree to write Zenia's biography.' Gianfranco raised a questioning eyebrow so she went on, 'No-one wants me to write it – not Concetta, not your father, not even Freddi. And they're the main players I need to have on my side.'

'But Zenia wants it written.'

'Yes. That's the only thing that's keeping me going. But writing the biography of a living person is proving harder than I expected. You're intruding into so many other people's private lives.'

'You wrote about Elizabeth Taylor, didn't you?'

'I did.' Alex was pleased that he'd remembered. 'But it was a celebrity biography – a cut and paste job. I didn't have access to any of her private papers or even her close friends. There were no ethical dilemmas; it was all in the public domain. Zenia's different.' Alex paused while a sliced steak on parmesan and rocket salad was put down in front of her. She picked up her fork and raised her eyes to look directly at him. 'What do you think I should do?'

'I think it's a story that needs to be told. There are too many lies and mysteries surrounding Zenia's life – someone has to try to tell the truth, even if it doesn't please everyone.' Gianfranco lifted his glass inviting a toast. 'Here's to your book. And to Zenia!'

Alex clinked her glass against his, watching his eyes smiling at her across the table. She smiled back and felt her guard slip a little. She would have to be careful. Very, very careful.

London seemed strange when Alex came back; noisier, dirtier, more crowded. Even Ladbroke Grove, where she'd lived since her divorce, looked alien as she got out of the taxi. The wet, grey street, the iron railings, the leafless maples, all refused to make themselves familiar. The big black front door with its five bell-pushes was just another door. And the apartment seemed smaller; three rooms cramped up under the roof with kitchen and bathroom squeezed under the eaves.

Alex could remember her mother's comment when she had first seen it, 'My God Lessie, for that price you could buy a detached house down the road from us with acres of garden!' But London had been where Alex wanted to be; London was where the work was. The thought of living near her parents on the outer hub of Milton Keynes made Alex feel nauseous.

After Alex dumped her suitcase in the bedroom the first thing she did was to go into the bathroom, take all the little blue pills out of the cupboard, press them out of their foil strips and flush them down the toilet. Lying awake at the hotel in Venice after her dinner with Gianfranco she had suddenly felt ashamed of relying on the chemical crutch for so long. Alex also wondered how much the pills might have contributed to her feelings of remoteness, as though she was viewing the whole world through a double-glazed window.

Still feeling bold and full of courage Alex opened the door into the little bedroom and switched on the light. Katy's room. Exactly as she had left it two years ago; the Michael Jackson posters on the wall, her certificates from school, a signed photograph of the Spice Girls on the dressing table. And on her bed, leaning against the pink pillows was the cuddly chimpanzee Steve had bought for her on one of his visits. After nine eleven, Alex had spent night after night curled up on this bed with the chimp clutched in her arms, weeping into the synthetic brown fur that still smelled of Katy. Alex wondered what the room would look like now if Katy was alive. Would all the childhood clutter of cuddly toys and pop posters have gone? Would she have painted it black, adopted the Gothic look, gone in for heavy metal and body piercings? Probably not. Katy was sensible, conventional, much more like Steve than herself.

Alex felt tired, over-wrought, but curiously exhilarated. There was the feeling of having stepped over some kind of threshold. She looked in the freezer at the array of Marks and Spencer's ready meals, didn't fancy any of them, and made herself some instant porridge. Tomorrow she would go shopping. She resisted the temptation to open a bottle of wine and took the porridge to bed, where she lay, exhausted and awake, writing up the notebook she had begun at the Kaštela.

I felt quite shaky as I watched those flecks of blue swirling, irretrievably, in the porcelain bowl, but I haven't taken any pills since the night before last and I haven't gone crazy yet, so maybe it won't be too bad.

Alex thought, too, of the village that Gianfranco
had taken her to, Cec, where almost every inhabitant had
been massacred, old people, women, children, babies, and
of the man with the dog, still camping out in the ruins. In a
flash of comprehension she realised that that was what she
too had been doing – camping out in the ruins of her for-
mer life. After a few moments she began to write again.

Jane was looking pleased when they met for lunch, and Alex noticed that her own ratings had improved as far as the Italian Bistro on the corner of Greek Street, so perhaps there was good news on the book.

'Can't get any of the real biggies interested,' Jane said, swirling about half a pint of the house Pinot Grigio round one of the extra large glasses they provided. 'The market for biographies is dire at the moment. And, of course, Zenia's a little obscure over here. But Thames and Hudson think it would sit very nicely in their list and the editor wants to meet you. Felicia Harries – have you met her before? No? Lovely girl. Young of course, but knows her stuff.' A pause. 'But the really big news is that Knopf want to publish in New York. I sent them the synopsis you emailed and they're talking sensible money. What do you think?'

'I worked with them before when they published my Caravaggio. I used to know the editors there, but twelve years is a long time – they've probably all changed.' Alex took a long look down into her plum red Nero d'Avola, breathing the fumes before taking a sip. Since she'd stopped taking the pills everything tasted different. No, that wasn't quite the right way to put it – everything had a taste. She smiled across at Jane. Suddenly, it felt very good to be here, drinking wine, eating aubergine Parmigiano and talking about books again, to be on the threshold of another contract.

'Why didn't you tell me you knew Freddi?' Alex asked eventually over a baked fig pudding with mascarpone.

Jane shrugged. 'It didn't seem important at the time. I went to school with her but I never knew her well. I don't think anyone did.'

'What was she like?'

'The original innocent abroad – totally ignorant about things – ridiculed – bullied I suppose – for being so naive. Badly dressed in out-dated clothes. Had a crush on an older girl at one point – followed her round like a spaniel. But then one day she came to school in a sports car with a very attractive man she'd met on holiday with her parents in Madeira. And then she was suddenly much smarter and better dressed.'

'What's her family background?'

'Apparently she was the only child of a successful barrister and his middle-aged wife, sent to boarding school at six. It sounded very bleak. I wasn't surprised that she'd allowed Zenia and the Kaštela to become her whole world.'

Alex sighed. 'I'm a bit worried about Freddi. I get the impression she's not very keen on the biography.'

'Fortunately Freddi's got no say in it,' Jane said briskly. 'Zenia's tied it all up with her agent. Even if she dies before the book's completed the estate will be meeting your expenses, providing they're reasonable of course.'

Alex wondered what would be considered unreasonable – a trip to Japan? Australia? Russia? Zenia had had exhibitions in all those countries. And probably lovers too. But there was one place that would have to be visited, the one place in the world she wanted to stay away from, as Zenia had known.

'I'll have to go to New York.'

Jane nodded. She was busy fiddling with her credit card and the bill. 'Knopf will want to talk to you in any case.' She looked up briefly. 'Let me know when you want to go and I'll arrange the tickets.'

'So how does it feel to be back in London?' Gianfranco asked on the phone. There was a faint Skype whistle in the background.

'Different. It doesn't feel like home any more. I can't work it out.'

'You've changed, that's why. Zenia does that to people.' He laughed. It was a very comfortable sound.

'Where are you at the moment?'

'I'm in Budapest with an orchestra. Bacalov. Have you heard of him?'

Alex wished she was more familiar with names in European music. 'An orchestra sounds classical. I thought you only played jazz?'

'I play contemporary classical sometimes. Bacalov's most famous for writing the music for *Il Postino* and I bet you've heard the theme even if you didn't watch the film – it was everywhere at the time,' Gianfranco said. There was a pause and then he asked 'How are you getting on with the research?'

'Slowly. I'm going to see a consultant surgeon tomorrow, one who specialises in gender assignment for children. It was difficult to get an appointment, I think he's quite busy, but I'm looking forward to finding out more about Zenia's...' Alex paused. What could one call it? Difference maybe? 'Zenia's condition,' she said after a moment. 'I looked it up on the internet and it's much more common than I'd thought.'

'I can't imagine what it must be like to be born without the proper body parts. Sexuality's difficult enough when you're a teenager.'

Alex remembered her own embarrassment, her conviction that her body was imperfect, her breasts too large, her hips too skinny, the coarse dark Italian hair that clashed with her blue eyes. What must it be like to be so very, very different?

'I suppose that's why there's so much surgical intervention. Trying to straighten out what somehow got corrupted.'

Gianfranco's response surprised her. 'I'm not sure I like the idea of surgical intervention – all those mutilated babies. I can't decide on the ethics of it either. Do you think Zenia would have been happier if they'd turned her into one sex or the other at birth?'

'I don't know what I think yet – I'm deliberately not making up my mind until after I've talked to the surgeon.'

'Let me know what he says. I'll give you a ring tomorrow night.'

The idea of speaking to him again gave Alex a small flutter of pleasure in her stomach. She suppressed it straight away and responded in a rather less enthusiastic tone than she'd intended, 'OK.'

'Till tomorrow night then. *Ciao ciao.*' He put the phone down abruptly leaving Alex feeling inexplicably flat and disappointed.

'Don't keep him long, he's got people waiting,' the receptionist said. She looked at Alex disapprovingly as though a woman in perfect health had no right to be there at all.

Then she pressed a buzzer and waved Alex through the door into one of the most cluttered offices she'd ever seen.

Alex had expected Professor Song Li to be either Chinese or Malaysian, but he was very western, forty something, with distinguished grey streaks at his temples and the cleanest hands Alex had ever seen. His accent was American. Alex, from her years of residence in the States, could identify New England in his voice, but nearer to Boston than New York. One part of her was ashamed of trying to pin him down so exactly.

'It's very good of you to give me your time,' Alex said. She switched on the MP3 recorder and sat down on the only chair not occupied by books or magazines. It was cheap plastic and shabby like the Professor's desk. Not a wealthy surgeon then, but a busy one. A pile of battered files was stacked on his desk, one was open in front of him and the telephone was already ringing.

He ignored it and waved a hand as if dismissing her concerns. 'I'm always willing to help advance understanding on this subject. It's probably one of the most misunderstood of all congenital conditions. Did you know that at least one in every two thousand babies has some form of gender anomaly?'

Alex shook her head. 'That sounds a lot.'

'Some of them are never picked up, unless they're an athlete, or have trouble with fertility. There are perfectly formed girls with XY genes out there.'

'The subject I'm writing about says that she was born a hermaphrodite. Can you tell me something about that?'

'Genuine hermaphrodite's are quite rare. I see maybe one or two cases where both male and female genitalia are fully present. Often it's simply an enlarged clitoris in a girl, or a smaller than usual penis and undeveloped testes in a boy, maybe a vestigial vagina.'

'So what do you do?'

'Well, these days we don't rush in like fire-fighters. We do DNA tests to find out whether the child is chromosomally male or female. And then we try to decide how best to equip the child for a happy and sexually fulfilled life.'

The computer played the jingle that announced a new email. Professor Song Li looked briefly at the notification and went on talking. 'Sometimes it's straightforward reconstruction or enhancement and that's very satisfying. A male child with an undeveloped penis used to be castrated and brought up as a girl because it was thought that gender wasn't determined until the second year of life. Obviously it used to be easier to construct a vagina than a working penis – I can't remember who came up with the phrase "It's easier to dig a hole than put up a pole", but that's been the general line of thought. And the psychology of gender was an area of total and quite brutal ignorance.'

'Oh?'

'There was a case in America some years ago where a young boy's penis was badly damaged during circumcision and he was brought up as a girl. But as he grew older, he absolutely refused to wear dresses, or play with dolls, or hang around with the girls. Eventually they realised that he couldn't be turned into a girl by upbringing and he was allowed to become male again. Modern plastic surgery gave him back his penis, but the psychological scars were almost too great to recover from.'

'Can I look the case up?

'I'll get my secretary to photocopy the study for you.' He scribbled quickly on a notepad. 'It involves a doctor called John Money, and it changed the way everyone thought about biological gender. Now, we don't act so fast, but it's often difficult to resist pressure from the parents. I had a young Spanish couple here recently with a baby girl who had otherwise perfect female genitalia that included a small penis where the clitoris would usually be. Taking it away would also have removed any ability she would ever have as a woman to get sexual pleasure. No orgasms.' He smiled briefly. 'We advised the parents to allow her to grow up and decide for herself whether she wanted to keep it when she was old enough.'

'And did they agree?'

'Nope. The shame for a traditional Catholic family was too great. But in the end they agreed that I could tuck the little penis under a fold of skin and stitch it down so that to the grandparents she would look normal, then when she grows older, all the options are still there.'

'It sounds sensible, but it must be very difficult for the child, growing up between sexes.' Alex couldn't even begin to imagine how hard it would be.

'We call it "inter-sex", and yes, it's a problem. There's a saying in our speciality: "nature loves variety; society hates it". There are a large number of young people out there growing up with indeterminate sexuality. How they make out seems to depend largely on the attitude of their family. Where it's openly talked about it's much easier, where there's secrecy and shame the outcome is not so successful.'

'My subject was born in the nineteen twenties, and I'm presuming that attitudes then would have been less enlightened than they are today?'

'Oh, very much so. Almost medieval. In most cases the anomaly was kept secret within a family, but where surgery was advised, it was always what I call the 'lop and chop' option, removal of the vestigial penis and any testes, and the creation of female genitalia.'

He moved his hands in a chopping motion as if to emphasise the words. Alex thought of what Gianfranco had said about 'mutilated babies' and shuddered.

'The notion was that a man wasn't a proper man without a proper penis,' the professor continued. 'And without testes it was thought that the female hormones would do their job in creating a near normal female.'

'But, if I've understood you correctly, gender is settled before birth and is programmed into our brains?'

'More complicated, but something like that. Individuals know from a very early age whether they are male or female regardless of their genitalia – it's up to us, as reconstructive surgeons, to create the body to fit the mind.'

The severe receptionist was hovering in the doorway. Alex was on her feet before the women opened her mouth to say,

'Your three o'clock appointment's waiting in the corridor, Professor.'

'One moment, Jenny, just one more moment.' He smiled at Alex. 'You see how hard she makes me work?'

Alex smiled back. The woman gave her a chilling look before retreating into the outer office.

'I just wanted to say that I have a very interesting client, a girl of eighteen who has opted to remain intersex. If she was willing to talk to you, would you like her to contact you?'

'That would be fantastic! I'd be really grateful.'

'You would, of course, make sure that it was all totally confidential?'

'Absolutely. I'll sign whatever assurances she needs.

It would be wonderful to be able to talk to someone in that position.'

'Of course she may not want to, but if she does, I'll get my secretary to mail you.'

Just as Alex was going out of the door the Professor suddenly called her back. 'There's a book you might like to read, the autobiography of a nineteenth century French hermaphrodite called Herculine Barbin. Started life as a girl, then told at puberty she was a man.'

'I'll look it up on the internet. What happened to her?'

'Not a good outcome; she committed suicide.'

~~~~~~~~~~~~~~~~~~
~~~~~~~~~~~~~~~~~~

Alex took a taxi from Milton Keynes Central to her parents' home on one of the baffling, symmetrical, ring roads that formed the town. They lived in a big detached house with mock classical porticoes, surrounded by a garden that, even after sixteen years, was still new and glaringly artificial. The emerald green turf, the half-grown trees and geometric shrubs looked disproportionately small against the house, and seemed to have no relationship with nature at all. Alex could never understand why her parents still lived there. Her father, Jim, had worked for a northern firm of accountants who'd relocated to Milton Keynes in the nineteen eighties. Since then her parents had repeatedly complained about living in the south, unfriendly people, everything expensive, and Alex had always assumed that when her father retired they'd move back to Yorkshire. But no, they remained in Milton Keynes. 'It's so convenient,' Alex's mother Barbara had said. Convenient for what? Alex had wanted to ask. They rarely went anywhere. There'd been a cruise to the Bahamas once and talk of a property in France, but their carefully rationed holidays were mostly spent on golf courses in Scotland, or on City Weekend Breaks in Europe. As far as Alex could gather, her father seemed to play a lot of golf these days and spend an equal amount of time watching it on TV. Her mother did part-time volunteering at the Citizen's Advice Bureau and went out to lunch with her circle of friends. Alex supposed they were happy.

They were both waiting for her at the open door when the taxi pulled up outside, so someone must have been watching from the window. Barbara was wearing a dark blue woollen skirt and matching jacket, Jim in one of his vast wardrobe of Pringles' jumpers. Barbara touched cheek to cheek as she accepted the flowers that Alex had brought – 'How nice to see you darling' – smelling of the same Elizabeth Arden fragrance Alex remembered saving up pocket money to buy her, years and years of birthdays ago. Jim kissed her cheek with a faint whiff of tobacco. He'd been trying, unsuccessfully, to give up smoking ever since he retired. 'Come in, come in,' he said, guiding her forward by the elbow. 'Your brother's here. Just arrived a few minutes ago. Perfect timing!'

In the hallway, her mother turned towards the kitchen. 'You go on in – your dad'll give you a drink – I'll just go and put the veggies on.'

Alex didn't have to enter the kitchen to picture the gleaming granite surfaces and stainless steel appliances, the bright blue timer beside the cooker counting down the precise order of doing things. Everything in its place, polished and tidy. And the hallway Alex was standing in was equally immaculate; boots, umbrellas, coats and bags all hidden behind doors discreetly concealed in the panelling – in fact, it looked as it had done the day her parents had bought it. It was the show-home, bought complete with contents, a designer interior that made a statement about its occupants. Alex remembered how thrilled her mother had been; thrilled and relieved that she didn't have to spend hours and hours in shops making decisions about furniture and carpets she might later come to regret. Barbara had never had any confidence in her own taste. Alex supposed that being brought up in a council house in Bradford, surrounded by patterned wallpaper and floral carpets, wasn't good training for the wife of a successful accountant.

As far back as she could remember, Alex's parents had always had an obsession with appearances. Most of her teenage rows with her mother had been about putting things away and the state of her room, a constant battleground. Her brother Bruce had been different. He didn't care about privacy and had just allowed his mother to go into his bedroom and sort it all out.

For Alex, coming to her parents' house was like taking part in a scene from a Mike Leigh production. She found herself wondering for the millionth time how she had been born to parents like this. It was a question she'd been asking since she was old enough to remember. She had never felt truly a part of this family. When she was about eight or nine she'd fantasised that she was adopted. Now, it just made her wonder what her unknown Italian grandfather had been like. Was he the one who had seeded her genes with this sense of being alien? There certainly didn't seem to be much of the Mediterranean in her half-Italian mother. When Alex looked at Barbara, typically English, typically Yorkshire, the only traces of her mother's exotic origins were perhaps in the coarse texture of the dark hair she kept neatly bobbed, a tendency to tan easily, a lack of height, big breasts and the stockiness she had always struggled with. And then there was her own name – had Barbara been making some kind of statement when, against all family protests, she had given her daughter an Italian name?

The wider family were so respectably conformist as to be almost a cliche. Alex had sometimes seen a glimmer in her grandmother's eye that had hinted at a woman who might have had a wild affair in wartime, but perhaps the reality of her mother's conception had been much more prosaic. And by the time Alex knew her grandmother, she had been outwardly conventional, married to a jobbing builder she'd met after the war, who'd accepted her daughter Barbara and was willing to bring her up as his own. Gran was so ashamed of her 'mistake' she never talked about it, and had pushed the product of her romantic error, Alex's mother, into marriage with her first serious boyfriend at the age of twenty.

'She was terrified I'd "fall" – that was how she put it,' Barbara once told Alex. 'She used to say, "Don't do what I did! You'll pay for it for the rest of your life." So I married your Dad. It was what you did back then.' The photograph was on the sideboard in a mock retro silver frame, a black and white sixties image of a bride in a very short lace dress, her shoulder length veil blown to one side in the breeze revealing the bobbed Vidal Sassoon haircut. Beside her, almost hidden in a snow-storm of confetti, the groom stood gawkily in a sharp jacket and pointed shoes, grinning inanely. Alex wondered whether, if Barbara had ever been able to get away from her own mother, and the small Yorkshire town where she'd been born, she might have chosen someone different, rather than the articled accountant with the safe job Alex's grandmother had so approved of. Alex knew her mother read *Hello!* magazine when her husband wasn't looking and sometimes thought she detected a note of envy in Barbara's voice when talking about friends with more exciting lives. There had been a moment, when Alex had told her mother that she was marrying Steve and moving to the States, when she'd seen a strange expression on Barbara's face and the first comment had been, 'Well! Aren't you the lucky girl!'

Alex had invited her parents to New York while she lived there, but it had been disastrous. Barbara had enjoyed the shopping, the tourist trips to the Statue of Liberty and the Empire State, but she'd confessed that the noise and bustle gave her a headache and the canyon-like streets brought on claustrophobia – she'd refused point blank to go down the subways and was afraid of being mugged in Central Park. Alex's father, Jim, had visited the Stock Exchange and been impressed, but otherwise condemned everything American from the food to the decor. Alex had taken them to a show, which her mother had enjoyed, but Jim had been bored by. Afterwards they went to spend a week at a golf hotel in Florida which was, according to the postcard they sent, 'just the ticket', apart from the fact that they'd had to leave two days early courtesy of Hurricane Ivan.

Both Jim and Barbara had spent less time with Katy than Alex had expected, in fact she'd been shocked by their lack of interest in their granddaughter. 'Of course we haven't seen much of her,' Barbara had said, 'so we don't really know her, not like Bruce's children.'

Bruce was in the lounge, breathing the same self-satisfaction as the gleaming black Audi parked on the gravel outside. But at least his awful wife wasn't with him. Suzie was apparently staying with her parents in Kent. Alex saw her mother give Bruce a sharp look when he said that, and something passed between them, a flicker of comprehension. So perhaps Bruce's marriage wasn't as perfect as Alex had been led to believe.

'You're working too hard,' Barbara said to him as

she put the flowers on a side table. 'Long hours. It isn't good. You should spend more time at home.'

Jim grunted. Whether in agreement or disgust Alex couldn't work out. He was switching on Sky Sports.

Over lunch Alex was asked, in an apologetic, almost perfunctory way, what she was working on. 'It's a biography of a contemporary Italian painter, a woman called Zenobia de Braganza.' Alex wondered what they would say if she told them she was writing about a hermaphrodite who had spent her life living with other women. 'She's very interesting. Lives in Istria, just across the Adriatic from Venice. I've just spent a couple of weeks there interviewing her.'

'Well, it's good to see you getting out and about again,' Barbara said, rather absently, as she searched for a mat to put the gravy boat on.

Alex resisted the temptation to laugh, looked at her father and was surprised to see a rather conspiratorial, amused expression on his face as he looked at her across the table, as if they were appreciating the same grim joke.

Closed lives, Alex thought. My parents live closed lives. The immaculate Volvo in the garage that rarely went further than the supermarket or the golf club, the Sunday Telegraph on the coffee table, the bookless living room. Had they ever opened any of the books she had written and then sent to them inscribed, 'To my mother and father, with love'?

Today it was roast chicken for lunch with apple sauce and sage and onion stuffing.

'It's free range,' Barbara said, as she put the oval carving dish in front of Alex's father. 'I get them from Waitrose and they're so worth the extra money, so much flavour! And none of those horrible antibiotics.'

'Aren't you confusing free range with organic?' Jim asked.

'Well, isn't free range organic?' Barbara asked, looking puzzled.

Alex hated seeing her mother baited by her father, but refrained from leaping into the conversation, knowing from experience that it would only cause her mother more embarrassment. Better to ignore it.

After the chicken had been carved and the overcooked vegetables passed round, her father asked the question Alex had been dreading.

'What are you doing for Christmas?'

Alex stopped chewing, took a sip of wine to give herself time to think and then said, 'I'm not sure. Probably going to be away again.' Last Christmas she had told her parents she was going to stay with friends in Cornwall and then had locked herself in the flat and unplugged the phone.

'You'll be going to your friends again then?' Barbara looked oddly relieved. 'It's just that your Dad and I have booked to go and stay with your cousin Shelley in New Zealand.'

She was fiddling nervously with her napkin. 'Do you remember Shelley and Martin? Your Aunty Greta's kids? Well, Shelley married a teacher and they've moved to Auckland. Greta hasn't been too good lately, so Shelley suggested she go out for some winter sun and she didn't want to travel on her own, not such a long way, so we said we'd go with her.'

'Good for you! I bet you'll really enjoy it. Everyone says New Zealand's lovely.'

'Bit behind the times though, like England in the nineteen fifties,' Bruce said. 'That's what I've been told anyway.'

'It'll be a bit different having Christmas dinner on the beach,' Barbara said. 'That's the only thing. And I'll miss seeing the girls open their Christmas boxes.'

Alex thought she detected a look of relief on Bruce's face as her mother said it. She knew that his wife Suzie didn't get on with her in-laws. Another source of conflict.

Dessert was tiramisu served up with an apology. 'I'm afraid it's only Marks and Spencer's,' Barbara said, and looked round the table nervously as if expecting a reprimand.

'M & S food's wonderful,' Alex said. 'I don't know what I'd do without it – it's such a godsend when you've got a busy life.'

'I wouldn't call your mother's life busy, exactly,' Jim said.

Alex saw her mother flush. 'Well, at least I don't sit around all day reading the *Financial Times!*'

'Now then!' Bruce said. 'No squabbling, kids!'

Helping her mother load the dishwasher afterwards Alex asked, 'Is everything all right with you and Dad?'

'Oh yes. Take no notice of a bit of "fratching" as your Gran would have called it. It's his retirement. I'm not used to him being around all day getting in my way. I used to have a cup of tea and put my feet up on the sofa with Radio 4, but I can't do that now.' She sighed. 'I realise it must be difficult for him of course. His work was his whole life you know. I'm trying to get him to do a bit of accountancy for a local charity, but he doesn't seem keen.'

'He needs something, otherwise you'll both go mad cooped up here together all day.'

Alex wandered over to the far corner of the kitchen where a glass door gave views of the garden. On the wall above the breakfast table was a collage of photos. Out of curiosity, Alex looked to see if any of them had changed since she was last here. She remembered the holiday snap of her parents arm in arm on some sunlit promenade – Florida? There was her Gran's eightieth birthday party, just before she died. Then her father's retirement celebration, black tie and champagne. And another familiar photograph, Bruce's eighteenth with herself and her brother at the barbecue, squinting at the camera. Then Bruce and Suzie's wedding photo, a meringue puff affair, Bruce in tails and a cravat that matched the bride's flowers. Innumerable photos of their twin daughters Faye and Jasmine, baby snaps, school mug-shots and then a posed studio portrait of two rather smug looking ten year olds dressed in matching Burberry prints which Alex supposed must be the most recent.

What had happened to her own wedding photograph, Alex wondered? And the photos of Katy? Had they gone in the dustbin, or been tucked away at the back of some drawer in the spare room? And where was her own book-jacket photo, taken in New York, head back, laughing, long hair drifting slightly in the wind that always blew through Central Park, the only photograph of herself she had ever liked and had given to her parents as a present, hoping they'd be proud of her. But perhaps it was in a frame, in pride of place on her mother's dressing table? Alex doubted it.

Looking at the collage Alex realised that what it represented to her was not a family unit, but a reinforcement of her own sense of exclusion, an absence of love. Alex didn't feel either loved or valued here.

'Lessie?' Her mother had come up behind her as she looked. Barbara hovered, lifted the glasses that hung on a cord round her neck and peered up at the photographs. 'I miss your Gran,' she said, briefly touching the photo with her finger. 'She was such a game old bird.'

Alex laughed. 'She was, wasn't she!'

Barbara sighed. 'You could never get the better of her though.' She glanced sideways at Alex. 'She ploughed her own furrow. A bit like you really.'

'Oh?'

Barbara looked flustered. 'Well, you keep yourself to yourself. Always did, even when you were a tot.' She smiled. 'We used to call you Little Miss Independent.'

Alex inclined her head. 'Yes, I suppose I was, still am. I don't like having to rely on anyone.'

'You can say that again! You'd no need to go getting a taxi from the station. Bruce would have picked you up, or your dad would have fetched you if you'd only said.'

'Sorry Mum. I didn't want to put anybody to any trouble.'

'Well, there's no need for a taxi back. Bruce says he'll take you.' Barbara took off her glasses and turned away, suddenly practical again. 'There's just time for a cup of tea before you go.'

In the car Bruce said, 'You should come over more, you know. It isn't fair. They're getting older.'

'Not that old!'

'Sixty-six isn't exactly young.'

'These days it is. Anyway, you stay out of my affairs Bruce and I'll stay out of yours. I take it life in Berkshire isn't as wonderful these days as everyone's pretending?'

'There's nothing wrong with my marriage. Suzie took the kids down to her parents because we thought it might be… distressing… for you to have them around at lunch.'

'Oh, for god's sake!' Alex yelled, then checked her-

self. They had only been trying to be considerate. 'Everything's distressing, everything, but I just have to live with
it. I'd have been delighted to see your kids.' They, at least,
Alex thought, would have acted spontaneously and brightened up a very difficult afternoon. 'Please, please, all of
you, stop treating me as if I was made of glass, or suffering
from some unmentionable, terminal disease. Katy's dead,
nothing can bring her back. But I have to go on living.'

Alex switched on the computer as soon as she got back. There was an email from Freddi. Alex opened it with some apprehension and was immediately surprised.

'I don't know what your plans are, but would you like to come out for Christmas? Zenia's visibly failing at the moment, hasn't got out of bed for more than a week, and she seems quite anxious to see you. Come whenever you like and stay over New Year if you can, we celebrate it well here.'

Nothing from Gianfranco. Not a telephone call, a text, or an email in over a week. There'd been contact almost every day before that – what had gone wrong? Had she said something out of place? Been too cool, too eager? Alex went over every remembered word of their conversations without being able to reach a conclusion. He had told her that the weeks before Christmas were a very hectic period for musicians, so perhaps that was it.

She sent an email, deliberately casual. 'Spending Xmas and New Year at the Kaštela. Maybe catch up with you at some point? If not, hope you have a good time.' Alex looked at the screen and kept the mouse hovering over the 'send' key. Should she? Or would it be better to wait until he contacted her?

One last chance. She clicked the mouse.

When Alex woke at 3am she immediately knew that something had changed. As she lay quietly in the darkness she realised that, for the first time since Katy's death, words were writing themselves in her head. She had been puzzling for days about how to begin the biography. Should she start with Zenia herself, or with Zenia's parents? Where did the story actually begin, with her birth or further back? And should she include her own search for the facts of Zenia's life in the book? Were readers really interested in the process of writing a biography or only the story itself?

Now, a possible beginning was starting to form in the darkness. Alex got up and went to fetch her notebook from the living room, propped herself up on the pillows and picked up her pen.

Zenia's story begins in 1920's Vienna, when a beautiful, ambitious young opera singer called Natalia Romanova, the illegitimate daughter of an Italian actress and a Russian diplomat, married Ferdinando, the youngest son of the de Braganza dynasty from Trieste. His family, respectable shipping magnates of Spanish and Austro-Hungarian descent, didn't entirely approve of the match, but as he was the youngest son he was allowed to have his choice of bride.

In 1923, a year after the marriage, their first child was born, but instead of the usual jubilation there was consternation and blame. Because the baby the midwife presented to Natalia had not only the normal genitalia of a girl, but a tiny penis as well. 'A minor imperfection,' the midwife said with a shrug. 'It is possible that it will correct itself in time. Don't fret yourselves. You have a beautiful daughter.' Zenia's father was sure that nothing like this had ever happened in the de Braganza family before, so he was forced to conclude that it could only be corrupted genes from Natalia's scandalous and exotic origins. But Ferdinando was still in love with his wife and didn't want her to be treated as a pariah by members of his family. The midwife was given a sum of money in return for her silence. Ferdinando was adamant. No-one must suspect. The 'little imperfection' must never be spoken of.

So the child was christened Zenobia after her paternal grandmother and dressed in frilled lace and pink ribbons, and Ferdinando gradually began to love his strange little daughter. But for Natalia the baby remained a secret source of shame.

Three years later another child was born, a son Bernardo, who was unambiguously male. For Natalia it was a reprieve, a rebuke to those who had suspected her of having bad genes. She loved Bernardo fiercely from the moment of his birth, and her sexually ambiguous daughter Zenia was pushed even more to the periphery of her affections.

As Alex read it back to herself, she wondered, not for the first time, how she could organise the past histories of her subjects so easily, but not her own.

The cheap airlines had stopped flying to Pula at the end of October, so Alex was forced to get a scheduled flight to Zagreb and hire a car for the long drive south to Visoko. In London it had merely been wet and cool, but in northern Croatia the temperature was only just above zero. There was snow on the hills and in sheltered places beside the road. A bitter wind was blowing in from further east and pewter coloured clouds were piling up on the horizon.

Closer to the Adriatic it was warmer. Alex turned the heater down on the car. She was finding her way more surely now, negotiating the narrow, bumpy roads with confidence. When she parked the car at the Kaštela, triumphantly without a scratch, and saw Lenka coming out of the gatehouse to greet her, it felt almost like a homecoming.

'We have put you in the Tomizza apartment this time,' Lenka said, after kissing her on both cheeks. 'Zenia thought you would like to be in a house named for a writer. And it will also be warmer. They have told us to expect snow tomorrow.'

'There's snow on the mountains above Zagreb,' Alex said.

Lenka nodded. 'That's where my family was, you know. I miss it sometimes, especially at Christmas.'

The apartment was close to Zenia's house, up a flight of stone stairs beside the memorial to the grieving mothers of Croatia. There were two rooms, a bathroom and small kitchen. The living room had thick stone walls, shuttered windows and a narrow balcony that looked out across the valley towards Rovinj and the distant sea. It was too cold to be out on it for more than a few minutes and Alex closed the glass door with a shiver, pulled the heavy tapestry curtain across and went to warm her hands on the wood burner.

A plaque on the wall beside the iron stove explained that Fulvio Tomizza was one of Istria's most famous authors, one of the Italian minority who had continued to live here after Tito pulled all the fragmented regions under the Yugoslav umbrella. Tomizza's novels celebrated

Istria, the text read, and he had won many international awards before his death in 1999. There was a collection of his books on the shelf, about eight titles. Alex wondered if Zenia had known him. More questions to ask. She took down *The Tree of Dreams*, because the title intrigued her, and put it on her bedside table.

After she'd unpacked Alex walked through the courtyard to Zenia's house. They were all collected in front of the fire, except Zenia, who was in bed, and Martin, who was obviously still keeping himself to himself. There were no guests at the Kaštela. 'It's just us,' Freddi said.

'Just the strays and gays,' Toby chipped in cheerfully and Alex noticed Freddi flush red with annoyance.

'Where are Jolene and Kelly?'

'Very odd,' Freddi said. Her expression brightened. 'When they heard you were coming they suddenly decided they were spending Christmas in France. Don't ask me why. They're a complete mystery.'

'Don't you know anything about them?'

'Not a thing! Jolene comes from Canada originally, though she won't talk about it, and I know she's lived in Ireland and France, but that's all. Kelly's equally puzzling. I can't work their relationship out at all. I've sometimes thought she's either a younger sister, or even a daughter, but I've no idea. Zenia says there's no point in speculating.'

Alex looked across at Toby who was staring down at the floor and remembered his comment about things not being what they seemed and she wondered if he knew more about Jolene and Kelly than he was admitting.

'Those ladies are both completely out to lunch,' Lenka said. 'I wish they would leave.'

Freddi sighed. 'I feel the same. The atmosphere is

always just that little bit heavier when they're around.'

Ludo bent forward to knock his pipe out on the fire grate. 'They will be leaving soon enough, I think,' he said quietly and then looked up at the ceiling as if directing everyone's attention to Zenia, whose existence was the thread that bound them all together, now slowly unravelling upstairs.

'Gianfranco's coming,' Freddi said, changing the subject.

Alex saw Lenka raise her head. Her own stomach lurched.

'He's been staying with his mother and stepfather in Switzerland. Apparently he's playing somewhere tonight, but said he'd drive down afterwards. He's hoping to get here in time for Christmas Eve.'

'The *meteo* is not good,' Concetta said. 'We are going to have snow.'

'We never have snow here,' Freddi protested. 'We're too near the sea.'

'But this year, I think we do.' Concetta pressed her lips together firmly.

'I hope he gets through.' Lenka's eyes were bright.

'He knows how to drive,' Ludo said. He was refilling his pipe, tamping the tobacco down with his thumb. 'And if he's coming from Switzerland he will have snow chains.'

As Alex made her way back to the apartment she caught a whiff of cannabis and, looking round in the direction of the smoke, she could see a hunched, dark figure on a bench below her balcony. It was Martin. He had a bottle of Concetta's plum slivovitz on the seat beside him.

He smiled up at Alex lazily. 'Want to join me?'

Alex almost said no, but then realised that she was still wide awake and not completely wound down after the journey. Martin saw her hesitation and grinned. He patted the bench. 'You'll need another glass.'

'And a blanket,' Alex added. 'It's utterly freezing.' She ran up the stairs to her room and came back with the quilt from her bed and a shot glass from the kitchen cupboard. She refused the proffered spliff. 'It makes me throw up.' Alex registered the scorn on Martin's face. 'Very sad, I know. Watching other people get stoned is one of the most boring things you can do, but better than an evening looking at the bottom of a toilet bowl.'

'How's the book?' He slopped a generous measure of slivovitz into the glass.

'OK so far. I've got an outline, it's just a question of research now, getting people to talk. The most difficult bit is finding out what really happened. So far there are several different versions of the same story.'

Martin laughed. 'I did warn you not to believe everything you were told by the oracle.'

'You and about a dozen other people! But the story of someone's life, the one they tell about themselves is sometimes more interesting than the real thing.'

'Sounds a bit philosophical for me.'

Alex felt the slivovitz speeding through her veins and arteries like electricity. 'And there are several mysteries I still haven't solved yet. Kelly and Jolene for instance.' She turned to look at Martin's profile. 'You're Canadian. Do you know who they are? Why they're here?'

'The last one's easy. Why are any of us here?' He glanced sideways at Alex. 'As Ludo says, we're orphans with nowhere else to go. Zenia's made us into her own very peculiar family.'

Alex waited as he took another drag on the spliff.

'As for J and K, I've no idea. Jolene's French Canadian, I'm not. The Quebecquois are natives of a foreign country to me. One thing I am sure of though – her name's not Jolene.'

'How do you know?'

He shook his head. 'Trust me.'

There were footsteps behind them. Alex turned her head and saw Lenka coming down the path. She stopped and did a double take when she saw Alex and Martin together on the bench. Alex noticed that Martin hadn't turned round. He remained staring straight ahead toward the lights of the valley, ignoring Lenka's approach.

'Hi!' Alex said. Her voice sounded brittle. 'Want to join us?'

The girl didn't reply and then suddenly turned and stamped away in the direction of the main terrace. 'You're a bastard, Martin,' she shouted as she began to descend the steps, the words blowing back behind her on a flurry of cold air.

'Why is she so angry with you?' Alex asked.

Martin shrugged. 'She wants me to take her to Canada after Zenia dies.'

'And will you?'

'Nope. There's no way I'd go back, never, not ever.'

The way he said it Alex knew she couldn't ask why. Instead she said, 'How did you meet Zenia?'

'She saved my life. Literally. I was back-packing round Europe with my girlfriend, we'd been to Morocco and we were both into some pretty heavy drugs. She overdosed in Naples and I knew I had to clean up somehow.'

He sighed and took another long gulp of slivovitz. 'A guy at the hostel I was staying in saw an advert on Gumtree for olive pickers in Istria, though it was Yugoslavia then, and that's how I arrived here. Zenia realised what the problem was pretty quickly.' He laughed, the unmistakeable giggle of the stoned. 'It wasn't difficult, I was out of my head most of the time. She sat with me all night when I came off the drugs and rolled me joints to ease the withdrawal symptoms. So now I'm addicted to the weed,' he waved the spliff in the air, 'but at least I'm not shooting up any more.'

'What will you do when she… when she's not here any more?'

'God knows. I might move further south, Greece maybe. I've never been there.'

Alex's feet were turning to blocks of ice. 'Will you take Lenka with you?'

'Probably not. She's got too many problems of her own, it doesn't make for a good relationship.'

'I suppose you're right.'

'Two bent twigs won't hold up a roof, my grandmother used to say.'

'Obviously a wise woman.'

'Pity she didn't pass any of it on to me.' Then he added, 'She only wants the visa you know.'

'Lenka?'

'She's a Roma. Most of them don't have proper papers, however long they've been here. She wants me to marry her so she can become official. But I won't, so she'll have to find someone else. That's why she's angry with me. That's why she's flashing her eyes at Gianfranco.'

Alex stood up and flexed her ankles. She realised she was shivering. Martin held up the bottle.

'Have some more of Concetta's anti-freeze!'

She shook her head. 'Sorry. I think I'd better go to bed.'

'Sure you won't have another?'

'Tempting, but no.' Alex wrapped up her quilt. A slightly maudlin tone had begun to creep into Martin's voice now. It was time to go. The last thing she wanted was more confidences about his relationship with Lenka.

'Goodnight Martin. See you in the morning.'

Alex had breakfast alone, drinking coffee and eating sweet pastries still warm from the oven. There were sounds of activity everywhere but no-one in sight. She could hear banging from the kitchen, Martin shouting at someone from the terrace, the sound of an axe on wood somewhere below the window.

Lenka came into the dining room while Alex was lingering over her second cup and said, 'Zenia wants to see you. Freddi won't say anything because she thinks Zenia's too tired, but I know there are things Zenia wants to say and it troubles her. She will not sleep until she talks to you.'

'I'll be careful,' Alex said. 'I won't stay long.'

Zenia was propped up in bed on a pile of cushions, the quilt pulled up to her chin so that only her angular face and an untidy mass of white hair was visible above it. The stove glowed white hot in the corner and the heat was almost unbearable.

'*Auguri*,' Alex said, sitting down on the edge of the bed. 'It's Christmas Eve and I've brought a present for you.'

'You have? For me?' Zenia's eyebrows rose very high on her forehead as if she was genuinely surprised that

194

anyone should bring her presents.

Alex put the small, heavy parcel on the bed and watched as Zenia lifted one trembling hand out from under the blankets. She tugged at the paper ineffectually until Alex began to unwrap it for her, folding the layers of tissue paper back to reveal the circle of stained glass inside. Alex had found it in an antique market in London, a perfect fragment of an old church window, in the rich medieval reds and blues she knew that Zenia loved. In the centre, a tiny shepherd with a lamb at his feet, was painted in miniature. Alex held it up to allow the light to play through it and watched Zenia's face as she followed the glittering reflections round the room like a child.

'It is beautiful,' Zenia said. 'Where did you find such a thing?'

'In a market,' Alex said. 'Would you like me to hang it in the window?'

'Please. But you shouldn't have spent your money on me. It is useless to give things to the very old – because soon we will be leaving them behind, you know.'

There was nothing Alex could say to answer that. She bent the wire around the window catch so that the light poured through the glass, daubing red, blue and yellow lozenges on the quilt, the white wall and the floor.

'And now, I must give you a present,' Zenia said. Her voice, usually strong and assured, trembled slightly.

Alex protested. 'You don't have to give me anything. I just wanted to give you pleasure. You don't give gifts to get things back.'

Zenia shook her head. 'I made up my mind that you should have this when you were last here. I don't have children to remember me, but when you write your book, then perhaps I will be remembered.' She pointed a shaky finger at the bookshelf. 'Over there on the bottom shelf. There is a package.'

Something square was wrapped in a plastic supermarket bag. 'This one?'

Zenia nodded. 'Bring it here.'

Alex lifted it out and put in on the bed.

'It is for you. My photograph album.'

Alex's stomach contracted. 'I can't take this Zenia. What about your family?'

'They have their own photographs, their own stories. This is mine, and it is for you.'

Alex turned the pages, full of excitement. She loved old photographs and these pictures of Zenia as a small child, with her mother and father, and her brother Bernardo, were wonderful. It was true, she needed them for the biography, to tell Zenia's story.

And there, over the page, was the woman without a face, her identity gouged out of the book. 'This one,' Alex said. 'Who is this?'

Zenia followed her eyes.

'That is Lucia.' There was a pause. 'She left me to go back to her child, you know, because they threatened that she could never see him again. She longed and longed for him. But after she went back, she was very miserable. She could not endure her marriage even for her son. We had bought each other lockets, when we were first lovers, and we put our faces in them as a pledge, cutting them out of the photographs. We were going to wear them forever.' Zenia sighed. Her eyes were flickering with images Alex couldn't even guess at. She sat quietly until Zenia began talking again.

'After she died, I was very angry and very unhappy. It was almost unbearable, you know.' She looked up at

Alex. 'I tell you this because you do know.'

Alex nodded.

'On the ferry from Rovinj to Venice, I tore the locket from my neck and threw it into the sea. But then I was sorry and I wanted it back, because...' She paused as if searching for words. 'Because it was the only photograph I had of Lucia and I had thrown it away...' Another pause. 'So I kept what was left of it...' Her voice faded and Alex thought she had finished. Then she said, very quietly, almost whispering, 'When I look at it I always try to picture her face.'

Zenia's closed her eyes, visibly exhausted. Her cheeks had sunk and her chin rested on the edge of the quilt.

Alex folded the album up and replaced it in the bag. There was a big label stuck on the plastic, 'For Signora Forbes', in the wild, black letters of a young child learning to write.

She stood up quietly. Zenia appeared to be already asleep.

Freddi was at the bottom of the stairs. 'Ah,' she said, looking at the package under Alex's arm. 'I see she gave you the photographs.'

'Is it all right for me to take them?'

'Of course.' Freddi's voice was brusque. 'She's giving everything away at the moment. Better than letting those bloody Antonellis get their hands on them.'

'Have they been back?'

'No. But they often come for New Year. Zenia never refuses them and there's always trouble.'

After she put the album in her bedroom Alex went into the kitchen. Concetta was slicing a squid at the table and the stove behind her was completely obscured by boiling saucepans. Through the strong, salty odour of fish, Alex could smell beans.

Ludo was peeling potatoes at the table.

'Can I help?'

Ludo passed her a knife. 'There's a bowl of apples on the shelf behind you.'

'This is for Christmas Eve?'

Ludo nodded, and Alex was surprised when Concetta replied, 'It is what we call a white meal – *La Vigilia.*'

'Italian customs,' Ludo interrupted. 'It's sometimes called the feast of the seven fishes because that's all you're allowed!'

'It is for purity,' Concetta said. 'When I was a child we used to fast all day. It's important to be pure for the Christmas feast the next day.'

Ludo winked at Alex. 'In that case, Concetta and I had better give up now, because after a lifetime of carnal sin we will never be pure enough to eat Christmas lunch.'

'Speak for yourself,' Concetta said. 'I am a respectable married woman and you are a dissolute old man.'

'Ah, Concetta, we both know each other better than that!'

Concetta turned to Alex and laughed. 'Don't believe a word from him.' She reached across the table and patted Ludo's hand. 'This might be our last Christmas together, old friend, so I think we had better eat and drink well and forgive each other our sins.'

Ludo turned his palm over and clasped Concetta's hand quickly and then released it. 'Where will you go?'

'To my sister in Trieste.' Concetta shrugged. 'My husband will give me trouble, but it can't be helped.'

Freddi was outside in the courtyard looking up at the sky. She was huddled in a woollen blanket coat made from coloured squares. 'Concetta's right,' she said, holding out her hand as a single white speck floated down from the grey cloud ceiling above them.

'You can smell it,' Alex said. The air was metallic, tasting of mineral salts and pine forests and glacial melt water.

'I suspect that Gianfranco won't make it. I tried to ring his mother but the telephones aren't working.'

'Not even the mobile?' Alex hadn't thought to check hers.

'They have batteries to power the antennae when the electricity goes off, but they always trip out at Christmas and Easter, because so many people are trying to ring home. You just get "network busy" or nothing at all.'

Alex took her phone out of her pocket, but there was no signal. It made her feel curiously vulnerable. The hills towards Slovenia were hidden behind the cloud.

'That's a blizzard,' Freddi said. She shivered and turned to go indoors. 'Are you going to Christmas Mass in the village tonight? Concetta and Lenka will go. Zenia always used to, but she's not well enough at the moment. I'll stay with her.'

'I'd love to go. Is it Orthodox or Catholic?'

'There's both, but Lenka and Concetta are Catholic. It's very pretty – they do the full Mass here – in Italy these days they've modernised it.'

Throughout the afternoon the cold crept in, settling around Alex's ankles and feet as she sat working on the remaining letters and files from the studio. Outside the window the sky was the purple grey of a bruise and an occasional dusting of white appeared miraculously across the marble terrace like a veil of icing sugar sifted across a cake.

Alex went through the photograph album making pencil notes about the identities of the people in it, but there were several she couldn't place and some she could only guess at. A big blond man with a laughing face, arm in arm with a young Zenia, could only be Ludo, but the other students in the group were strangers. And then the faceless woman leaning on the balcony railing. Curious to have a closer look, Alex slid the mutilated photograph of Lucia from its slot and turned it over. A dedication had been pencilled on the back in tiny, elegant script; 'con te vivo una favola' – with you I live a fairy tale. Alex returned the photo to its place. How could Lucia have known that, like so many old fairy tales, it would not have a happy ending?

At the very front of the album, pasted inside the cover, was Ferdinando and Natalia's wedding photograph, bride and groom sitting nervously on chairs in the photographer's studio; Natalia in white, almost hidden behind a gigantic bouquet of flowers, Ferdinando small and slim beside her. Behind his chair stood a formidable lady in black bombazine with a widow's toque and veil on her tightly curled hair. Her hand gripped Ferdinando's shoulder with all the possessive authority of a parent. This was presumably his mother, the Zenobia that Zenia had been named for. Behind Natalia a slim girl, whose facial features matched Ferdinando's, stood submissively. Was this his sister Therese, mother of Antonio? There was no sign in the photo of Natalia's mother, the actress of dubious morality.

Alex put her head round Zenia's door, but she was snoring peacefully on the pillows. Freddi, reading in the chair beside the bed, frowned at Alex and put her finger to her lips. Alex nodded, smiled, and went down to the kitchen.

Ludo was still sitting at the table and Concetta, taking a break, was sitting playing *Scopa* with him, a bottle of slivovitz between them. Alex put the album down and waited until they'd finished the game. Concetta, after some thought, and some prompting from Ludo, confirmed the identities of the faces in the photograph.

'Natalia told me that Ferdinando's mother, the old Zenobia, was a formidable woman, very strong. She had five sons and a daughter, but three of the sons died in the first war.' Concetta spoke grudgingly, as if each word was being extracted under duress, but at least she was talking. Alex waited for her to go on.

'Her eldest son was a banker in Vienna and she lived with him after her husband died from the influenza in 1919. But she didn't live for many years after that photograph was taken; she already had the cancer and it was only her temper that kept her alive. Zenia was perhaps only three or four when she died, but the old harridan lived long enough to see the next baby and, when they told her it was a son, Bernardo, she said, "Thanks be to God", turned her face to the wall and died.' Concetta crossed herself and then she got up, retied her apron, and returned to the pans on the stove, turning her back with finality.

~~~~~~~~~~~~~~~~~
~~~~~~~~~~~~~~~~~

The power, which had been flickering all day, went off just after six thirty. By the glow of the stove, Alex managed to find the candle lantern and the torch helpfully provided on a shelf beside the door. When she went outside, snow was falling more purposefully through the darkness and no longer melting from the ground the moment it touched down.

In the dining room Lenka had a taper and was lighting the candles on the long table. 'Doesn't it look nice?' she said. 'Toby did it.' Branches of pine sprayed silver and gold were laid in the middle decorated with ribbons and clusters of red berries. In the centre was a pyramid of fruit, apples, oranges, lemons, persimmon and pomegranates, piled almost to the ceiling with trailing gold and silver ribbons wound around from apex to base.

Every place setting had its own terracotta candlestick made in the shape of a figure. 'Ludo makes these,' Lenka said, and then tossed her head. 'He says they are the spirits of Christmas, but of course he is a heathen.'

Alex picked one up, a boyish, pagan figure with horns on his head and the legs and feet of a goat, dancing and playing a flute. 'This is Pan,' she said.

'Gianfranco,' Lenka giggled, and then added in a

gloomy tone. 'We've set his place, but he will not be here.'

Lenka moved along the table, pointing to a seat further up on the opposite side. 'This is yours.' Alex's candlestick was a female figure in a long flowing gown with a star for a halo and small cosmological symbols around the hem of the gown. 'You are the north star,' Lenka said. 'Ludo made it specially.'

The pole star, the navigator's aid, a fixed point. Alex wondered why Ludo had given her that.

At the head of the table, Siamese twins of brother and sister were twined together in a loving embrace. It could only be Zenia's place. Lenka followed her eyes. 'This will be the first time she hasn't sat at table with us for Christmas. Freddi was hoping she might come down, but she seems happy now to stay in her room and sleep. Concetta says she is practising for the final sleep.' Lenka rubbed a hand across her face. 'I can't think of it you know. This place without Zenia.' Tears were glittering on her cheeks in the candlelight. Alex put her arm around the girl, but there was nothing that could be said. Lenka's shoulders were unyielding. She moved away from Alex towards the kitchen. 'There are things still to be done.'

'Is there anything I can help with?'

'No. Concetta and I will do it.'

In Zenia's bedroom Freddi, Toby and Alex sat around the stove and listened to her steady breathing by candlelight.

'The power situation gets worse every year,' Freddi said. 'Especially since the war.'

'What was it like here before?' Alex asked.

'Fantastic!' Freddi's face suddenly became animated. 'Pula was a big tourist destination, hotels everywhere. Tito had a holiday place on one of the islands off the Istrian coast before he died. We were always full. And there were two artists' communities just north of here, both thriving. Ludo worked in one of them before he came to live with Zenia.'

'Where did you go during the fighting?' Toby asked.

'To London and New York. But at least we had somewhere to go. Zenia couldn't bear to turn the television on after a while, seeing all the suffering, the ravaged villages, the concentration camps.'

'Martin stayed though,' Toby put in.

'Yes, he stuck it out with Ludo. And Zenia paid some people with connections in the military. There was a bit of looting, some vandalism, but no destruction here. Other people weren't so fortunate.'

'I saw what happened to the statue at Cec,' Alex said.

'I heard that her sculpture in Belgrade was blown up too,' Toby added.

Freddi nodded. 'Zenia's politics have always been complicated. It takes real skill to deal with both sides in a civil war. I don't understand any of it.'

'Probably better for you not to know,' Toby said.

'Have you thought any more about going to Berlin?' Freddi asked.

Toby shook his head, then turned to Alex. 'I had an offer from a couple of Croatian artists working in a studio there, but I don't fancy it. I'd rather go to Rome or London – Zenia's agent's looking out for me.'

There was a silence. Both Freddi and Toby looked strained and miserable.

Then Toby stood up and said, 'I'll go down and ask Concetta what time she's serving dinner. It must be nearly ready.'

After he'd gone Alex sat quietly with Freddi in the candlelight listening to the muffled sounds coming from the kitchen far below.

Freddi looked towards the bed where Zenia was now so deeply asleep she scarcely seemed to breathe at all.

'She looks so beautiful. So peaceful.' Freddi's voice sounded unsteady.

Zenia was lying on her back and the way her flesh sank back from her face exposed the powerful bone structure. Alex could see the arch of her cheekbones, the large eye sockets fringed with those incredible eyebrows. In the silence, watching Zenia sleep, it seemed to Alex that it was the right moment to ask Freddi the question she needed to ask, but had never found the opportunity. Freddi never seemed to be alone, was always rushing, busy.

'Sometime when you can,' Alex said, 'I'd like to hear about your relationship with Zenia.'

Freddi looked startled, as if this was something she hadn't been expecting to be asked. She drew back in her chair. 'I'd really rather you kept me out of this.'

'I'm not sure I can,' Alex said, perplexed. Had she blundered, been tactless, tackling Freddi now? 'You're part of the story of Zenia's life. You must have realised?'

Freddi shook her head. 'It's all too private – I can't talk about it.'

'Then I won't ask.' Alex felt very uncomfortable. 'But if you reconsider and you do want to tell me something, will you write it down and send it to me? Email, letter, anything. I'd rather hear your story than anyone else's version.'

Freddi sighed and ran a hand through her hair. 'I agreed to your coming here for Zenia's sake,' she said. 'Because she wanted it. But it's not what I want at all.' She made a helpless gesture towards the bed. 'I've always let her have her own way, done what she wanted.'

Alex wondered how Freddi would manage when, soon, she would have to make her own decisions, make her own way.

The Christmas Eve feast felt sombre, perhaps because of the darkness and silence of the power blackout and the three empty places, not just Gianfranco and Zenia, but Concetta too. She had appeared from the kitchen with a tray and, when Freddi moved forward to take it from her, said, 'I will sit with her tonight.'

Freddi hesitated. 'I'd planned to do that. She'll eat for me. It's important to make sure she eats.' She held out her hands as if pleading for the tray, but Concetta held on to it.

'You cannot make Zenia do anything she doesn't want to do,' Concetta said. 'She has always been like that, all the time I have known her, since she was a young woman. And what she needs now is peace.' Concetta moved towards the staircase door with the tray and disappeared through it.

Freddi shrugged, but she was biting her lips as she sat down and Alex thought that there were tears in the corners of her eyes. It puzzled Alex once again, how Freddi deferred to Concetta, was almost nervous of her. And it seemed now that some kind of battle for ownership was going on.

Martin for once ate with them, sitting opposite Ludo and saying very little. Alex was grateful for Toby who kept up a flow of chatter, ignoring the blatant hostility that seemed to flow towards him from Martin at the other end of the table, only equalled by the fact that Lenka was blanking Martin out totally.

As if tainted by the atmosphere the food too seemed less appetising than Concetta's normal fare. The baccala, langoustines and cured swordfish seemed bland. The tiny clams in the spaghetti tasted slightly gritty, only the monkfish baked with apple and holy basil had any flavour. The panettone trifle made with marsala and mascarpone, decorated with glace fruit, stayed intact as it was passed round the table. Ludo was finally persuaded to have a little, and Freddi insisted on Alex having a taste, but no-one else seemed in the mood for festive puddings.

'It's one of Zenia's favourites,' Freddi said sadly looking at the abandoned trifle. 'We have it for her. None of the rest of us have much of a sweet tooth, I'm afraid.'

When Alex went down to the terrace at eleven o'clock, wrapped in her thick winter coat and wearing fur-lined boots borrowed from Freddi, she was surprised to find Martin standing there with Concetta.

'We're just waiting for Lenka,' he said. 'Toby's decided to keep Ludo company beside the fire.'

'I didn't have you down as a churchgoer,' Alex said.

'I'm not,' he said. 'But I can't let you all go down to the village in this weather on your own.'

'I didn't have you down as chivalrous either.'

'I like to surprise people,' Martin said with a sardonic grin.

Lenka came out hurriedly, tying a scarf around her head and trying to button up her coat at the same time.

Martin handed her a torch and Alex noticed that they said nothing to each other.

'*Andiamo!* Let's go,' Martin said, leading the way down the path that led towards the village. The night was totally dark. No street lights were visible below them, no moon or stars over their heads. Occasionally flurries of snow showed in the beams of the torches.

The houses in the village were closed up, shutters locked, the occasional dim glow at the bottom of a door to show candlelight or firelight in a room. The air was acrid with wood smoke.

The interior of the church was lit by hundreds of candles, hanging in chandeliers, grouped in tall candelabras, on the altar in massive silver holders, or smoking in sconces on the walls to illuminate the Stations of the Cross. On the floor and on every conceivable ledge, tea lights flickered. The soft, pulsating light imbued the painted icons around the walls with warmth and a sense of mystery. In the corner, the mother and child sitting among the carved donkeys, sheep and cows, seemed almost real, and not the chipped plaster figures that Alex imagined would be revealed in full electric light.

During the Mass Alex stood with Lenka on one side of her and Concetta on the other listening to their strong responses. Concetta's order of service lay unopened on the ledge of the pew, since she knew the words by heart. Alex glanced occasionally at Martin's profile, on the other side of Concetta, noticing that he was silent like herself, a stranger to the Latin Mass.

Why was he here? Alex had to ask the same question of herself. She could be tucked up warm in front of the fire with Ludo and Toby, or keeping vigil with Freddi in Zenia's room. Was it curiosity about another culture?

Or something else, something she was fighting not to acknowledge, a primitive need for spirituality.

She watched some of the young women crossing themselves in front of the statue of the Virgin, a little curtsey before the Queen of Heaven and her son, and heard Zenia's voice asking, 'Do you have children?' Alex had said no then, but she would have answered differently now.

Concetta was watching the women too. 'That one,' she said, nodding her head towards a very young girl with a black lace shawl over her head. 'Last month she had a baby who died. Now she's asking the Virgin to keep him safe for her in heaven.'

Would it have helped, Alex wondered, if she herself had been able to have faith in simple religion? But she had never, even as a child, been able to believe anything just for comfort or convenience; she needed to believe it with her head too. The chipped plaster Madonna in her blue robe was a less convincing figure than Zenia's bereaved mother, howling out her rage and grief, pushing her dead child forward into the face of the world, offering up her dripping breasts, her torn dress, her everlasting tears.

Alex turned towards Concetta and met her eyes. They exchanged a look and, just for a fraction of a second, Alex thought she saw both understanding and compassion in the older woman's gaze.

Outside the snow was piled over the street cobbles almost as high as Alex's boot tops. Lenka made a snow ball and threw it at Martin who turned as she pitched, so that it exploded harmlessly on the back of his jacket. He ran, bent swiftly and fielded a fistful of snow that landed on her shoulder making her shriek with childlike excitement.

Concetta laughed at them. 'It's a long time since we had snow in this place – not in all the years I've lived here.' She stirred the surface of it with her boot. 'For me, God can keep it!'

At the Kaštela, Ludo had made a hot punch from fruit juice and spirits. The alcohol content made Alex's eyes smart as she put the glass to her lips. But it warmed the chilled core that had grown steadily colder and more solid inside her, on the way up from the village.

Freddi came down when she heard them return. 'It's time to give out the presents,' she said. She seemed happier, more composed than she had been before they left.

'And I will be *Babbo Natale*,' Ludo said, 'if someone else will crawl under the tree and give the presents to me.'

Lenka immediately crouched down beside the lowest branches and began to pass the packages to Ludo.

Alex hoped her own small gifts would be acceptable; a hand printed silk scarf for Freddi, cigars for Ludo, Fortnum and Mason's chocolates for Concetta, a set of charcoal pencils for Toby, the latest Prada fragrance for Lenka. Martin had been difficult, impossible, but in the end she'd settled on Bob Dylan's autobiography. If he didn't like it, that was just too bad. But he smiled and nodded and began turning the pages straight away, Alex suspected only to annoy Lenka, who had given him a beautiful woollen designer scarf, which he had added to his pile with scarcely a glance.

Alex was touched that so many of them had given her something. She had a glazed clay plaque from Ludo, again with the figure of the North Star on it, a small bottle of slivovitz and a jar of chestnut conserve from Concetta, chocolates and Panforte from the others, and a book from Freddi, the *History of My Travels in Istria*, by a 19th century Turk, translated into Italian, with exquisite black and white etchings.

'It belonged to Zenia,' Freddi said, touching it with a finger tip. 'But I think it needs a new owner now.'

It was after one o'clock when Alex fell into bed in the dark, clutching the hot water bottle Concetta had insisted that she took with her. She didn't remember blowing out the candle, or falling asleep.

Alex woke to hear the dripping of a tap, then realised that it was water dripping from the roof onto the terrace below. The room was full of grey light, but it felt warmer, her nose above the blankets no longer frozen. Her digital clock said eight thirty. The bedside light clicked despondently, so there was still no power.

Alex wrapped the quilt around her and shivered into the bathroom, then back into the living room to re-light the stove which she'd forgotten to stoke before she went to bed. The ash was still hot and it caught quickly, roaring up the metal chimney encouraged by the wind that was now rattling the shutters. Outside, on the terrace, the snow sagged over plant pots and balustrades and slithered from the branches of trees. A steady trickle of water was flowing down the steps. In a few hours the snow would be gone.

There was still no mobile signal, so at least she had an excuse not to send any Christmas messages to her family, though paradoxically Alex felt suddenly that she would have liked to do so. She wondered where Gianfranco was, and realised how much she'd looked forward to seeing him again. She slapped the thought down fiercely.

Alex spent a couple of hours going through the last

box of Zenia's letters. It still troubled her that someone had been through the box before her. She was conscious of an absence in the letters, too ephemeral to pin down, like something you glimpse out of the corner of your eye that disappears when you turn your head to look at it. Something was missing. Someone had edited out a chunk of Zenia's life. But who, and why?

Freddi, in order to protect the privacy of her relationship with Zenia? One of the Antonellis? God knows they must have a thousand reasons. Neither Lenka nor Toby had been around during the period covered by the box, but what about Martin, or Jolene and Kelly? Then Ludo and Concetta? Did either of them have anything to hide? There were no letters from Concetta in the box, a few from Zenia to her, mainly giving instructions about arrangements at the Kaštela, listing the people she was bringing and dates of arrival. No letters between Freddi and Zenia at all, but if you lived with someone you didn't write to each other. Maybe this was one mystery she would never solve. And perhaps it was all her imagination, perhaps no letters had been taken out at all.

Alex went down to the kitchen for a late coffee around half past eleven. Freddi, Concetta and Lenka were all busy with vegetables and saucepans and the most savoury smell was coming from the oven of the big iron stove.

'That's Bambi,' Freddi said, 'with chestnut stuffing.'

'I hope you like it,' Lenka said. 'I know the English don't want to eat any animal that looks cute.'

Concetta looked up from the sink. 'If God hadn't wanted them to be eaten, he wouldn't have made them taste so good.' It sounded like a reproof.

Alex laughed. 'I love venison. It's really expensive in England, so I don't get it very often.' She breathed in the odours of rich gravy and crisping meat. 'Can I help with anything?'

Her assistance having been declined in every department, Alex made a pot of coffee for everyone, boiling the kettle on a kerosene ring, and they all sat down to drink it. Lunch, Freddi said, would be late, between two o'clock and three, so that it would stretch through the afternoon and do for both lunch and supper.

As if they had smelled the coffee, Ludo and Toby appeared, squelching through the slush on the terrace. Freddi produced a tin of Amaretto biscuits from the back of the cupboard and Toby had fun setting the wrappers alight and watching them float upwards towards the ceiling until they expired in a little puff of ash.

There were footsteps outside, which Alex thought must be Martin, but then the door opened and there was Gianfranco, his cheeks red with cold under the fur flaps of his ski hat. Lenka jumped up straight away with a cry of delight and surprise. Concetta exclaimed, 'Gianni!' and held both of her arms out to him.

But Alex was almost certain that, as he came through the door, hers was the face he looked for first. He gave her a small, odd, smile before he stepped forward into Concetta's embrace.

Lenka was already making more hot coffee, Ludo pouring slivovitz.

'Come and sit by the stove,' Freddi said. 'You look chilled to the bone.' She helped him out of his padded ski jacket. 'We thought you weren't going to make it!'

'So did I!' Gianfranco held his raw hands over the stove. 'It was snowing a complete blizzard after I left Trieste, but the main road through Slovenia wasn't too bad - at least it was ploughed. But once I turned off, the side roads were almost impassable and then some idiot in a BMW four-wheel drive forced me off the road near Iršca. Stronzo! I spent the night in the car, then this morning it had begun to thaw a bit, so I persuaded a farmer to give me a hand to dig the car out and got as far as Praška before I was beaten by the drifts. I walked the last couple of miles.'

'Four or five, more like,' Ludo said. 'Did you not have chains?'

'I do. But you can't use them when the snow's so soft.'

Alex noticed that all the time he was talking he kept glancing at her. She knew her face must be flushed with the pleasure of seeing him again, but she kept her head down towards the table.

'I'm afraid I haven't any presents,' he said. 'I had to leave everything in the car. If it carries on thawing maybe I'll be able to get it back tomorrow.'

'Zenia will be delighted you could come,' Freddi said.

'Is she in her room?'

'Hasn't left it for a week. I'm very worried about her.'

'I'll see what I can do, as soon as I get out of these wet boots.' Gianfranco stood up, coffee cup in one hand and with the other he poured the slivovitz into the coffee. 'Where am I staying, Freddi? I'd like to have a quick shower and a shave before I see Zenia. I've a feeling I probably look and smell as though I've just spent twenty-four hours in a car!' He ran his hand over the stubble on his chin.

'You do,' Lenka said, flirtatiously, 'but we don't mind.'

Freddi ignored her. 'We've put you in St Jerome, because I know you like the murals.'

'Good. I'll go and get changed.' He picked up his jacket and hat, grinned at the kitchen generally and went out of the door.

'Now we will have fun!' Lenka said.

And she was right; the atmosphere was at least ten degrees warmer than it had been before his arrival. Even the candles on the table seemed to flicker more brightly. Gianfranco carried Zenia downstairs wrapped in a blanket and settled her into the big chair at the head of the table. She looked rather vague, as if looking at everyone from a distance, but she smiled and seemed happy to be there and was soon enjoying the latest Italian jokes as told by Gianfranco.

'Have you heard the one about the three workmen who saved Berlusconi's life?'

Zenia's eyes were wide. 'No! There are workmen who would save his life?'

'You're supposed to wait for the punchline, Zenia.'

But then, as if taking part in a parallel conversation, she asked him: 'Do you have a lover?'

The tanned skin of his cheeks flushed to a slightly darker tone.

'My sex life is none of your business Zenia!'

'You will grow old and lonely.'

'Better alone than with the wrong person. Have you ever compromised?'

'Certainly not!'

In his company Zenia seemed almost her old self, sitting in her chair, wrapped in woollen shawls, her eyes bright and piercing, tossing her head with some energy.

Lunch wasn't finally over until after seven, when the last crumbs of panettone had been swallowed and the Vin Santo and grappa passed around several times. Gianfranco carried Zenia back up to bed and then came down again to sit beside the fire. He looked across at Ludo and said, 'Are you ready?'

'Of course.' Ludo reached down beside his chair and picked up a box. Inside it was a small accordion, the kind that Alex had seen buskers playing. He pulled it apart between his palms and then pushed it together again, making a wheezy discordant sound. Then he waved across to where Martin was turning his chair to face the fire. 'And Martin has brought his guitar.'

'Great!' Gianfranco opened a rather battered leather instrument case and took out a clarinet, which he polished and fitted together with the speed of an expert. He waited until the others were ready and then blew a note. Taking it as a cue, Martin began tuning his strings.

'So,' Gianfranco said, after Martin had finished, 'What shall we play?'

Ludo looked up. 'I've been teaching Martin some Croatian songs.'

Martin nodded, pronounced some word Alex didn't understand, and instantly the three of them began to play, Martin less confidently than the rest, picking his way through the chords, but Gianfranco and Ludo both playing with panache.

Then, suddenly, Lenka opened her mouth and began to sing, in a raw, haunting voice that made all the hairs on Alex's arms stand up. She couldn't understand the words, but the tone of loss and longing didn't need any translation. Alex watched Lenka having a musical dialogue with Gianfranco, the voice answering the clarinet and then waiting for the next phrase, Gianfranco's little nods of approval, and felt a terrible jealousy. How wonderful it must be to be able to sing like that! Instantly, she forced the thought down. It was stupid and juvenile to have those kind of thoughts.

But Alex continued to feel uneasy. About nine o'clock, she filled her hot water bottle in the kitchen and slipped off to bed, without anyone noticing that she was gone. From her room she could still hear the clear notes of the clarinet and Lenka's voice raised in some kind of gypsy lamentation that made her want to weep.

〜〜〜〜〜〜〜〜〜〜〜〜〜〜

Only Alex, Freddi and Toby appeared for breakfast.

'Martin and Lenka have gone off with Gianfranco to get the car,' Freddi said. 'The roads are almost clear this morning.'

'I hope it's still where he left it,' Toby said.

'How's Zenia?' Alex asked.

'Tired – she rather overdid it yesterday.' Freddi flicked her a look. 'There's no point in trying to talk to her.'

'There are one or two things I need to have cleared up, but they can wait. Do you know if the Antonellis are coming?'

Freddi shrugged. 'Antonio hasn't said they aren't. That's all I know.'

Alex went for a walk afterwards, down the steps towards the village, but turning back on the outskirts. Threads of wood smoke rose from the chimneys, but the hamlet still had a grim, closed look about it. This, Alex supposed, was its winter face, a profile of endurance, averted from the weather. As she walked back, she heard the sound of a car engine and the old Audi roared past her up into the car park, Lenka in the passenger seat beside Gianfranco and Martin chugging behind in the station wagon. They parked side by side on the gravel.

'That was interesting!' Martin said as he climbed out.

Alex smiled. 'You made it though.'

'Just! There are still a couple of awkward drifts if you haven't got four-wheel drive.'

Gianfranco was heaving a bag out of the boot and passing a couple of plastic carriers to Lenka. He grinned at Alex and she felt herself smile back. The sun was just visible like a ghost behind the thin cloud over the Adriatic, threatening to break through.

'It says on the radio that the road to Rovinj's open,' Gianfranco said.

'Fancy a trip?' Martin asked. 'Or have you had enough of travelling?'

'Maybe. I wondered whether Alex would like to go. You haven't seen it yet, have you?'

'No. I've only been to Pula, a brief glimpse when I flew in the first time, and then when I went to catch the ferry. It would be great to see Rovinj.'

'I'd like to go,' Lenka said. 'I haven't been out of this place for weeks.'

'Maybe after lunch?' Gianfranco was looking at Martin, who nodded.

'OK, if the weather's still fine.'

Alex felt dismayed at the thought of going anywhere in this foursome, but didn't know how to refuse. It seemed that this was how it was going to be.

In the back of the Audi with Lenka, Alex concentrated on looking at the landscape on either side of the road. It wound down through the valley, onto the narrow coastal plain beside the bay, and then westward towards the point where Rovinj sat facing the Adriatic, looking towards Venice. The small town was just a cluster of brightly coloured buildings on a dome of rock sticking out into the sea like a circular island attached to the mainland. A tall church spire rose dramatically from the centre.

'That's the Basilica of St Euphemia,' Gianfranco said over his shoulder, as if he'd been watching the direction of her gaze in the rear view mirror. 'It's a pity, but we probably won't have time to see it today; it gets dark so early.'

The town was surrounded by a circular wall of houses, four or five stories high, all painted in different shades of ochre, with slim, Italian-style shuttered windows. Gianfranco parked the car in a public car park close to one of the entrances that tunnelled their way into the cobbled streets of the '*centro storico*'.

There was a surprising amount of activity for a late Boxing Day afternoon. Some shops appeared to be open and there were people in the main piazza and lights in the windows. No power cuts here.

'There's something I want to show Alex,' Gianfranco said as they stood in front of the archway that opened into the old town. 'So I suggest we all meet up back at the car about five thirtyish?' He was looking at Lenka. 'Martin's got my mobile number if you want to be a bit later.'

'Can't we come?' Lenka asked.

'Sorry.' He sounded genuinely regretful. 'Family business.' He smiled, as if to soften the refusal.

'I've got a better idea,' Martin said. 'There's a good bar on the quayside where they tie up the fishing boats, just next to the clock. I think it's called the Viecia Batana? Let's meet up there, then it doesn't matter who's late.'

'I want to show you the house,' Gianfranco said, as soon as they were out of earshot of Lenka and Martin. 'Where Zenia lived with Lucia.'

Rovinj in its winter, post-war trappings seemed drab, with the exhausted appearance of a seaside town off-season. The streets seemed to consist of shuttered houses and hotels, boarded up bars and empty art galleries. But Alex could see that in summer, with the striped awnings down, the café tables out on the pavements and the sun romanticising the cracked stucco, it would all seem very different.

Through the archway into the old town, cobbled streets wound their way up towards the church. They were so narrow, the houses almost touched. Every now and then a small space would open out between them and there would be a shop or a bar, potted plants and, in some of them, washing strung out across the balconies. Gianfranco stopped in front of a bakery, closed 'for holiday' according to the tattered notice on the door. Above it were two windows in a peeling pink wall and a rusty balcony, facing across the tiny piazza with views towards the sea. 'That's where they lived, though I think it was probably in rather better condition then.'

It looked smaller than Alex had expected. How had Lucia coped after living in the Pardini palazzos of Venice? And the little vignette that had been drawn for her by Angelina, of Lucia being dragged away by her father, had presumably happened just here, on these damp, uneven cobbles. A plastic carrier bag outside the shop had been torn apart by seagulls, spilling bones and vegetable peelings onto the ground.

Gianfranco kicked a mouldy orange into the gutter. 'The rubbish collections don't work too well here, these days.' He sighed. 'This was so beautiful once.' He was looking towards a palm tree growing in a terracotta pot, trailing ragged brown branches like the sails of a ruined mill. 'Over there.' He nodded towards a boarded-up building on the corner with a café sign over it. 'That was the bar James Joyce used to visit when he was here. It used to be full of tourists. And Zenia of course! Apparently she used to sing for them when she was short of money and they would buy her drinks. When she brought me here as a child, people were always asking her to sing and she always did. It used to make me cringe with embarrassment, even though she had a really good voice.'

Alex looked around her. 'Will it ever recover, do you think?'

'I hope so. Maybe never the international destination it used to be. Who knows?' He turned away, putting his hand behind Alex's elbow. 'Come down to the sea. Let's find somewhere to talk. My mother told me an interesting story I think you need to hear.'

A cold offshore wind funnelled through the narrow streets as they walked steeply downwards. Suddenly, ahead, Alex could see an archway between the houses that walled the left-hand side of the street, and through it an expanse of grey and white water. Gianfranco led Alex lightly down a flight of steps, slippery with weed, onto a small rocky outcrop, the stones still wet and patrolled by hungry gulls. They sat down in the lee of the wind on a ledge of grey rock, furred with baby mussels. It was quiet, apart from the suck and hiss of the tide and the gulls quarrelling with each other.

'Has Zenia ever talked to you about someone called Elena?'

'Never. Though the name crops up now and then

in some of the letters. I wondered who she was, but no-one's mentioned her.'

'That's interesting.'

'Who was she?'

'You know we speculated that my father might have some kind of hold over Zenia?'

Alex nodded.

'Well, I think that Elena is it. According to my mother she was a beautiful, rather needy, Croatian girl who modelled for Zenia in the early days and was employed as a kind of assistant, organising exhibitions and things like that. Zenia was hopeless at organisation – still is!' Gianfranco paused to smile and then went on, 'Zenia was in the process of restoring the Kaštela and getting tourists to come and stay and getting in a hopeless muddle, particularly with her taxes. Then she had a lucrative offer to go to America for a lecture tour. Elena persuaded Zenia to let her run the Kaštela and handle everything while she was away. Apparently Zenia signed papers that, in effect, gave Elena the Kaštela, though she doesn't seem to have realised that – she thought it was some kind of lease. My mother thought it was something to do with the way that Zenia had acquired the property – she paid the people who had emigrated, but under Tito that didn't necessarily give you rights – particularly as a foreign national. Ownership often depended on who was living in the property, and Zenia wasn't at the time.'

'So what happened?'

'Elena promised to pay the tourists' money to Zenia in a Swiss bank account after she'd taken her cut, and the bills would be paid out of Zenia's money – my mother didn't know the precise details, but that was the general idea.'

'It sounds very dodgy.'

'It was. Elena stopped paying anything to Zenia, put it all into her own account and she ran up huge debts with local suppliers, didn't pay any of the bills. Concetta finally told Zenia what was going on and she asked my father to investigate and sort it all out.'

Alex was beginning to see how much Zenia had relied on Antonio for all her business transactions. Hadn't she said that she had asked Antonio to buy the Kaštela for her in the first place?

Gianfranco went on, 'My father threatened Elena with the police when he discovered the fraud, but she said that she'd make a big scandal if he did, something to do with an affair Zenia had been having with a politician's wife. But he managed to keep it all quiet. Zenia got the Kaštela back, but not the money. She was broke for years. But, and this is the interesting thing, my mother said that Zenia made a will leaving the Kaštela to him as a reward for what he'd done for her. That was before she met Freddi.'

'Now I understand why Zenia puts up with so much. Does the will still stand do you know?'

'I've no idea. Zenia's always making them. She's quite impulsive.'

'So what happened to Elena – does your mother know?'

'She says Elena married some rich guy with a hotel in Dubrovnik – she's still around somewhere. Whether she'd talk to you…' He shrugged expressively.

'Probably not. I'll need to check dates and details, but that shouldn't be too difficult if there's official paperwork.' Alex smiled at him. 'Thanks for telling me, it explains a great deal. And thanks to your mother for remembering.'

'You'd like my mother. She's had a very tough life, but she always manages to keep her sense of humour.'

'Will I ever get to meet her?'

'That depends. I hope so.'

Alex took a deep breath and with a rush of courage asked, 'You stopped telephoning or texting – why?'

'I thought I might be making a nuisance of myself. Was I?' He looked directly at her, raising one eyebrow.

'No. Did I give that impression?'

'Sometimes.' Gianfranco looked down and began dipping the toe of his trainer into a small rock pool. 'You're difficult to read face to face, but at a distance… And it's hard to gauge someone's mood in a text message.' He glanced up at her again.

'Sorry. I didn't want you to think…' Alex stopped, unable to say what she meant, but he read it anyway.

'We're both too defensive. I'm afraid my last relationship broke up so badly, I've been very wary of getting into another. Does that make sense?'

Alex nodded.

And then he reached over and took her face in his hands and kissed her. His lips were warm and soft and her own seemed to enter willingly into a conversation with them, mouth opening to mouth, as if they were familiar lovers. She felt herself begin to tremble, and her stomach contracted with what she recognised as desire and something else. Need. The need for physical contact with another human being, the touch of skin on skin. The need for love.

She pulled away from him for a moment, shaking with the intensity of it. He was looking at her, his eyes only inches from hers, reading her expression, and then he ran his fingers gently down her cheek.

'This is dangerous territory for both of us, isn't it?'

Alex didn't trust herself to reply. She turned her head and put her lips to his fingers.

~~~~~~~~~~~~~~~~~~
~~~~~~~~~~~~~~~~~~

It was dark as they drove back up the narrow treacherous road to Visoko. Rounding a corner Gianfranco's car came suddenly behind the bright tail lights of another vehicle travelling more sedately upwards. His headlights illuminated the gleaming black rear door of a Range Rover with a Milanese number plate.

'I know that car,' Gianfranco said, without any pleasure. 'That,' he said, 'is my father.'

In the car park Antonio's chauffeur was opening the door for his employer, who stepped out, dressed in a dark overcoat and black shoes, clutching a briefcase, as if he had just come from a board meeting. The chauffeur was folding a rug and collecting luggage as Antonio came towards them. He ignored Lenka and Martin, bowed to Alex with a little nod of acknowledgement and then held out his hand to Gianfranco.

'What possessed you to travel in this weather?' Gianfranco asked, as his father shook his hand and clapped him on the back in proprietorial fashion.

'I have to be in Milan for New Year. Caterina is having a big party, some very important people. So I thought I should come to see Zenia early. She is far from well, I gather.' He turned away towards Lenka as he spoke, as though the question was addressed to her and she immediately began to answer.

As Lenka spoke, Gianfranco bent his head towards Alex and murmured, 'Far from well but not at death's door yet.' His voice sounded as if the words were being forced between clenched teeth.

On the pathway Antonio led the way with Lenka, still discussing Zenia, followed by Martin and the chauffeur carrying what appeared to be a ridiculous amount of luggage for a brief visit.

Alex and Gianfranco walked together at the rear.

'I get the impression you don't have an easy relationship with your father?' Alex said.

'I can't pretend to feel much warmth towards him. We're such opposites in temperament, politics, everything really. I used to be grateful to be included in the family, but when I grew up I realised that was Zenia's doing, not his. He hasn't done well where sons are concerned. He and Cesare don't get on, and there was a still-born baby boy with Caterina's mother, which, according to mine, broke up that relationship. Since then nothing. His last wife was Swiss, but she died from cancer a couple of years ago.'

'So he only has you and Cesare?'

'He would have liked an heir for the empire. Caterina's probably the most like him of us all, but she doesn't count, being a girl.'

The happy relaxed atmosphere of the evening before was completely absent. At dinner everyone was being frigidly polite. Conversation was impersonal, centred around world news, the political situation in Rome, the weather. Concetta insisted on eating upstairs with Zenia. Freddi looked stressed and miserable. Alex felt obliged to make polite chit-chat with Antonio across the table to help her out. Ludo and Toby remained silent, and Gianfranco seemed preoccupied. The only person who seemed happier and more bubbly than normal was Lenka, who tried to flirt with Gianfranco all through supper, and Alex found it very hard to endure the way her dark, almost black, eyes lit up every time he turned in her direction, the visible tautening of Lenka's body when she felt his eyes on her.

Alex struggled with this awareness. Gianfranco, on the other hand, was treating Lenka with the friendly amusement with which he treated everyone else. He had a way of relating to people, Alex noticed, that seemed friendly and open, but was also defensive. A charming exterior that held people at arm's length. The only person he treated differently was Zenia. With her, he was more volatile altogether.

After dinner Gianfranco and Ludo excused themselves, as if by a mutually arranged plan, and Lenka and Toby began clearing the table. Antonio got up and took the chair at the head of the table next to Freddi, and it seemed to Alex from his body language that he wanted some conversation with Freddi on her own.

Alex stood up, 'It's getting late, I really should...'

'Oh, no, please,' Freddi said, her eyes wide with panic. 'Do stay and have a night cap. Some slivovitz? Another wine? I've got some French chocolate if you'd like a hot drink?'

Alex hovered reluctantly.

'And you Antonio? A grappa?'

He inclined his head in agreement, shooting a look at Alex that made it clear that her presence was unwelcome.

Alex sat down. 'Slivovitz for me please, Freddi.'

Freddi was standing at the drinks table, with her back to them, when Alex spoke, but she saw Freddi's shoulders relax. She turned and came across the room carrying the drinks. 'You said you wanted to talk to me,' she said, handing Antonio his glass. She put Alex's slivovitz down beside her with a wry smile that Alex interpreted as relief.

'Has she made any decisions yet?' Antonio asked abruptly.

'None that I know of.'

'Time is getting late. She needs to arrange everything now.'

Freddi shrugged. 'You can't tell her anything. Zenia is just Zenia.'

'Do you happen to know how many wills she's already made?'

'No. Does it matter?'

'It might. God knows what fool she's left everything to. Is her lawyer still old Paricelli?'

'No. She quarrelled with him over something. She's with a local lawyer called Barsetti now. He practises in Pula. Apparently she knew his father in Trieste when she was a child.'

'Then I'll contact him when I get back to Milan.'

'Isn't that a breach of confidence?'

Antonio's eyebrows rose. He made an elegant gesture with his right hand. 'I am her next of kin. It will be left to me to sort out her affairs when she is dead, just as it was in life. They cannot object to that.'

'I can,' Freddi said. Her cheeks were flushed. 'Zenia is still very much alive and in charge of her own affairs. It is, frankly, none of your business.'

Antonio drained his grappa glass and put it carefully on the table. 'That is where we differ. It is very much my business.' He stood up. 'It has been a long day so I will say goodnight and I will see you in the morning. Signora Forbes.' He gave a little bow to Alex, almost clicking his heels, 'and Signora Baker Thompson. Tomorrow I will see my cousin and we will find out how things are.'

He turned and left the room. Alex realised that Freddi was silently crying.

'He's a poisonous man,' she said. 'I can't bear it if he inherits all this… He's a soulless hypocrite.'

Alex wanted to agree with her, but was also conscious that she might need some of his approval for Zenia's biography, particularly if he was likely to inherit any of her manuscripts. She was tempted to confide her personal feelings to Freddi to comfort her, but she remembered her mother telling her sternly when she was a child, 'Walls have ears!' She closed her lips on all she might have wanted to say.

'It's difficult to know who you can trust,' she said to Freddi.

'No-one,' Freddi said. 'I'm the outsider here. The interloper. That's how they see me.'

'Even Concetta?'

'And Ludo, and the family. Fourteen years I've been with her and they still don't accept me.'

Alex didn't know how to contradict such evident truth. 'Don't Zenia's wishes count for anything with them?'

'I think they've watched her making bad decisions all her life and they all feel they know what's best for her better than she does. It doesn't matter while she can still speak for herself, but afterwards…'

'What you and Zenia have is very special,' Alex

said. 'It shouldn't be discounted.'

Freddi almost smiled.

'Thanks. But he won't care, and in the end neither will they.'

There was silence. Freddi was staring into the fire.

Alex sighed and put down her glass, still half full. 'I must go to bed. It's been such a long day. Let me know if there's anything I can do tomorrow?'

Freddi didn't look round. Curled in the chair with her feet drawn up, she seemed very young and vulnerable.

'Goodnight Alex. Sleep well.'

Alex woke up late with a start. Nine o'clock. How could she sleep so long? By the time she'd showered and dressed and walked down the steps to the dining room it was almost ten. Alex could hear raised voices and as she cautiously pushed the door inwards she realised that she was walking in on a scene.

Freddi was standing with her back to the door, rigid, with one hand on a chair. Alex could see Antonio's face in the overmantel mirror, a smooth, controlled mask.

Freddi was speaking. 'I won't have you upsetting her. How dare you go up there when she's scarcely awake!'

'She is not upset. A little troubled perhaps. But these things must be settled.'

'She's distraught!' Freddi shouted.

Alex had never seen her so out of control.

'She's supposed to be kept calm – peace and quiet, the doctor said. He was adamant. She could have a stroke – a heart attack – how dare you come here and do this to us!'

'I am merely doing my duty to the family, to find out how things stand. It is very important that everything is properly tied up.'

'Important for you! Property is all you care about

– you don't care for her at all.'

'That is untrue,' Antonio's voice had an edge to it like a knife. 'She is my cousin and I care more for her than you think.'

'I would like you to leave,' Freddi said. 'Now.'

'You don't have that authority,' Antonio said calmly.

There was a movement on the other side of the room. A man's voice said, 'Doesn't she?' Alex saw Concetta step through the kitchen door, and standing behind her was Gianfranco. 'I think you're forgetting the common courtesies,' he said as he came into the room. 'It isn't your house yet.'

'But it is Zenia's, and when she asks me to go, I will go.'

'So when she told you to get out, earlier – oh yes, I was listening – you obviously didn't understand her? Am I right?'

'How dare you!' There was anger now in Antonio's voice. 'I warn you, if you take her side,' indicating Freddi, 'you will forfeit my support. There will not be a single *centesimo* for you.'

'As if I cared for that.'

There was contempt on Antonio's face. 'I know very well how much you can earn from music. How are you going to live when she isn't there to give you handouts?'

'I earn enough.'

Alex realised, looking at his clenched fists, that Gianfranco was shaking with anger.

He went on, 'Not for you maybe. But enough for me.'

'You think there is some morality in being poor?

You are wrong. Poverty makes men into thieves.' Antonio looked round the room. He turned his head and for the first time saw Alex standing in the doorway. 'Signora Forbes. No doubt you are recording all this for posterity?' He walked towards her. 'You had better be careful what you write, otherwise you will be receiving a writ from my lawyers.' He nodded to her and swept past and out into the courtyard.

'I'm going to send for the doctor,' Freddi said. 'She won't want me to, but I'm worried about her. I've never seen her so upset. She told me to telephone her lawyer and she insists on seeing you – I've no idea why. She won't tell me what she intends to do.' Freddi looked at Alex. Her eyes were accusing. 'She tells you things she's never told me.'

Alex felt guilty. 'Sometimes it's easier to talk to a stranger.' The biographer, Alex thought, was always the observer, the outsider, the one whose job it was to be objective and impersonal. But how was she to do this in Zenia's case, when she was getting more and more involved? Drawn into the story and in danger of becoming part of it? Wasn't this what anthropologists feared? That the very act of observation affected the behaviour of those observed, the chain of events?

Gianfranco followed Alex up the stairs. Propped up in her bed, Zenia looked agitated. Her hands constantly clutched at the bedspread, crushing it and then letting it go. Her head moving from side to side on the pillow.

'Why does she want to bring me a doctor? There is no cure for what I have. I am going to die. But, please God, not until I have arranged everything for my children.'

Gianfranco sat on the bedcover and stroked her hand. 'Freddi said you wanted your lawyer.'

'Andrea Barsetti. He is a good man. I am going to do what Signora Forbes suggested.' Her eyes flickered across Alex's face. 'I am going to make a kind of "*usa frutta*" for Freddi. I had thought… my cousin…' She made a helpless gesture. 'But your father has betrayed me now a second time and that I cannot forgive.'

'What did he want?'

'Everything. He wants to control my work, but more than anything he wanted me to sign a paper saying I rejected publication of my life story. It is because of what he did in the war, I think. But I also fear that there is something else.' She turned her head and addressed her next words to Alex. 'Some of his connections from the war have done terrible things here in Croatia. Antonio likes to stay in the shadows. Your book may shine a little beam of light where he does not want it to be seen. You must be careful.'

The door opened and Concetta came in carrying a tray. She nodded to Gianfranco and Alex and turned towards the bed. 'It is time for your breakfast, *cara*. Your visitors must go.'

'But I want to see you afterwards,' Zenia said suddenly, waving a trembling hand towards Alex. 'After I have had a little sleep. You and I must talk before it is too late.'

'Too much talk is not good for you,' Concetta said with a frown as she put down the tray on the bed.

Zenia looked up at her with a very sweet expression, and said firmly, 'Soon, *cara*, there will be no talking at all. So let me do it when I can.'

It was quiet in the dining room. Lenka had taken Antonio a tray to his room, and the chauffeur ate alone in the kitchen. The atmosphere was sombre. Freddi had a white, pinched look to her face and her eyes were a record of sleepless nights. Even Concetta looked troubled.

Gianfranco's mobile rang just as she was serving up a gigantic *torta di mele* swirled with cream and vanilla sugar. He got up from the table and went outside to take the call. When he came back in he looked as though he'd just been given bad news. 'I'm afraid I've got to go,' he said, with a wry twist of his mouth, looking towards Alex. 'Someone's fallen ill at the jazz club in Turin and they want me to step in.'

'What a pity!' Freddi said. 'We were looking forward to you being around for a few days.'

Lenka's mouth had turned down at the corners and Alex suspected that her own had also drooped.

Alex was walking back towards her room just as Gianfranco appeared with his weekend bag over his shoulder, carrying two instrument cases. He stopped and smiled down at her. 'Sorry,' he said, 'Just as it was getting interesting.'

Alex turned and began to walk towards the car park with him. 'Back to texting and emailing then?'

He laughed. 'I suppose so. As a musician all you seem to get are long distance relationships. The music always has to come first.'

Alex noticed that he had used the word relationship. She thought for a moment then she said, 'I suppose one day we might be in the same place at the same time long enough to get to know each other properly.'

'Is that on the wish list?'

'Yes.' She risked a quick glance sideways. He was smiling.

'Good.' He opened up the boot and packed the bag and the instrument cases carefully under rugs. Then turned and took her face in both hands and kissed her. His lips were warm against her cold face.

There was the crunching sound of feet on gravel. They drew apart and Alex turned her head to see Lenka standing with a shocked expression.

'I came to say goodbye,' she said, and then turned and walked furiously away.

'I don't encourage her, you know,' Gianfranco said regretfully. 'She's only trying to make Martin jealous.'

Alex wasn't sure, but she agreed.

'Watch over Zenia for me,' Gianfranco said. His face was very serious now. 'There are too many people trying to influence her to do things for their own benefit.'

'I'll try. But it's not easy.'

He got into the car, waved and then she watched his car swerve down the steep gradient below the gate, brake lights flaring in the low, afternoon light.

Toby put his head round the door about 4pm and said, 'She's awake and wants to see you.'

Zenia looked brighter, less troubled after her sleep.

'Where have they put you this time?'

'In the Tomizza apartment. Did you know Fulvio Tomizza?'

'Ah, Fulvio,' Zenia said. 'I knew him a little. A nice man. He understood about art. Writers don't always understand about painting – they want to make it into a narrative – a story. But sometimes it is not. Sometimes it is about colour and space and the way a line moves across the surface. It is another language I have tried all my life to learn. And perhaps now it's too late.' She was silent for a moment and then glanced across at Alex. 'Why did you ask about Fulvio?'

'I'm reading *The Tree of Dreams* – it was in my room.'

'Yes, that was the best of his novels, I think. Art is just the fabric of dreams – it is like dreaming when you are awake – you know the phrase "*sognare da sveglio*"? Only now I seem to be dreaming all the time – and I don't know whether I am asleep or awake. Does that make sense to you?'

Alex nodded. She could still remember being a child, not being able to distinguish between what she imagined inside her head and what was outside it – both seemed equally real. Perhaps it was like that again when you were very old?

'Anyway, what I want to tell you is that I have sent for my lawyer to make the trust. And I want you to be a witness to it. All the others, you see, will be remembered in the will, but you are not part of the family, so you will be allowed to sign. And I am relying on you to make sure everyone knows what I wanted to happen. That man is a snake! Madonna! I should never have trusted him, but you know, when people are family…' Her voice died away as if from exhaustion.

'You said earlier that he had betrayed you twice. What was the first time?'

'Did I not tell you? It was when he told my mother, after he had seen me swimming with Bernardo. It was after that that my mother came to my room and demanded to see my body. She was very angry. It has often puzzled me. Perhaps she had forgotten my "little imperfection"? Or perhaps she hoped that it had gone away. She had never troubled me about it until then. I tried to cover myself, but she was too strong for me and I was not prepared. I was astonished that she should do such a thing. She swore at me and then she went away. I think I cried.'

Zenia paused. Her eyes were fixed on the distance as if watching pictures moving in front of them.

'The next week she took me away – she didn't tell me where we were going – I thought it was a holiday, or perhaps to see a new school. But it was a private clinic in Vienna. The doctor – I will always remember him – he wore an armband with the Nazi swastika on it. My mother spoke German with him, which I couldn't follow, and then she left me there and told me I must do what they told me to do.'

There was a long silence, as if Zenia was making up her mind whether to go on or not. Then she ran her tongue over her lips and began to speak again.

'They castrated me. First they cut off my little penis and then they gave me radiation to kill the hormones. Or they thought that was what they were doing. Then they gave me other hormones to make my breasts grow. I was to become wholly woman. But my mind was always a man's mind. All that they did to me was to take away any pleasure that my body could give me. From that day on there was only a longing – a hunger for loving that could never be satisfied. And there were times when it was so much agony that I could hardly bear myself at all. I hated my mother for doing this to me. And I hated Antonio – because I was sure then that he was the one who had betrayed me to her.'

Zenia sighed. 'But it was all a long time ago when we were children and somehow you must learn to forgive.

Otherwise you will go mad. Your parents are only human beings and they make mistakes. When you grow up you have to forgive them for these things. Maybe if it hadn't happened I would never have become an artist. So perhaps in taking away one thing, they gave me something else. I don't know.'

There was nothing Alex could say, in the face of a private tragedy so enormous, that would have any meaning at all, or be of any use. And for an instant she knew how inadequate people might feel when confronted by her own story. There were no words that could be said. Alex held out her hand and Zenia took it.

'Once in New York, after I had quarrelled with someone dear to me – I had a dream – a nightmare. I was still a child and they had pinned me to the bed – holding me down by the arms and legs. Someone had taken a poker out of the fire and they were burning my little penis off. I could feel it burning and burning, and I was screaming, but no-one could hear me. I woke with such pain between my legs as you could not believe. And I got up and I just wanted to go down to the Brooklyn bridge and throw myself off. So I got in the car and I drove down there, but as I was standing on the edge looking down, this big black man came across the bridge pushing an old supermarket trolley full of plastic bags with a dog sitting in the basket at the back. He was scavenging through the litter bins for half eaten take-aways and cigarette ends people had thrown down. Somehow I couldn't jump off with him watching me, so I waited. But he came up to me and held out a rather battered cigarette he took out of his pocket. "Don't do it," he said.' Zenia imitated the man's rough American voice. '"What you got in your life can't be so bad you don't want to see the good things a-comin'." He had a broad southern accent – Texas maybe. "Are there any good things coming?" I asked him. "Sure thing," he said, standing there in his rags, unwashed, probably without a cent in his pocket. "The whole world's a candy store – you just gotta get in there with a cart."'

She paused and laughed, a dry, self-mocking laugh. 'He was crazy, of course. A loony-man. But he stopped me from killing myself and I have always been grateful for that. All the best things in my life came to me after that day. I had my first big exhibition, I met Paulina, I found the Kaštela. And I realised suddenly that in his crazy way he told the truth – life is not just to be suffered. You have to go out there and go after what you want with the biggest basket you can find. To be passive is to be a victim – and I will not be a victim!'

As Alex stood up to leave, Zenia said, 'They will try to stop you writing this, you know, after I am dead. But you mustn't let them.' Zenia reached out and clutched her arm. 'Promise me!'

Alex grasped her cold, shaking hand and promised.

The atmosphere at the Kaštela was gloomy after the departure of Gianfranco. Zenia kept to her room and Freddi was preoccupied and unusually silent. It was almost a relief for Alex when it was time to go. Freddi, her eyes swollen with crying, came into the bedroom while Alex was gathering her belongings together .

'I meant what I said you know. I don't want you to mention me in this biography.' She seemed distraught, pushing her fingers through her hair, moving nervously around the room. 'I know what Zenia wants and I can't

stop her or you. But you have to leave me out of it, just as
I asked, please. I don't want you to use my name.'

'Are you sure, Freddi? You've been such an important part of her life. I've got to mention you even if it's just
to say, "Freddi Baker-Thompson, her companion for ten,
fifteen years", however long you've been together.'

'Fourteen. Fourteen wonderful, difficult years. The
heaven and hell of living with Zenia. There are always two
ways of looking at things with her.'

'But that's what I need from you. No-one else can
tell me how that feels.'

'Absolutely not! Do you know what people might
say?'

Looking at the genuine distress in Freddi's face,
Alex capitulated. 'OK. I'll try to keep you out of it, Freddi.
But it won't be the same.'

Freddi turned and left the room without saying
anything. Alex heard her feet running down the steps back
towards the tower and then the slamming of the door.

Alex felt sick. First Concetta, now Freddi. If the
two people closest to Zenia didn't want to co-operate, how
was she ever going to write a comprehensive, credible, account of Zenia's life?

Alex hadn't been back in England more than three days, when she had a phone call from her doctor.

'How are you Alex?'

'Fine. Absolutely fine.' The surprise in her voice must have been very audible.

'You weren't expecting to hear from me?'

'Is there something wrong?'

'That's what I'm hoping to find out from you. At the practice, we're a little worried that we haven't heard from you for a while, and you haven't picked up your repeat prescription.'

'I stopped taking the drugs.'

There was a pause at the other end of the line. Alex could hear papers being moved.

'Are you sure that's wise?'

'The only things I need, you can't put on a prescription.' Love, Alex thought. A little happiness.

'I would feel a lot better if you came in to see us and had a chat about it.'

Alex sighed. 'No, really. I'm fine. I haven't had any side effects from not taking the pills. I'm sleeping better and I'm working on a new project.'

'That sounds wonderful.' The sound of a pen scratching on a pad. 'But I would still like to see you. I could fit you in sometime this week? When would suit you?'

'Look.' Alex felt weary. 'It's really, really, good of you to care enough to check up on me. But I am as OK as it's possible to be at the moment and I'm not in danger of jumping off a bridge.' She gave a wry laugh. 'Don't worry. If I start getting depressed again, I'll call. I promise.' Then she put the phone down firmly and sat looking at it for a moment. The call had unsettled her. Was she fine? Or was it an illusion? But if she couldn't decide that for herself, there was certainly no point in going to a doctor.

Alex dug out one of her old address books and rang a contact in New York.

'Hi, Matti. It's Alex here. Alex Forbes.'

There was a short incredulous silence and then a squeal of recognition. 'Alex? It's really you? Oh-my-god! We haven't heard from you in – well, not since – how are you?'

'I'm fine. Working on another book. Are you still writing for the *Tribune*?'

'No. I'm not working at all.' There was a pause. Alex could hear her hesitating, picking her words. 'I'm post-natal.'

'That's great. What did you have?' Alex was careful to keep her voice steady and upbeat.

'A little boy.' She could hear Matti's relief. 'We called him Carl after my father. Ten pounds two ounces. Can you believe? I blew up like a balloon. I was so big I didn't see my feet from June through to September.'

Alex laughed, trying to imagine five feet two, seven and a half stone Matti giving birth to such a monster.

Her happiness made Alex feel immensely sad. It was time to broach the subject she'd rung for. 'I need to pick your brains, Matti. Or maybe your address book. Who would I talk to if I wanted to find out about the painter Frank Harrison? Could you find out for me. I thought your father might have some contacts through the gallery.'

'Is this for your new book? I'll do my best. God, it'll be good to get my brain round something other than measuring formula. I'm turning into a moron.'

'It's the hormones. Your brain starts to function again after about a year.'

'Thank God for that. Did it ever get you down, too?'

Alex hadn't thought about those hot, frustrating days in New York for a long time. She hadn't coped with pregnancy well at all. Her body had felt clumsy, she was always hot and sweating, the apartment didn't have air-conditioning and sometimes she felt she would suffocate. Everyone said it was one of the hottest summers they'd ever experienced. Alex, swollen and bloated with this alien life form growing so tenaciously inside her, had taken endless cold showers, lain on the bed with the fan full on her damp skin, struggled up and down the stairs with shopping, while her brain had turned to mush. When she tried to work, the words had wriggled about on the screen like insects refusing to be pinned down. She felt panic at the prospect of not being able to work at all – would changing diapers and feeding babies consume the whole of her life?

Steve's mother had crowed with joy when he told her she was to be a grandmother, and then turned up at the apartment with cots and car seats and high chairs and expensive baby clothes, none of which were what Alex would have chosen. She felt that the baby was being taken away from her before it was even born. And her mother-in-law seemed determined to keep her stored in cotton wool. 'You've got to take it easy,' she kept saying. 'Not go racketing around town when there's no need. You don't want to tax yourself. It's important to get enough rest.'

Alex was sick of rest. Sick of being in the apartment. Afraid the baby, when it was born, would be possessed by her mother-in-law who seemed obsessed by the sex of the baby, determined it should be a boy. 'What did the midwife say?' she would ask, ringing up almost the moment Alex returned from her antenatal appointments (Did Steve tell her the times and the dates?). 'Do we know what the little fella is going to be yet?' She seemed horrified that Alex didn't want to know in advance. Alex was sure her mother-in-law had tried to persuade Steve to find out, without telling Alex. She dreaded having a boy.

But then came the moment when the midwife said, 'You have a beautiful little girl,' and handed her Katy, who was from the first moment all her own.

Alex hadn't been prepared for that rush of joy and overwhelming love when Katy was put into her arms. The moment when those blue eyes (Steve's eyes) had blinked open in the bright light of the delivery room and fixed on her face, and then the baby had turned and nuzzled her breast, instinctively seeking the nipple under the surgical gown that was stained and damp with the milk that had leaked out during labour. It had seemed like a miracle.

Alex sat at her desk, still holding the telephone, and wept for it.

But then, afterwards, had come the boredom. Looking after Katy's physical needs didn't occupy her brain at all and Alex began to long for stimulation. Feeding spoonfuls of baby cereal while watching daytime TV; sometimes she read a book while she fed the baby, feeling guilty – wasn't she supposed to use this time for 'bonding'? Alex began taking Katy out to galleries, pushing the buggy round while she slept, and it was there standing in front of Caravaggio's *Musicians* in the Met that she began to wonder whether she could tell his story. While Katy slept she wrote. While Katy played she read. A friend who had a child the same age agreed to have Katy one morning a week so that Alex could spend time on research in the New York Library. It was salvation. Putting words on paper made Alex feel a different person. She could cope with broken nights, the mind-numbing domestic routine, even the visits of her mother-in-law, if she could only do that.

But it didn't meet with approval. Steve's mother had taken to turning up unannounced at their flat bringing unsuitable clothes and toys, expecting to be welcomed, angry to find Alex out and about with the baby. Once, Alex had come back from the park to find her sitting on a chair in the lobby, utterly furious.

The worst thing was not being able to complain to Steve about his mother – he was stubbornly loyal and Alex could see, now that she had Katy, that the mother and child bond counted for a great deal. Steve would never take her side against his mother. She would just have to suffer it, in silence if possible.

Except that it wasn't.

The publication of the book had gone a long way to help – Alex now had her own life, independent of Steve and his mother, and she had Katy, which gave her status and power within the relationship. Looking back, Alex could see that this had made her reckless.

She sat for a moment longer, thinking of the most shameful episode of her whole life. The one she still could not forgive herself for. The action that had caused everything that followed.

It was a gallery opening party. Steve had been at home baby-sitting Katy. Alex had drunk rather too much champagne and a group of them had gone back to the apartment of a journalist friend whose name Alex could no longer remember. Bill had been there – a painter who's exhibition she'd reviewed a few weeks earlier. He'd been phoning and chatting and they'd had coffee occasionally and lunch once. He knew she was married with a child, knew she was unhappy. She knew he wanted her.

Somehow, during that evening, she'd found herself in the spare bedroom, flinging off her clothes and having violent, ruthless sex with Bill. Afterwards, lying there exhausted and replete, she had sobered up and seen clearly – too late, much, much too late – what she had done.

Dr Song Li had kept his promise to arrange a meeting with his young client, though it was email addresses only, no surnames and an early evening interview at a wine bar in Richmond. She could spare about half an hour, she said.

Chris was sitting at the bar, and Alex guessed who she was almost straight away. She was dressed in jeans and a white shirt, her hair short in a female kind of way, but something about the length of her torso, the way she sat, the set of her shoulders, was very masculine.

She turned her head as Alex approached and grinned. 'Hi! You must be Alex.' She held out her hand to be shaken. A big, square hand. 'Do you realise we've both got genderless names?'

'I'm afraid mine's short for Alessandra.'

'Oh. I'm just Chris. My parents thought it might be a good idea to call me something ambidextrous.'

Alex climbed up on the bar stool beside hers and ordered a glass of wine from the waiting barman; 'Dry white – ABC – anything but chardonnay, please!'

Chris raised her eyebrow in a question mark.

'The backlash to Bridget Jones.'

'I didn't see that movie.' The way she said it made Alex feel very old. 'I'm a half of lager kind of person. I don't like wine.' She waited until the barman had set the glass in front of Alex and then said, 'Dr Song said you wanted to talk to me about some book you're writing.'

'I'm working on a biography of a painter who was born a hermaphrodite in the nineteen twenties. I'm trying to get some insights into her life and your consultant thought it might help to talk to someone in the same situation.'

Chris frowned. 'I don't think anyone can really know how it feels unless they've been through it themselves. It can be hell. Stupid people treat you like a freak. But it's normal at the same time, normal for me anyway.'

'How did your parents cope?'

'You'd have to ask them, but they've been fantastic compared to what I've heard about other people's. It's always been talked about and they've always encouraged me to think of myself as a third sex, rather than an aberration of the other two. And they let me make my own medical decisions. But I'm lucky they had money and could send me to a private school – can you imagine being on a council estate and going to the local comprehensive? I've met kids at the clinic who've had the shit kicked out of them – one even tried to top herself.'

'It must have been difficult at school though?'

'What do you think?' She shrugged. 'Being different's hard for kids. Being told you're special doesn't help either. Dr Song's really good though. He's formed this group on the internet – you can chat to other inter-sex people – read their experiences. It's all very private – you have to be a member to get access – keeps the wierdos out.'

'What's the hardest thing?'

Chris hesitated and then said, 'Relationships – you tell the bloke as early as you can, but you still don't know how he's going to handle it in bed. You can take that literally if you want.' She giggled. 'But then there's the assholes who are just dating you out of curiosity. That's really hurtful.'

'So you're attracted to men?'

'Not exclusively. I fancy girls too. It gets complicated.' Chris held out her glass to the barman for a refill. 'There are times when it gets you down. I've been lucky to have so much support.'

'Dr Song Li told me you're doing A levels this year – do you know what you're going to do with them?'

She answered straight away. 'Performance arts. It's the one career where being able to be both sexes is an advantage. You can wear masks and be anyone you like. And all the actors I've ever met are so accepting of anyone who's a bit different.' She giggled again. 'Can you imagine me being an accountant? And they'd never let me near a class full of children!'

Chris had told Alex that she was meeting friends at about eight and it was already a few moments past the hour on the bar clock.

'I'd better go and leave you to your evening out,' Alex said. 'Thanks for talking to me. I'm really grateful.'

The girl shook her head. 'I don't think talking to me's going to give you much idea, really. We all handle this in our own way. No-one's experience is the same. Mine isn't going to help you understand hers.'

'Oh but it has,' Alex said. 'A lot.' This girl was going out into the world courageously open about her intersexuality, whereas Zenia had had to conceal a great deal. Chris was being allowed to keep her dual identity, but Zenia had been maimed by her well-meaning mother. Alex hoped that Chris would find happiness without having to go through the torments that Zenia had endured.

'Bye.' Chris held out her hand again. 'Good luck with your book. Let me know when it's out – I'd be interested.'

Alex's final conversation with Freddi had left her shaken and pessimistic about hearing from her again. But, a couple of weeks after Alex arrived back in London, Freddi's email address popped up on the screen.

I just wanted to thank you for your help in persuading Zenia to make the trust. You don't know what that means to me. You must have thought me very ungrateful. I'm still anxious about the biography and still believe that Zenia was extremely ill-advised to agree to it (I blame her pushy agent Andrew Kir for that). But I've realised that, if the biography isn't published, Antonio will have won control over Zenia's life-story and reputation, and I can't let that happen. I haven't changed my mind about wanting you to keep my name out of the book though, however awkward that may be. But, in the light of Antonio Antonelli's recent interference, I think you should know the facts about our relationship – I don't want to be misrepresented in any way.

I met Zenia when I was eighteen and working at a gallery in Cork Street. I was studying a course in art history, and didn't know quite what I was going to do with my life. When Zenia came into the gallery, I thought she was extraordinary – the most fantastic person I'd ever met. We went to lunch and then lunch turned into dinner and then we went on to a party at Jeffrey Archer's and she was introducing me to all kinds of people I'd only dreamed of meeting.

After that she kept coming into the gallery with presents – lovely things like the Nigerian mask on the wall in the bedroom, or it might be a pound of wild boar sausages she'd found in a deli in Soho. She would come to my flat unexpectedly with several of her friends and bottles of wine. Or ring up in the middle of the night needing to be rescued from somewhere or other. Once she was in a garage and had filled up with petrol only to realise she had no money with her!

I resisted being involved at first because I had never thought of having a relationship with a woman – it had never occurred to me – and particularly one so much older than myself. I'm not a lesbian. Absolutely not. So I thought, how can I love a woman? It disturbed me. I had boyfriends too – of course I had. I was very pretty. But none of them loved me as Zenia did. None of them turned my world upside down like Zenia. So in the end I just gave in. And I've loved her ever since even though it's sometimes hard. She's selfish, infuriatingly illogical and egotistical and used to having everything her own way. That's what I meant by the heaven and the hell of living with Zenia.

Please don't make assumptions about our relationship. And please don't hang it out to dry in public for people to wink and make snide remarks about. It's been the one really precious, worthwhile thing in my life and I want to keep it intact. That's why I don't want my name mentioned.

There's another reason too. My parents don't know about Zenia – at least only part of the truth. They think I'm living here as her personal assistant. They're very conventional and I want to avoid giving them any distress.

There was a text from Gianfranco. 'I'm in New York next week playing at the Village Vanguard – when are you thinking of being there?'

Alex texted back, 'Probably next week. Just have to set up a meeting with someone.' Matti had sent the information Alex needed within days. Frank Harrison himself was dead, but he had had a wife called Toni, Alex thought probably the 'T' of the letters, and she had proved to be still very much alive. Alex wondered whether she was the 'painter's wife' who, according to Angelina, had caused so much trouble in Zenia's life. Matti's contact at the gallery had come up with an address, telephone number and a recommendation which they'd already mailed to Toni. She indicated that she'd be sympathetic to the contact, so all Alex had to do was arrange an appointment.

'Great!' Gianfranco inserted a smiley face into the text. 'And you won't need a hotel; I've got the key to Zenia's apartment. Will email address.'

Alex felt a slight ripple of panic and her fingers froze on the keypad. She knew what he would expect to happen if they shared the apartment – what she also knew would happen if they were in such close proximity. It was too soon. Much too soon.

After a moment she texted back. 'Will be staying at the Chelsea where Zenia used to live. Already fixed up. Will let you know when I'm going to be there.'

But as soon as she'd sent it, Alex felt regret. He would interpret it as a rebuff. Which it was. 'I need to concentrate on Zenia without emotional complications', Alex told herself, knowing that it wasn't exactly that. She was running away. Besides, she argued, there were other things she had to deal with in New York and they were things she could only confront alone.

'God, what's wrong with you? I would kill for a really good fuck,' Josie said, putting her feet up on the spare chair, out of sight of the barman, and swilling her red wine round the glass. Divorced, childless, outspoken, Josie was one of the few friends Alex had kept up with, whose company she still felt comfortable in.

'So what's the problem with this Italian of yours?'

'Nothing. That's the problem.' Alex thought for a moment, trying to find negatives. 'He hates to fail, so I suppose he's a perfectionist. He says music has to come first, so he's probably selfish, and I think also commitment phobic, all good reasons to stay clear.' Alex paused. 'The trouble is, I fancy the pants off him.'

'Mmmmm.' Josie took another swipe at the hummous with a triangle of pitta bread. 'You're scared that you might actually want a relationship with him.'

'What about you? It takes one to know one.'

Josie shrugged. 'I've slept with too many men. Some of them I don't even remember. I woke up one morning, there was a dent in the pillow and the whole bed smelled of man. I got up to look for him and the loo seat was up, there was cigarette smoke in the kitchen and an empty coffee mug, but no sign of him anywhere. That was the saddest sight of all, that coffee mug, on its own on the corner of the table.'

She picked up her glass again. 'If you pass this one over, Alessandra Forbes, I'm warning you, there may never be another chance.'

'Well then, we'll just have to grow old and drunk together,' Alex said, lifting her glass and clinking it against Josie's. '*Salute!* Here's to an immoral old age.'

Alex wasn't sure what she'd expected Zenia's agent to look like. Andrew Kir, according to the internet, was an old Etonian, but Alex suspected that he came from an Eastern European background. He was immaculately dressed with a politician's smooth, watchful face. His voice was beautifully modulated, quick to adapt to any nuance in a protagonist, ready with an apt response. Alex had deduced quite a lot from the fluidity of his voice on the phone, but she hadn't expected him to be also slightly gossipy.

'How's the old reprobate?' he asked.

'Fading away.'

'That doesn't sound like Zenia.'

'It's true though, she seems remarkably accepting at the moment. When I first met her she was full of anger and willing to fight to the last. Now she sleeps most of the time.'

'How very sad! Still, I suppose we can't choose how we go. And Freddi? How is she taking it? We don't talk about it on the phone.'

'Hard, I think. And there seems to be some kind of battle going on with Concetta over who's in control of

Zenia's care.'

'A lot of jealousy there, my dear. A lot of water under the bridge. Concetta's been with Zenia for forty years, much of it working unpaid. And probably her lover too at some time or other.'

Alex felt quite shocked. 'Do you think so?'

'Why ever not? What else could explain such devotion? When I was staying there once, Concetta's husband arrived on the doorstep, drunk of course, brandishing a hunting rifle and accusing Zenia of taking his wife away from him. The language was apparently terrible – I was glad I didn't understand it. I'm afraid my Italian is confined to art history and fine dining.'

'But surely – Concetta's a devout Catholic?'

'Oh, if it's sexual deviancy you're after, Catholicism is the creed for you – nothing that can't be wiped out by a good confession.'

Alex was liking Andrew less and less, but kept her facial expression under control because she needed his approval and help. She told him she was going to New York and asked for a list of contacts he thought might be useful. 'I've found the Harrisons through a New York friend, so I'm arranging to meet Toni when I'm there.'

'That's good. Sadly, Frank is dead. And his work has rather slipped out of fashion. A mention in your book might stimulate a little interest. You know he painted them nude?'

'Toni and Zenia?'

'People used to refer to them as his two wives. I never saw the painting though – rumour has it that it was destroyed when Zenia was thrown out. You know Frank threw all her belongings out of the apartment window into the street? All hearsay. It was before my time.'

He smiled. Alex found it rather unpleasant.

He went on, 'Her life has been quite scandalous you know – the kind of thing the tabloid press love to report. Of course it's very good for business, but I do hope your biography isn't going to be like that. We're looking for something rather more elegant.'

'Of course. I don't do tabloid.' Alex tried to keep the anger she felt out of her voice. She thought about the difference between the public view of Zenia's life and the view from the inside. Zenia's whole life had been a search for love, both the giving and the receiving of it. To reduce her important relationships to the status of grubby 'affairs' made Alex feel nauseous.

'Zenia really loved those women you know.'

'But, my dear, she was so promiscuous!'

Words were themselves promiscuous, Alex reflected. Promiscuity used to mean 'mixing easily' in her A level science class, a reference to the desirability of chemicals to interact creatively. But in common speech it meant something different and derogatory – the immoral acquisition of multiple partners.

New York felt familiar from the moment Alex stepped out of the taxi outside the hotel. The canyon-like street, strident winter cold, the roar of traffic, the hooting and lane-changing, people careering down the sidewalk – the energy hit Alex like an electric shock. Apart from the disintegration of her marriage, those years in New York had been the happiest in her life. Why had she ever gone back to England after her divorce? In full flight from Steve, like a wounded animal retreating into its hole, she had gone 'home' only to discover that it wasn't.

The Chelsea's quirky flamboyance, all paid for by Zenia's agent, was a new experience for Alex. Her knowledge of it was superficial. She had once been to a book launch inside, and she had heard, (who hadn't?) the legendary stories of the writers and artists who'd lived, as some of them still did, on its upper floors; among them Thomas Wolfe, Mark Rothko, Jack Kerouac. It was supposedly haunted by the ghost of Dylan Thomas who drank himself to death there, though he'd actually died in a hospital. And Zenia had once been part of that legend, until Paulina had left her the Village apartment in her will.

As Alex walked into the foyer, she was almost stopped in her tracks by the display of paintings; an assault on the senses of abstract and figurative, blatant acrylic colours, pale pastels, sombre oils, all jumbled together on the walls and up the ornate staircase. Alex wondered if there were any of Zenia's portraits there. She asked the man behind the reception desk, but he shook his head. 'I have no idea,' he said. 'But you could walk up and look – it's twelve floors though.' He smiled broadly at the expression on Alex's face. 'I could ask the owners. They'd remember her – they remember everyone.'

Alex's room was at the front – bigger than the average hotel room, with a muddle of sixties furniture; a coffee table shaped like a palette, yellow and red plastic chairs that looked impossible to sit on and a gigantic bed with a sunburst headboard, each cast-iron ray topped with a coloured plastic ball. The mattress sagged. But there was hot water in the taps, wi-fi, and the view from the little wrought-iron balcony was spectacular. It would do for the moment.

Toni Harrison's voice on the phone had been very English, overlaid by a slight American intonation. She had sounded cautious, reluctant, persuaded by Alex's mention of the gallery owner's name and his recommendation. But face to face Toni was more welcoming. She lived in a stylish modern apartment block in Manhattan with panoramic views of the Hudson river and New Jersey that Alex calculated must have cost at least a couple of million dollars. Frank Harrison had done well out of art. A gigantic abstract in black and orange and red against a blue background, filled the whole of one wall in the sitting room and there were other paintings scattered around the room.

Alex was asked whether she'd had a good trip – how

did New York seem after being away from it? – and without giving Alex time to answer the question, Toni volunteered that she'd lived here so long she could hardly imagine being anywhere else. Alex was invited to sit down on a big white leather sofa and offered tea or coffee or something stronger? She chose tea and it was brought by a small Hispanic girl in a grey uniform. Toni sat opposite, neat in pale green trousers and matching cashmere sweater, a yellow chiffon scarf around her neck, sipping a glass of mineral water. Her eyes were very bright and, from the flow of trivia she'd kept up since Alex came through the front door, she seemed naturally talkative.

'As I told you on the phone,' she said brusquely, 'I'll try to help you, but I'm not going to tell you anything that might reflect badly on my husband or myself. If Frank was still alive he wouldn't have wanted me to speak to you at all.'

'I appreciate that. And I do understand your need for privacy.' Alex tried to sound as reasonable as possible. 'I just need to ask a few questions to try to establish whether the version of events I've got from Zenia and other people is correct.'

'You can ask,' Toni's voice was robust, 'but I don't guarantee to give you an answer!'

Alex felt daunted, but she put the first question from the list in her notebook. 'I gather that Zenia lived with you and your husband for a while in New York. Was it here?'

'No, of course not!' Toni laughed and waved a hand dismissively. 'We didn't have much money then – we had an apartment in Brooklyn – brownstone, fourth floor, no lift. You know the kind of thing. Zenia was supposed to be Frank's assistant.'

She paused for a moment and Alex, fearing she was going to dry up, said, 'You met in London?'

Toni nodded. 'It was Zenia's idea to come out here with us. But there was always so much competition. And she would get in such a rage if he got an exhibition and didn't include some of her paintings in it.' Toni seemed to be picking her words carefully now. 'But he couldn't always – their work was very different – not just in style but in quality – her work was very rough then. And the gallery owners often didn't want her. New York is a hard place to break into and Frank saw Zenia just as an assistant, a kind of satellite, rather than an artist in her own right and I think she found that very damaging. So it was a rather explosive relationship.'

The next question was more difficult. 'I know it's personal, and maybe painful to you, but there are letters between you and Zenia that seem to indicate a close rela- tionship between the two of you that also caused conflict.'

Toni's tongue slid cautiously around her lips and her grip tightened on the water glass as she formulated her reply.

'You know…' she began and then paused to put the glass down on the table. She sat back on the sofa and sighed, so that Alex thought she wasn't going to answer. But Alex stayed silent, watching the woman's face as she gazed out of the window, her eyes flickering. After a few moments Toni began again. 'Zenia was very much in love with me at the time. My marriage to Frank was going through… a difficult phase. He had a lot of affairs. It was the sixties – everything was suddenly very free back then.' She stopped talking again and looked down at her empty hands, twisting a ring with a big blue stone around on one of her fingers. Then she looked up at Alex and her eyes sparked briefly. 'Of course I cared for Zenia. How can you not? When someone like that loves you, and you're un-happy…' She paused and her face contorted as if she was dealing with unwelcome memories. 'Zenia wanted me to go away with her to South America. I think we fantasised about Brazil. But then Zenia's mother arrived from Italy. She was ill and needed treatment – this wasn't long before she died and Zenia had offered to get an operation for her here in New York and look after her.'

'That can't have been easy. I gather Zenia and her mother didn't get on at all.'

Toni gave a twisted smile. 'That,' she said with emphasis, 'is an understatement. There were fights – real fights – they were both people with violent feelings. In the end Frank threw them out.'

'Because of Natalia, or because of Zenia's relation-ship with you?'

Toni was silent for a moment. 'It was a long time ago, so I don't remember details very clearly, but a bit of both I think. Natalia hated me.'

'Reading the letters and talking to Zenia, the break-up seemed to cause her a great deal of pain.'

'I think it did – she went a little crazy for a while. But what did she expect? I loved Frank, in spite of every-thing, and I wanted to have children – we patched it up and he started to make money. It was never easy, but we were happy enough.'

Toni picked up the glass and took a sip. 'He did a painting of the two of us, you know, before he gave up figurative art completely. Would you like to see it?'

Alex followed her into a small study off the hall-way. Tony indicated a canvas on the wall above the desk. It was composed of blocks of earth colours – browns and ochres and pale cream, semi-abstract planes that seemed to represent a building with a big window. At the window, just visible, gazing round the upright edge of a half drawn curtain, was a woman, and just below, at the corner of the building, in the centre of her sight-line, was another woman staring back. 'That's us,' Toni said. 'Zenia and me.'

'Zenia's agent told me that he'd once painted you both naked in bed together.' Alex had wondered whether she could ask this question, but felt able to risk it.

Toni looked angry. 'Absolutely not. What a poisonous individual! Zenia would never take off her clothes for a man. Not after what happened…'

'She told you about Vienna? The clinic?'

'Of course. I don't know how her mother could have done that to her. No wonder they didn't get on.'

There was a photograph on the desk of a young couple – the man blond-haired, wearing sunglasses and clutching a bourbon glass, smiling broadly at the camera. The slim girl beside him in a mini skirt had a sleek helmet of black hair cut level with her ears, pale lips and big, sooty eyes. 'That's Frank and I at one of the openings,' Toni said. 'He did really well here – he was from northern England, gritty, macho, working class, no bullshit. They loved him.'

At the door Alex said, 'I will be discreet in the book, but Zenia's insistent that she wants to tell the truth. Do you want me to use initials? Or a pseudonym?'

Toni sighed. 'What would be the point? These days with the internet people can find out in two minutes. But I don't want anything prurient. Nothing that would upset my children. My son's a professor of economics at UCLA and my daughter's got her own PR company in Chicago.'

'It won't be sensational, I promise you,' Alex said. 'I'll send you the draft pages so you can see what I've written. I need your permission for quotes from your own letters in any case. But I'll be careful.'

'Thank you,' Toni said, holding out her hand. 'It's a relief to find someone so sympathetic. I was afraid you'd turn out to be some kind of tabloid journalist.'

'It's not easy writing about someone who's had such an unconventional life,' Alex said.

Toni gave a short, curt laugh. 'Zenia could never do anything the easy way. She chose to live in a kind of war zone with everyone and everything around her.' Toni looked wistful. 'How is she now?'

'Dying. But still very lively. She's living in Croatia – Istria – with someone called Freddi. She's been happy I think.'

'Good. I would want that for her.' Toni opened the door. 'It's been interesting meeting you. I'll wait for your pages, but I'm not looking forward to reading them I'm afraid.'

Alex sat on the bed with her notebook on her lap, open at a blank page. Her fingers trembled as they held the pen against the paper. After she'd left Toni Harrison's apartment, Alex had sat in a bar for a while, too agitated to eat lunch, drinking a better than remembered Californian wine, trying to make up her mind about what she was going to do next. Did she have the courage? She had to find the courage. How could she face Zenia again if she didn't? And if she waited any longer, maybe she wouldn't do it at all. It was only a short walk from the apartment, along Twelfth Avenue.

Now, in the quiet of her hotel room, listening to the tick, tick of the radiators, and the faint hum of traffic beyond the double glazing, Alex forced herself to shape the words on the page, to fix the moment when she had chosen to confront the blank space at the centre of her life. It seemed important that it should be recorded.

'*They call it Ground Zero,*' she wrote. '*Which makes it sound like a military exercise or a battle zone. But perhaps that's how they want you to think of it. Nothing prepares you for the enormity of the space – a gigantic gap as big as the absence I'm learning to live with.*'

Alex had been surprised to find that there was a viewing platform you could climb onto to look down into the pit; surprised to find heaps of debris still in it and earth-moving lorries crawling around like huge dung beetles. How many more years would it take to clear?

'*The scale of it is beyond comprehension,*' Alex wrote. '*When I lived in New York the two towers and their satellite buildings still stood there. Now they're gone and my daughter has gone with them. I hope she died quickly. That has haunted my days and nights – the suffering and the agony that drove people to fling themselves from windows ninety stories up. It's the knowledge of what she might have suffered that still aches inside me. But Steve worked on the eighty-ninth floor of the south tower, so perhaps it was instantaneous. I comfort myself with that.*'

The barriers and steel screens erected around the site were decorated with photographs, poems and objects people had left at this improvised shrine. There were hundreds and hundreds of them. Alex had been almost ashamed of bringing Katy's furry chimp over on the plane with her, but now she took it out of her bag and placed the chimp with its back to the barrier. And then, on an impulse, she took the tattered photo of Katy out of her wallet, found a safety pin at the bottom of her make-up purse and pinned the photo to its fur. It felt absolutely right that Katy should be remembered there with all the others.

'Afterwards I walked back along the street crying.
No-one looked at me – I suppose they're used to tears here.'

The afternoon sun was slanting through the windows now, finding a gap in the buildings on the opposite side of the street. Alex, suddenly exhausted, put her pen and notebook on the bedside table and lay back against the pillows.

Alex seemed to have been asleep for hours when the hotel phone beside her bed rang. She picked it up automatically, not sure for a moment where she was. 'Hullo?'

'Sorry. Did I wake you?' A man's voice speaking Italian, pleasurably familiar.

'Gianfranco.'

'In person. Is it a bad time?' He sounded hesitant.

'Where are you?'

'In the hotel lobby. Should I go away?'

'No!' Alex struggled to sit up on the quaking bed. She spoke louder than she'd intended.

He laughed and the anxiety went out of his voice. 'I'll take that as a sign of hope then, shall I?'

Alex laughed too and they were both silent for a moment. Then Alex said, 'Have a drink in the bar while I shower – I'll be really quick.' She was already halfway to the bathroom. 'Mine's a white wine.'

It was the first time Alex had seen him in a suit – dark and formal with an open-necked shirt. She felt that looking so good should be illegal. It was unfair.

'I'm dressed for the gig,' he said, interpreting her expression. 'Though we're not on until late – the second shift. I thought we might have some dinner first, if you'd like to?'

'I will admit to being hungry. I skipped lunch.' Alex looked at her glass, the straw colour of the wine, the beads of moisture on the outside of the bowl, aware of his eyes on her face, half-amused, half something else – she couldn't meet them because of what she knew would be there – affection, knowledge, and Zenia's uncanny ability to read her thoughts and feelings. Alex was reluctant to have them read.

She braced herself to look up and smile at him. No, there was something else in his face she hadn't listed. Sadness. That was unexpected. Was it her fault?

'I was going to invite you round for a meal at Zenia's, but when I couldn't get you on the phone…'

'I'm sorry – I switched the mobile off this afternoon and forgot to switch it on again. Is there anywhere you'd like to go?'

'There's a small bistro just round the corner from the gig. It gets pretty full, but we could check it out? Shall I get a cab?'

The bistro was tiny, run by New York Italians, and it was full. But as they stood, checking for spaces, someone at the back started shouting, 'Hey! Frankie!'

A large black man in a white shirt with broad blue braces, stood up and began waving his arms towards them. 'Over here!'

'It's the band,' Gianfranco said. 'Are you up for this? We can go and find somewhere quieter if you like?'

'No, it's fine.' Alex was curious to meet the musicians he played with.

They pushed through towards the back corner

where three men had abandoned their half-eaten meals and were already organising an extra chair to make a table for four into one for five.

'Hey!' The man in the white shirt said, putting up his hand to high five Gianfranco. 'So,' turning to inspect Alex, 'who's the lady?'

'This is Alex,' he said in careful, accented English. 'Alex, this is Gene. He's the drummer.'

Gene took Alex's hand and squeezed it in a muscular grip. 'Come and sit down. Meet the other guys. This one's Bart. He's the bass player.'

A tall, thin man, middle-aged, wearing a flat cap, stood up and reached across the table to take her hand, murmuring, 'Pleased to meet you,' as he grasped her hand with calloused fingers.

The third member of the trio half rose and made a mock bow, putting his hand out for her to shake. 'Bojo. I'm the piano man.' And then to Gianfranco, 'We're just finishing up, so you guys can have the table to yourselves in a while.'

'Don't hurry for us, please,' Alex said with a quick glance at Gianfranco.

'They probably want to go and have a little smoke before the gig,' he said and grinned at Bojo, who winked back.

Alex ordered a pizza and Gianfranco pasta *al pomodoro*, both of which came quickly.

The talk across the table was of music, mutual acquaintances, and they talked fast in a loose slang that Alex struggled to follow. It was interesting, watching the easy friendship they had with each other and which also included Gianfranco. She had somehow expected there to be some edge, some hostility, after his opinions on America and its politics. But he had presumably been telling the truth when he said that it was only a sector of American society he hated and its foreign policies.

'Don't you sometimes feel exposed being British?' He had asked her one evening at the Kaštela. 'Surely there are places abroad where a British passport isn't welcome? All that colonial legacy?' Was there anywhere left in the world, Alex thought, where anyone, regardless of nationality or ethnic origin, could be wholly welcome without some uneasy resonance from the past getting in the way?

At the Vanguard, Gianfranco settled Alex at a small table in an alcove reserved for the band. The club was crowded and noisy. A mixed audience, a lot of middle-aged men, some couples who looked like tourists and a handful of smart young New Yorkers. A few years ago she could have been one of them, in the days when she and Steve had gone out together, Katy on a sleep-over at a friend's, in the days when life was normal, when the only shadow was a needy, interfering mother-in-law.

The lights in the club dimmed, the spotlights on the band stand were turned up, and the musicians walked in. Gene first, bowing to the applause, taking his position behind the drum kit, picking up the sticks and adjusting the cymbals. Then Bart, tall and thin, lifting the double bass from its prone position on the floor. Bojo, broad and magnificent, his dark skin shiny under the lights, bowing low to increased applause. He paused in front of the microphone.

'Good evening, ladies and gentlemen, guys and dames, good to see you all enjoying yourselves, because things just got even better. We're going to take the roof off this place tonight!' More cheers, whistles and applause. Bojo extended his left arm to where Gianfranco was waiting beyond the reach of the spotlight. 'Because, all the way from Italy, we got Frankie Antonelli on the tenor sax and clarinet. Give a big welcome you-all for Frankie Antonelli!'

There was wild applause as Gianfranco stepped into the lights and bowed to the audience. He flicked a glance towards Alex and picked up the saxophone from its stand, removed the cap from the reed and hooked the instrument onto the black strap that hung from his neck. He settled his fingers on the pads and waited for Bojo to take up position on the piano – a quick glance at the drummer and the bass player – the tap of a foot – and then there was a blast of sound as they all launched into the music at exactly the same moment.

It was obvious, even to Alex's limited musical knowledge, that this was seriously good. She simply hadn't realised the level at which Gianfranco played. She watched as he wrestled with the saxophone, coaxing sounds from it she hadn't thought a saxophone could make. And she felt the sheer joy that emanated from him as he played, waves and waves of it passing across the room, inviting the audience to jump and shout and tap their feet and whistle and ululate.

The musicians were so integrated, the drums, the piano, the bass and the sax, it seemed sometimes as if they were reading each other's minds. Did Gianfranco's empathy come from this kind of musical awareness? Then the piano and the sax were playing games, a few bars of complicated tricks on the white and black keys from Bojo, challenging Gianfranco to improvise even wilder sequences on the sax, and then they would look at each other and laugh as if to say, well, that's one over on you! But then the other would come back with an answer, constructing a crazy house of musical cards until, bang, a big thump on the drums and all four of them would launch into a reprise of the main theme.

Alex gave up trying to understand it and let herself be carried off on the excitement of the music. Then, suddenly, Bojo announced a change of mood. 'Ladies and gentleman, we're going to slow things down a bit. We're going to play you something from the great Billy Strayhorn – a ballad called Chelsea Bridge.' Gianfranco put down the sax, and picked up a clarinet from its black case, the same instrument he'd played at the Kaštela. The piano rippled, the drummer hushed on the cymbals and the warm clear notes of the ballad floated out across the room, stilling the audience, who put down their glasses and sat without speaking or moving.

Alex was holding her breath, watching the concentration on Gianfranco's face as phrase after perfect phrase breathed from the clarinet and melted away into the shadows at the back of the room. It felt personal, as though he was speaking directly to her.

When the last note died into silence, the audience erupted, stamping, clapping, shouting for more. Even the band were clapping. Gianfranco just bowed, keeping his head down towards the floor for a long time, acknowledging the applause. And as he straightened up and turned to put the clarinet away in its case, he looked directly at Alex and held her eyes just for a moment.

After the gig was over, some of the audience swarmed forward towards the band stand. Alex watched them from her sheltered alcove. Gianfranco was surrounded by people waving CDs for him to sign. Several of them, Alex noted, were very attractive women. One in particular seemed to be treating him in a rather familiar way, touching his arm and chatting in a provocative manner while he signed her CD cover. She stayed around while he signed other autographs, as if she was waiting for him. Was she one of his girlfriends? God knows, he must have them. She was surprised how bad that felt.

She saw Gianfranco look in her direction and wave for her to come over. She went with a cold sensation in her stomach. As she came up he turned away from the woman and said, 'Ciao, cara,' and kissed her on both cheeks, whispering in Italian into her ear, 'What took you so long? Couldn't you see I needed to be rescued?'

The cold feeling began to thaw. As Alex emerged from his embrace she saw the other woman's face darken and her open, flirty manner begin to fade. She smiled a brittle, rather venomous smile towards Alex and said, 'I was just telling him how good he is – Wow! The way he played that thing tonight.'

'Are you ready to go?' Gianfranco said in Italian. 'I just need to pack up the instruments.'

'Fine. No hurry. You still need me to ride shotgun?'

He grinned suddenly. 'You got the message.'

'So, are you Italian too?' the woman asked.

Alex shook her head. 'No, I'm English. You're obviously a fan?'

'I go to all their gigs. They're great guys. But I guess I better be going.' She began to move away reluctantly, smiling at Gianfranco and waggling her fingers provocatively. 'See you again soon.' She backed away towards the exit.

'Thank God for that,' Alex heard him say behind her. She turned.

'Don't you like the fan club?'

'We call those sorts of fans "grippers",' he said. He was hauling a red cloth through the innards of the clarinet. 'Because they grip your arm and insist that you talk to them.'

Bojo came up and banged him on the back. He grinned at Alex. 'You better come here again,' he said. 'This boy was playing out of his socks tonight!'

'You mean he doesn't play like that all the time?' Alex was glad to watch Gianfranco squirm a little.

'You take no notice of them,' he said, in that imperfect, accented English. 'Listen to them and you never speak to me again. They destroy my character.'

Bojo laughed. 'We won't dub on you Frankie – not in front of a lady who loves jazz.'

He grasped Alex's hand. 'Nice to meet you. Maybe we see you again.' He didn't sound optimistic, so Alex guessed either he was being tactful, or that Gianfranco didn't turn up with the same woman too often.

The two men said goodbye and Gianfranco asked a waiter to call a cab.

'They seem really nice guys,' Alex said. 'Do you play together regularly?'

'Only when I'm in New York. They're the resident trio here. Brilliant musicians – the sadness is, hardly anyone outside New York, or even outside the jazz scene, has heard of them.'

'Why do they call you Frankie?'

'I think they find Gianfranco a bit of a mouthful – everyone gets a nickname here. That's mine.'

'Do you mind?'

He shook his head. 'I quite like it.' He put his hand on her shoulder. 'I think that's our cab. Do you have to go straight back to the hotel?'

'Not specially. Why?'

'Come and see Zenia's apartment, the one Paulina bought for her. We can have a nightcap. You could have stayed, you know,' he said. 'I am capable of behaving myself, whatever you may have heard about Italian men!'

'But perhaps it wasn't you I was afraid of,' Alex said playfully and then blushed.

The way he smiled at her made Alex aware that tonight, for the first time in many months, she needn't sleep alone if she didn't choose to. In the cab, he touched her hand lightly with his fingers and her stomach turned over with a mixture of fear and anticipation.

Zenia's apartment was on the edge of the Village – top floor with old wrought-iron balconies and a clanking lift with a metal grille you had to pull shut manually. Inside the apartment the lighting was subdued, table lamps and uplighters, illuminating the same kind of clutter of antique furniture and eastern rugs that characterised the Kaštela.

'It looks better at night,' Gianfranco said. 'By day you can see the cobwebs and the peeling paint. But it has lovely views.'

The kitchen was narrow and high ceilinged, with old fashioned wall cabinets and an enamel cooker. But on one of the surfaces there was a gleaming chrome-plated Gaggia coffee machine and, standing beside it, a fridge the size of a Cadillac. Gianfranco opened it and took out a bottle of Prosecco. 'Zenia always has a good supply. There are two or three cases in the cupboard. We might as well drink it while we can.'

He pulled the cork out with only the briefest pop and glugged the fizzy wine into two glasses. 'Who did you see today?'

'Toni Harrison. Zenia lived with Toni and her husband before she met Paulina. I gather it was all rather complicated.'

'Things always were with Zenia. *Salute!* He clinked his glass against hers. 'Was she helpful?'

'More than she intended I think.' Alex paused, took a deep breath. 'And then afterwards, I went to Ground Zero.'

He came and stood beside her and put his arm round her, resting his chin on her hair. Alex had been afraid she might cry, but found herself quite dry-eyed and in control. 'I didn't think I'd be able to do it, but now I'm wondering why I didn't come before. It felt so right.'

He tightened his grip on her and she raised her face and let him kiss her, dizzy with wine, and music and emotion.

He let her go almost immediately and said, 'Come into the sitting room – there are things I want to show you.'

In the big room he switched on a wall light to illuminate a large portrait on the wall that had previously been lost in the shadows cast by the other lights.

'This is Zenia's portrait of Paulina,' he said. 'What do you think?'

The monochrome painting showed a tall, etiolated figure with a pale, narrow face, framed by a series of tight, slate-grey curls that seemed fixed to the skull even as the woman turned towards the viewer, three-quarter face, caught in mid-movement, her angular body arrested between poses, like a bird mid-flight, slightly off-balance. Her eyes were wide open and bewildered, her lips just closed on words already spoken, her hands committed to canvas mid-gesture. There was fear, surprise, the suggestion of a neurotic tic, a restlessness, totally at odds with the static image on the canvas. The rich, unhappy Paulina Rothermeyer.

'Would you like to hear what Zenia had to say about her? I've got it on my netbook.'

Alex was glad that she hadn't had time to empty her bag after her visit to Toni. She took the computer out, put it on the coffee table, found the MP3 file and soon the room was echoing with Zenia's voice.

Her name wasn't Paulina of course, that was the name I gave her. Her father had called her Palomina after a horse. Can you imagine? My little filly he used to call her. And she also had Spanish blood – Paulina's mother was a dancer who had come from Valencia to California to find work after her own parents had died. And then she met this German immigrant who kept a shop and the dancer married him, gave up dancing and had Paulina. The German shopkeeper wanted his children to grow up and have respectable occupations, but he gambled with the horses and there was no money and so his wife started teaching other children to dance as well as her own and Paulina, who was very beautiful, began to get jobs in the theatre and soon she had a part in a film – just a small part, but there would have been more. She had good clothes and went to Hollywood parties. And then J.D Rothermeyer saw her and he wanted her. You will know his name? He was one of the richest men in America at that time. When everyone was jumping out of their office windows, he was charming their widows, buying their houses and their cars and their businesses for a fraction of their true value. No-one knows where his money came from in the beginning. He arrived in New York from Eastern Europe with a suitcase and ten years later his name was everywhere.

By the time he met Paulina he had imported Mama and Papa and brothers and sisters and they were all living in New York in the apartments he had bought for them in a grattacielo on Central Park. His own apartment was at the top of the building looking out over the whole of the city. J.D.'s family did not want him to marry Paulina. They were Jewish and she was not. They called her a Shiksa – and however good she was to them, it was never good enough to be one of them. She had even become a jew to please them, and so that she and J.D. could be married under a canopy. But in her heart she was always a Spanish Catholic. We used to go secretly to mass together at Xmas and Easter and it made her happy to do that. She would confess and get absolution and for a while she would be at peace. She was terrified that she would die without a priest and she made me promise that I would get a priest for her somehow if she was ill, so that she would not die without the last rites. But, of course, I was not there when she died and the family – they would never allow a priest through the door. I have a mass said for her at Easter every year. The Church tells us that such souls as hers are in purgatory and it makes me very sad. I do not believe myself, but Paulina did and she must have died in fear of spending eternity in limbo. My darling Mouse – there was so much fear in her life.

Even when I made love to her – she was so very happy, but there was always fear. The first time we were in bed together – such love and such delight – and then afterwards she got out and knelt on the floor and prayed for forgiveness – as if such love could be sinful – how can it be wrong to love someone and express that love with your body? We live in a crazy world that can call the love of one person for another an evil thing.

As the voice died away, they both stood in front of the portrait, arms around each other, without speaking. Then Gianfranco said, 'Concetta told me they went through a ceremony of marriage.'

'How?'

'In the little church at Visoko. Secretly. They made vows, exchanged rings and blessed each other with holy water. Concetta said that she was a witness.'

'She's begun to talk to me, you know. But I don't think she will ever tell me the whole story.'

'Probably not. Concetta's the keeper of the secrets. Has been for the past forty years. She's not going to give up the job yet.' He looked down at her. She thought he seemed unsure of himself. 'It's very late. Would you like me to call you a taxi, or would you like to sleep here?' he asked.

'With you?'

The arm around her shoulders tightened. 'Yes.'

It was decision time and Alex was aware that her body, somehow unhitched from her mind by wine and the unsettling nature of his proximity, was making the decision for her. Suddenly bold, Alex reached up to kiss him. 'It's so long since I made love with anyone, I'm not sure I can remember what to do.'

'That's all right,' he said easily. 'I could do with a

bit of revision myself.'

'I thought you would be well practised. There must have been a lot of women. I saw the way they looked at you tonight. The woman who came up and wanted you to autograph her CD. You must be aware of the effect you have on them?'

He laughed. 'Yes, but it wears off. I went a little wild when I was a teenager, like a kid let loose in a chocolate shop. But it helped not having much money, you can't go too far astray… And it never seemed right to sleep with a woman and then walk away as if she was a restaurant meal – I watched how my father treated my mother, and other women, and the damage it did. I've never wanted to be like that.'

'I'm glad. But I wouldn't have blamed you for taking the opportunities. It's not good to be too much alone.'

'You don't die from loneliness, but it certainly doesn't make you a better person.' With one hand he slid her silk blouse from her shoulder and began to press his lips into the hollow of her neck, moving gently downwards.

Alex could feel herself begin to shudder with desire. She slipped her hands under his shirt, across the smooth flesh of his back, feeling the muscles and the bones of his spine with her fingertips. Josie, she thought, would be proud of her.

Afterwards she went to the bathroom feeling sore. She'd been celibate for far too long. Alex looked at her face in the mirror and smiled at her own reflection. Her skin was glowing, her eyes bright – she looked pleased with herself, even smug. Then she had a thought. Neither of them had mentioned contraception. It hadn't even occurred to Alex to think about it. Or presumably to him, since he hadn't taken any precautions either.

Her fingers gripped the edge of the basin. She tried frantically to remember where she was in her cycle, but without a diary it was useless. Where, she wondered, did one get the morning-after pill in New York? Presumably the Chelsea hotel reception would know. No point in worrying now. Alex went back to bed and curled up against Gianfranco's warm body. He was already snoring peacefully. For the first time in two years, she actually felt something that was just a little like happiness.

In daylight, as Gianfranco had predicted, the apartment appeared less luxurious. There was dust on the surfaces, in the folds of the curtains and even on the fine filigree of spiders' webs around the electric light fittings. The rooms had the musty, stale odour of old clothes and tobacco smoke. Alex found mouse droppings on the kitchen surface when she went to investigate the complexities of the coffee machine. The Gaggia made noises as if it might blow up at any moment. It reminded Alex of the pressure cooker her mother had bought and then only used once because she'd been so afraid of it. Gianfranco went out for bread and pastries while she coaxed the machine into life, and then they had breakfast together in the sitting room with cold winter sunlight slanting in through the windows from the street.

After breakfast they made love again, more slowly this time, looking at each other's bodies, exploring them gently, building desire caress by caress until the final release which left them both exhausted. They showered together, giggling like children, enjoying the sensual delight of soap on skin, no longer erotic, but a kind of confirmation of intimacy. This was not just sex, there was a chasm under Alex's feet with a label on it that said, 'The Future'. She wasn't sure, yet, whether she wanted to jump in. With Gianfranco she could detect no such hesitation. When his eyes looked at her with teasing affection, it was as if he was simply biding his time, waiting for some signal from her.

As Alex straightened her wet hair with the comb from her flight kit, still in her handbag, she could hear a mobile ringing in the bedroom and Gianfranco answering it.

He came into the bathroom looking serious. 'That was Freddi. Apparently Zenia's had another stroke, and at first they thought she was all right, but then during the night she got rapidly worse and the doctor says it could only be a matter of hours.'

'How's Freddi?'

'Much as you'd expect. Holding together, but she sounds a bit desperate. I think we should go. What commitments have you got here?'

'Nothing I can't postpone.' Alex had intended to go and see Matti, wander round the Metropolitan, check out galleries and locations relating to Zenia. The agent had given her a list of places and people. It would have to wait. 'What about your gig?'

'I'll have to dep it out. No problem there. There's hundreds of musicians in New York just waiting to jump into someone's shoes.' He smiled grimly. 'In the music business one man's misfortune is another's lucky break.'

There were seats on a direct flight to Milan. Gianfranco re-scheduled his ticket, Alex put in her credit card, hoping that this too would be paid for out of the kitty. They took a cab to the Chelsea to collect Alex's suitcase and then went straight to Newark airport.

At Milan, tired and jet-lagged, they took a train to Vicenza to pick up Gianfranco's car, skipping lunch to drive to the Kaštela. It was already dark when they arrived. The lights were on in almost every house, but everyone was gathered in the dining room, huddled round the fire, even Concetta. She hugged Gianfranco and smiled at Alex. 'Freddi's sitting with her. Go up. I will make you coffee and some bean soup.'

Alex could hear the sound of Zenia breathing before she entered the room – the painful effort of air being sucked in, before being expelled with a hoarse rattle.

Freddi got up out of the chair as they came in. Her eyes were wide with lack of sleep. She looked terrified. 'Zenia's in a coma,' Freddi said. 'It sounds awful, but the doctor said she's not in any pain.'

Gianfranco sat on the side of the bed and took Zenia's hand. 'She feels cold.'

The stove was so hot Alex could feel herself sweating under her jumper.

'The doctor said… it… could happen at any time.'

'How long has she been like this?'

'She fell the day before yesterday when Lenka was taking her to the toilet. We didn't realise straight away. The stroke affected her arm and one side of her face, but she was quite lucid, even managed to talk a little. The doctor was very pessimistic though, that was why I rang you. He said her heart was very weak. Then, yesterday evening she became confused and all night she was wandering among the dead; talking to her mother and to other people in a kind of Italian I didn't understand.'

'Veneto?'

'I don't know. But this morning she was too deeply asleep to rouse and she's been slipping deeper all day.'

Concetta had come into the room. 'I've put out

some food downstairs.' She touched Freddi's arm. 'I'll sit with her. Go down with them; you must have something to eat. And then you must have some rest. I will call you if there's any change.'

Freddi didn't argue, but came reluctantly, pausing in the doorway to look back at Zenia, almost invisible under the bedcovers heaped up around her.

After eating the soup, Alex was so tired she was barely aware of the room that Toby took her to. Gianfranco followed soon afterwards, bringing his own luggage. He stood in the doorway.

'Do you mind if we share? I don't think I want to sleep alone just at the moment, but I'll go away if you prefer.'

'I don't want you to go away.'

'Good. You look absolutely exhausted.'

'I am. Not much sleep over the past few days.' She caught his eyes and they both smiled.

'You go to bed. I'm going up to sit with Zenia. Freddi and Concetta are there, but I'd like to be there with them. There isn't much time left.'

Alex nodded. Part of her would have liked to be there too, but she knew that these last moments were for Zenia's most intimate friends and family. Her presence, the biographer in at the death as it were, would be totally inappropriate. After Gianfranco left, Alex fell asleep almost straight away. Sometime in the darkness of the early hours, his cold body crept in beside her and he curled himself up against her back.

'Zenia's gone,' he said in her ear.

Alex turned over and put her arms around him and they held each other until they fell asleep together.

Zenia looked unusually peaceful laid out on the bed. Concetta and Freddi had dressed her in a tunic of peacock coloured silk with a silver-buckled belt. Concetta was brushing her hair. The stove was off now, the windows open to let in the frosty air.

Two men from the village clattered through the dining room and up the stairs during breakfast, looking at everything around them with avid curiosity.

'They are making the coffin,' Concetta said matter-of-factly. 'The funeral is the day after tomorrow.'

'So quickly?'

'If someone dies at home it must be within three days.'

Antonio and Caterina had spent the night in Trieste and arrived in the chauffeur-driven Range Rover just before lunch. Antonio had brought with him a tall, thin man in a dark suit and a long cashmere overcoat.

'What's happening?' Alex asked Freddi in the kitchen. She looked tired and unfocussed.

'I don't know – he told me on the phone he was bringing his lawyer. So I rang Zenia's this morning and he's arriving sometime this afternoon. There's going to be trouble I think.'

Concetta gave a hoarse, grunting laugh. 'There is always trouble with him. *Scusami*, Gianni,' she said to Gianfranco. 'But your father is not a good person.'

'I've always known what kind of man he is. But he's my father and it's too late to change that.'

Alex would have liked to say that maybe he had been good to Zenia, giving her legal advice and sorting out her problems, but perhaps that had all been motivated by self-interest, a desire to get his hands on Zenia's property. Though maybe it wasn't as crude as that. Who knew what threads of guilt and debt held them together from their shared childhood? Who had betrayed whom?

'Is Cesare coming?' Alex asked.

'Unfortunately not. Apparently his mother is also dying. She can't be left, so Cesare and Angelina are staying in Venice.'

'It is just as well,' Concetta said, clattering lids at the stove. 'We will have too many people as it is. And where is Toby? He went to the supermarket early to get things for me and now he has disappeared.'

'Perhaps he's gone to pick up Zenia's agent,' Gianfranco said. 'I heard him on his mobile phone this morning to someone called Andrew arranging something.'

'It's possible,' Freddi said. 'Andrew's chosen not to stay here. He's in one of the big hotels down on the coast. I don't know why. He's never done that before. Lenka has his apartment ready and now she's angry.' She sighed. 'Everyone's behaving strangely. This place is falling apart.'

'Once the will's been approved it will be better,' Gianfranco said.

'But it won't be the same without Zenia,' Freddi's eyes were glossy with tears. 'She's the cement that glued us all together – without her we're just separate people with separate ideas about what we should do.'

Lunch was a very subdued meal. Toby still hadn't reappeared, causing Concetta to swear loudly in the kitchen about a shortage of bread. Lenka and Martin were sitting at the bottom of the table, but Martin was avoiding any kind of interaction at all. He concentrated on his food, glancing round the table occasionally. Jolene and Kelly gave the impression of having quarrelled. They didn't speak to each other or to anyone else, but kept their heads down towards their plates. Ludo sat beside Concetta, unusually silent. Alex thought he looked frail. Zenia's chair at the head of the table was empty, but Alex noticed that Concetta had laid a place for her.

Zenia's lawyer arrived just as they were finishing lunch. He was a small, earnest man in his early forties, with heavy-rimmed glasses. Alex thought he would be no match for the Antonellis' advocate, a man whose clothes and shoes exuded wealth and confidence. During the meal Signor Bonduelli spoke only to Antonio and Caterina, looking down his long, thin nose at everyone else around the table as if to make it clear that he rarely kept such low company.

As soon as the table had been cleared after the meal, Antonio stood up.

'You may all be wondering why I have brought Signor Bonduelli with me. But the reasons are very simple – he is an expert on the Croatian law of settlement. I have heard that my cousin made a new will two months or so ago with Signor Barsetti. Is that so?'

Barsetti nodded.

'And I am going to ask him to produce that will so that my own lawyer can judge whether it is legal or not. We think not.'

'This is obscene!' Freddi said. 'The will shouldn't be read until after the funeral.'

'There is no time to observe etiquette,' Antonio said. 'Signor Bonduelli has an important meeting with the Minister of Justice in Zagreb tomorrow. It is important that everyone knows exactly where they stand. Because if, as we believe, this new will is invalid, I am going to ask everyone to leave this house.'

'You're presuming a great deal!' The muscles of Freddi's face were contorted by anger.

'I'm not presuming. I know.'

'But perhaps Zenia has left you a few surprises?'

'I don't think so.' He laughed.

'First of all,' Antonio went on, 'all of you who are not concerned with my cousin's will should leave the room. Signora Forbes?'

'But I am. I was a witness.'

Antonio looked annoyed. 'You two!' He pointed to Jolene and Kelly. 'You have outstayed your welcome.'

'They are beneficiaries in the will,' Freddi said calmly. 'In fact, everyone in this room has been mentioned.'

Andrea Barsetti cleared his throat politely. 'Signor Antonellli. If you would allow me. I would like to read out the will of Signora de Braganza.'

A rather sardonic smile hovered around Antonio's mouth, but he inclined his head in agreement.

Barsetti sat forward in his chair and adjusted his glasses. He held the cream pages scattered with black script up in front of him and began to read. 'This is the last,' he paused after the word as if to emphasise it, 'will and testament of Zenobia Maria Theresa de Braganza. Made on the 27th of December 2003 in the presence of Andrea Michele Barsetti and Dottore Tomas Viviani, witnessed by us and by the Signora Alessandra Forbes.' He went on to read the clauses Alex already knew; that the Kaštela was to be left to Antonio Antonelli for the benefit, during her lifetime, of Freddi Baker Thomson, in order to preserve it as a museum in memory of Zenia and her work. There were small legacies to all her friends; a painting to Ludo, the gatehouse to Concetta for her lifetime, a sum of money to Martin. But as he read, Alex watched Antonio's face and the strange little smile that tugged at the corners of his mouth. It made her feel uncomfortable. Why was he smiling, when this will was taking away his power to possess and control Zenia's property? What did he know? Why was he so sure that this document could be set aside?

Antonio's lawyer was listening carefully and, as Barsetti began to go through the details of the minor legacies, he suddenly held up one beautifully manicured hand. 'This is all very good, and very well-intentioned, but I must remind all of you that, although Signora de Braganza was an Italian citizen, her property is in Croatia and is governed by Croatian laws of inheritance. One of those laws is that the testator or testatrix should be of sound mind and have sufficient mental competence to make a will and fully understand the implications of their depositions. We believe that in this case, those terms have not been met.'

Barsetti interrupted. 'There can be no problem there, because one of the witnesses is Dottore Viviani, Signora de Braganza's physician.'

Signor Bonduelli took an envelope from his inside pocket and slid out a letter which he opened carefully. 'I'm afraid that Dottore Viviani has retracted his signature.'

'He's what?' Freddi sounded stunned.

It was Antonio who replied. 'He said he only signed because she was an old friend and he didn't want to offend her. But that she was no longer mentally competent to understand the complexities of what she was doing.'

It was true, Alex thought, that Zenia's mind had weakened in the last weeks. But on that day, just after Christmas, she had seemed very strong, very determined. Alex could swear that she had been as much in her right mind as anyone else in this room, and very sure about what she was doing. Zenia had sat up in bed dictating her wishes aloud to Barsetti who had written them down verbatim. Alex remembered being surprised that hand-written wills were not only legal here, but commonplace. The old doctor had sat on a chair beside the bed and listened. Alex had heard Antonio describe him as an old fool and for once she had been inclined to agree with him. Tomas Viviani was tall, stooping under the door frame, with sparse white hair growing down to the collar of a shabby suit that carried traces of whatever it was he'd had for lunch. His face was long and mottled, and the skin sagged over prominent cheekbones beneath eyes that were vague and glossy with moisture. He had abundant moustaches, tinged with yellow and rather uncared for, that looped down on either side of his mouth almost obscuring his lips. But he had been good with Zenia, holding her hand, talking to her gently in a voice that had a slight tremor. There was an air of kindness about him as well as senility. Now, Alex wondered what pressures Antonio had brought to bear on him to revoke the authority of his signature as a witness.

Zenia's lawyer looked as though he was being asked to eat ground glass. There was a frigid silence.

'Unfortunately,' Signor Bonduelli said. 'I think it likely that the Croatian court will not accept this will in the light of Dottore Viviani's letter. And, since this new will, and the beneficial ownership it attempts to create, is invalid, it is Signora de Braganza's previous will that stands. I will now ask Signor Barsetti to read this document, though I would mention that we have already had it vetted by a lawyer in Zagreb.'

Barsetti reached out a hand towards the paper. Everyone was looking at him. He shrugged and raised his eyes to heaven as he took the document.

'But how do we know that this is the previous will?' Gianfranco asked.

'Because I have all the others, my friend.' The lawyer took a thick pile of aging brown and cream papers from his briefcase and put them on the table. 'You may examine them if you wish. *Guardate pure.*'

Barsetti counted them and made a note of the dates on a pad. 'I will need to have a closer look in due course,' he said. 'But they do seem to be in order. They have all been registered.' He paused and Alex noticed that the knuckles holding the pen were white with effort. When he spoke again his voice was harsh as if he was struggling to keep it under control. 'If I had realised how little time… how ill the Signora was… I could have got a physician from Zagreb.' He glared at Antonio Antonelli and then at Freddi as if it was their fault that he had been made to look a fool in front of a Milanese lawyer.

Freddi had her head in her hands and Concetta was looking at the floor, Ludo staring out of the window. Out of the corner of her eye, Alex saw Martin, who had been standing against the doorpost at the back of the room, turn and slip out into the loggia. Lenka looked up in alarm and half rose. For a moment, Alex thought she was going to follow him, but then she subsided in her chair again

Alex turned her head and saw Gianfranco looking at her. His face was sad, but there was also a flicker of humour.

'Trust Zenia to have a corrupt doctor,' he murmured.

'Can it be challenged?' Alex whispered back.

Gianfranco shook his head. 'I don't think so. This is Croatia. If there are any doubts, the courts will go with the family and the physician.'

Antonio turned to his lawyer. 'Salvo, I think you had better read the will aloud.' And then he stretched out his legs and leaned back in his chair with an air of complete satisfaction.

'Very well.'

Alex could hardly bear to listen to the dry legal voice intoning what was, in effect, an eviction notice for everyone. In this will the Kaštela was left to Antonio absolutely, although he was to be liable for Zenia's debts. But there was one surprise; the contents of the Kaštela and Zenia's residual estate were left to Gianfranco.

Alex saw the look of sheer astonishment on Gianfranco's face.

He looked across at Freddi and said, 'Of course, you'll choose whatever you want to keep.'

Freddi shook her head – not in refusal, Alex thought, but in disbelief.

'She made this will before she met you,' Gianfranco said. 'You have to remember that.'

'But there are other properties, not covered by this will,' Barsetti interrupted. 'And I have to tell you that in her lifetime, December to be exact, Signora de Braganza transferred her London house by deed of gift into the name of Signorina Baker-Thomson, and her apartment in New York to her cousin Gianfranco Antonelli. These transfers are legally correct and have already been registered in England and America.'

Alex heard another sharp intake of breath beside her. But Antonio was already talking again.

'Those depositions will be overturned,' he said. 'She was no longer in her right mind. We have the letter from her physician.'

'I think not,' Barsetti said. His voice was silky smooth. 'These transfers would be very difficult to challenge. Both properties,' he went on, 'came into my client's possession after the date of the will you have produced and, since they are not covered by Croatian law, the beneficiaries can opt to have any legal challenges heard in America and the United Kingdom. The courts there would, I think, take a dim view of a physician who signs a will and then changes his mind. Perhaps it is he who is not competent? It would be a very interesting case, but I have no doubt what the decision of those courts would be.'

'Don't you think you have enough?' Freddi asked Antonio. 'Would you even try to disinherit your own son?'

Antonio blinked. He glanced towards Gianfranco and made a gesture with his hand, but before he could speak, Caterina had leapt to her feet and was standing in front of Gianfranco.

'Hah!' she said. 'It's well seen that you've spent your life currying her favour. Are Cesare and I to get nothing? How did Zenia know you really were her cousin and not some bastard son of your mother's many lovers?'

'She didn't,' Gianfranco said. Alex noticed that his fists were clenched tight. 'But she left it to me anyway.'

Antonio held up his hand. 'So, as I've already made plain, I want everybody out of here as soon as the funeral is over.'

'I intend to take legal action,' Freddi said. 'I know the law here and you can't do anything until the will has been validated by the court.' She nodded towards Barsetti. 'I want to register an objection. Zagreb, I think,

Andrea?'

Barsetti nodded. 'And while that is pending, nothing must be changed. And nothing must be removed from the property until we have a legal ruling.' He looked from Antonio towards Freddi and Gianfranco.

Antonio was visibly annoyed. Caterina turned and slammed out of the room. Antonio stood up to follow her. 'I will win, of course,' he said to Freddi as he was leaving. 'You are merely buying yourself a little time. And it will cost you a great deal.'

~ ~ ~ ~ ~ ~ ~ ~ ~ ~ ~ ~ ~ ~ ~ ~ ~

Alex waited until later in the afternoon, when she knew Concetta would have finished her work, and walked down to the gatehouse. She knew that this could be her last chance to talk to Concetta. After the funeral tomorrow, who knew where everyone would be? Alex knocked on the door, which was slightly ajar, but there was no reply. Hesitating for a moment she pushed it open and went inside.

'Signora Tonone? Concetta?'

The room was dimly lit, the shutters closed against the afternoon light, but what Alex could see was very fussy. There were embroidered doilies and napkins on every surface. The shelves were lined with little lace fringes. There was a collection of ornamental dolls in one corner, lamps of brightly coloured glass, pieces of lurid majolica, bouquets of artificial flowers in jugs and vases of gilded, floral porcelain. The room smelled of polish and wood smoke.

'Signora Tonone!' Alex could sense Concetta's presence, a disturbance in the air perhaps, or some animal awareness that the silence around her contained another person's heartbeat, the sound of their breathing.

A door in the wall swung open – Concetta must have been standing behind it, because Alex hadn't heard any footsteps.

'What do you want?' Concetta said abruptly.

'I need to talk to you about Zenia.' Alex hesitated and then said, 'Why do you dislike me so much?'

Concetta stepped into the room and closed the door behind her. 'I don't dislike you. But I don't think you should be here. You should not be writing this book.'

'But Zenia herself wanted it written.'

Concetta shrugged. 'I told her again and again that she was a fool. Zenia was like a child. She did not know what it would be like to have everything – all her life – put out there for everyone to see.'

It seemed odd to Alex that Concetta referred to Zenia as a child. To Alex she had always seemed very adult and aware – someone who had thought through all the implications of her conduct and made informed and courageous decisions about how much she was willing to tell.

'What do you think of that man?' Concetta asked, with a jerk of the head towards the Kaštela. Alex knew by the contemptuous emphasis on 'that man' that she was referring to Antonio.

'Probably the same as you do,' Alex said guardedly, though it made her grind her teeth with frustration. She longed to express her hatred and detestation, but knew that she might need Antonelli's cooperation. For Zenia's sake, she mustn't give him any excuse to suppress the biography. Concetta didn't want the book written either – could she be trusted? Zenia had wanted her story to be told and Alex was determined to do it.

'Antonio is a bad man,' Concetta said. 'He was always trying to get his hands on Zenia's money – the only reason he has come here all these years is to ask for money. I heard him last Christmas, talking to her. He is a bully,' Concetta said vehemently. 'And a coward!' She almost spat the words. 'In the war he shot himself in the leg so that he could come home to his mother. That is the kind of man he is.'

She put a hand on the table and looked directly at Alex. 'He betrayed her brother Bernardo to the fascists after the war. Innocent people were massacred because of him. Such a thing cannot be forgiven!'

'But I've been told that it was actually Zenia who betrayed Bernardo, even though it was an accident. That's what her mother believed.'

'*Vaffanculo!* Poisonous lies! Do not let anyone tell you those things.'

'What happened?'

'Antonio's family were fascists; Bernardo was with the communists up in the mountains. There had been a meeting between the two of them, some family business, and it was after that meeting that the fascists marched up to the village where Bernardo was staying and shot everyone. It could only have been Antonio. He knew where Bernardo was.'

Antonio was certainly a smooth politician, and Alex could credit him with any amount of underhand business dealing, but Zenia had thought him too weak to have soiled his hands with anything as sordid as a war crime. A snake, yes, but not a murderer.

'But didn't Zenia take Bernardo food and messages? And she once told me that she had been captured too, but she escaped!'

'That was all a fantasy of Zenia's, to be a *communista*. She wanted to be a boy up in the hills with the partisans, not at home in her mother's house rolling bandages and knitting balaclavas.'

'But Zenia didn't believe her cousin Antonio had

betrayed Bernardo. She told me it wasn't true.'

Concetta shook her head.

'Because she would not believe it. She thought someone made up the story for malice. And Antonio and his children were the only family she had left. You do not understand the importance of family in Italy. If I asked her she would say that no-one knew for certain what happened up there in the mountains. There was a lot of killing. Who can tell who was responsible for the death of Bernardo? But it was obvious that the fascists were responsible.' Concetta paused.

'The son of one of the men Antonio fought with in 1946 is on trial for war crimes he committed here in Croatia in the civil war.' Her eyes were fierce. 'These families go into the shadows, but they still have power. The fascists are always there. Antonio will be able to do what he wants with the Kaštela – it's a base for him to expand his business interests here. I have heard that he has bought a lot of empty property in Zagreb and Pula, even a hotel in Dubrovnik. He is a Judas! I know. I know in my heart.' She struck her breast with her fist twice in quick succession.

'Bernardo's wife believes that Zenia betrayed Bernardo.'

Concetta's face changed. She sighed. 'Poor Signora Angelina. Zenia's mother Natalia hated Angelina – she treated her like a maid. But Angelina was very kind. Very good to me. Even after I married, she still wrote to me every New Year. But when I came to live here with Zenia the letters stopped for a while. And then of course, she had such trouble because of her son.'

'Tell me about Salvatore.'

'He was only two years old when Bernardo died. They lived with Natalia, Signora de Braganza, but it was not very good. She spoiled Salvatore, let him do just what he wanted. After that Angelina could never control him. By the time he was eighteen he was really wild. And then when Natalia left him all her money… It was a great mistake.'

'Gianfranco told me she left nothing to Zenia.'

'Nothing. And it should have been hers, because the money came from her father's brother, who was a banker in Vienna. He left money to Natalia when he died so that she and Zenia would be cared for. But after America, Natalia made a new will leaving everything to Salvatore. And of course when he died in the crash, it all went to Angelina. Poor Zenia never saw a single lira. The two of them haven't spoken since Salvatore died. Thirty-two years of not speaking.'

Concetta waved her hand towards the dining table. '*Sediti*. Sit down. I will make some coffee.' She began to fill a small espresso pot and set it on the gas ring. Then she reached up to the shelf and took down a bottle of slivovitz and two glasses. She put them on the table with a bowl of sugar and the coffee cups.

'It is time we were plain with each other,' Concetta said. 'Because I think that perhaps you are going to become part of this family now.'

Alex blushed. 'Why do you say that?'

'I have watched the two of you. And I know him very well.'

'Do you disapprove?'

'No. Though I had rather he would marry an Italian girl.' She filled the coffee cups and sat down opposite Alex, unscrewing the cap on the slivovitz and pouring a shot into each glass.

'*Salute!*' she said.

Alex raised her own glass and clinked it against Concetta's. '*Salute!*'

'But it does not change the fact that I do not like this book you are writing.'

'I was hoping you would help me to tell the truth. That was what Zenia wanted. But sometimes the stories are so muddled, and everyone has a different version. You've known her longest and I was relying on you.'

Concetta looked silently at Alex with sharp, dark eyes for a while before she spoke. 'Ah,' she said at last. 'Truth! Why do we value it so much when sometimes a lie can be so comforting? And so useful! There are truths in Zenia's life that will not bear telling.'

'Like her relationship with her mother?'

Concetta nodded. 'Years ago, when that American woman came here to write her book, I took some letters from the studio. Letters between Zenia and Natalia.'

'Why?' Alex was shocked.

'They were sad, angry letters full of poison.' Concetta paused for a moment. 'Natalia couldn't accept Zenia as she was – and she blamed her for Bernardo's death and couldn't be persuaded otherwise. For Zenia it was terrible – to be rejected by your mother… So, when her mother accused her of killing Bernardo – Zenia sent letters of hate and then her mother sent terrible letters to her too. There is no hatred like that between a mother and daughter, because there are also such deep ties – it is a hatred that has roots that curl themselves round the heart and strangle it. Sometimes I thought it would destroy her.'

'What did you do with the letters?' Alex could hardly bear to hear the answer.

'I burned them, to prevent Zenia looking at them again and again, and to prevent that other woman having them.' Concetta's eyes flickered briefly. Was she telling the truth? 'It was better that no-one should ever see them.'

Alex could have wept. But it was no use. Concetta had her reasons. She had lived all her life to protect Zenia and she would go on doing it.

Concetta was speaking again. 'Did you know that Angelina telephoned to her just after you left at New Year?'

'No. But I'm pleased that she did,' Alex said. 'When I saw her in Venice she said that they had been enemies long enough and she wanted reconciliation.'

'It was sad,' Concetta said. 'Zenia was too ill to talk. She listened to Angelina for a while and nodded and then she gave the phone to me. I told Angelina, but she was very, very upset. She had left it for too many years.'

'It's sad she's not coming to the funeral.'

'Ah. Elvira's health is just an excuse. She hates that man,' again the wrench of the head towards the Kaštela, 'and she can't bear to be under the same roof.'

So much hatred and trouble. Alex took another gulp of slivovitz, thinking that if she stayed here much longer, she would become an alcoholic.

'So what will happen now?'

'Antonelli will get the Kaštela and he will turn it into a tourist village. You will not recognise it. Ludo is going to his neice and I am going back to my sister in Trieste.' She looked sadly round the room. 'Who knows where Jolene and Kelly and Toby will go? But they are young.'

'Lenka?'

'Lenka will stay and work for him. He has already asked her. Haven't you noticed him talking to her every time he comes here? She gives him information and he promises that there will be a job for her. She says she is to be the housekeeper. He will probably give her my house. Martin has also been asked to stay.'

'It's all very sad.'

Concetta shrugged and set her glass down on the table. '*Sai com'è!* It's life!'

As Alex was leaving, Concetta said, 'There is something else that you should know.'

Alex turned to look at her.

'On the day that Antonio left, the first time you came, I saw Jolene with the box of letters, carrying them up to his apartment.'

'Jolene? Whatever would she want with them?'

Concetta gave a gruff laugh. 'Oh, she has secrets, that one. Since she first came here. I hope you find out. There were too many people clinging to Zenia's kindness. But you could never tell her.'

Alex walked straight along the path and down the steps to the rooms below the terrace which Concetta had told her were occupied by Jolene and Kelly. It had originally been a stable for ponies and sheep, Concetta said, but Zenia had converted it into two single rooms. They weren't quite big enough for guests and you had to go outside to the bathroom, so they were used to house extra help in the summer. 'The young ones don't care,' Concetta had said. 'They come from Australia or Spain, looking for an adventure.'

Jolene's door was open. Alex knocked, not really knowing what she was going to say, especially if Kelly was there. But it was Jolene who came to the door and opened it wide for her to come in.

'Excuse the mess… We're packing.'

'Where are you going to go?'

Jolene stood with her arms wide and shrugged. 'God knows.' She ran a hand through her wiry hair. 'I was hoping… I believed… that she'd left me some money so I could go somewhere… We'd talked about the South of France – I'd love to set up a painting school there – a kind of retreat. Zenia seemed to think it was a good idea when we talked about it.' She sounded bitter.

Alex decided there was nothing to lose by plunging straight in. 'A couple of months ago, when I came the first time, a box of Zenia's letters disappeared. Concetta told me that she saw you taking them back to Signor Antonelli's room. I know there are letters missing from that box. Did you take them?'

Jolene was very still for a moment and then she nodded.

'Why?'

'I couldn't let anyone else see those letters…'

'From you to Zenia?'

'And from other people.'

'What was in the letters Jolene? Why did they matter so much?'

'I hated her.' It was said with considerable venom.

Alex felt puzzled and frustrated. 'Then why did you come here?'

'She owed me… for a childhood. Zenia stole my childhood.'

'Will you tell me?'

Jolene cleared a space on the bed for Alex to sit down beside her. 'I was brought up by my mom. She was on her own and it was a struggle for her to manage after my dad walked out. She got typing jobs from an agency and she was always going on about her lost chances – how she'd wanted to go to art school. She was very bitter. Then she got this job as Zenia's assistant, when Zenia came to Canada for that lecture tour she was always going on about. Mom went everywhere with her and then to the States afterwards. She dumped me with my grandma out in the backwoods so that she could go off with Zenia. Dear God…'

Her voice was choked with emotion, but Alex couldn't tell whether it was anger or tears.

'…and believe me there was too much God in that house! She was a hard woman, my grandma. She could chop logs with her teeth, as the saying goes. You'd get more love out of a brick wall.'

'What about your mother?'

'My mom never came back for me. Zenia helped her get a place at art school and then she met some guy in Chicago and that was it. I was lucky if she ever remembered my birthday.'

'What brought you to Europe? Kelly talked about secrets the first evening I was here.'

'I was pregnant with Kelly and I knew they'd never let me keep her.'

So that was the relationship – Alex felt that she should have guessed.

'I took some money and a passport and came over here. Changed my name. I worked in bars, swept floors, sold sketches on the street, painted people's dogs, lived in squats with drunks and weirdos, but finally one day I was walking past this big gallery in London and I saw Zenia's name on the poster outside and I thought I'd go in and take a look.'

Jolene paused. She was twisting her skirt in her fingers, plaiting the material in jerky, nervous movements.

'Zenia was there and I spoke to her. Very polite.

But after I came out I got real angry and I wrote her a letter. There were other letters too. She owed me. Big time. And then eventually she asked me to come here.'

'And when you took the box you got those letters back?'

'Yep. And some others. When I went through it there were letters to my mom from Zenia and some of her replies – letters that upset me a lot. Zenia could be very cruel – she only saw herself – she didn't care what she did to people.'

Alex sighed. 'I can't blame you for taking your own and your mother's letters. I'd probably have wanted to do the same.'

'They belong to me,' Jolene said. 'I checked. And I don't want you putting anything in the book about this either.'

'No. A bit of blackmail wouldn't look too good.' Alex stood up. 'I'll see you at the funeral tomorrow, Jolene. After that, well, I wish you luck, you and Kelly both.'

<div align="center">~~~~~~~~~~~~~~~~~~~</div>

'So, you've found out why Jolene was here, but have you solved all the other big problems?' Gianfranco asked as they lay in bed that night, exhausted and jet-lagged but still sleepless.

'Not really.' Had Concetta actually burned the letters between Zenia and her mother? Letters that might have answered some of Alex's questions about that relationship. 'The only people who know the truth are dead. From what Concetta and Angelina told me, it seems certain that it was Bernardo who told Natalia that Zenia was developing into a boy rather than a girl. I'm presuming that her mother had chosen to ignore her "little imperfection" until Bernardo started talking, innocently as children do, and then of course, Natalia must have realised that she would have to do something. But the issue of who betrayed Bernardo and was responsible for the massacre is anyone's guess. Concetta says it was Antonio; Angelina believes it was Zenia. We probably won't ever know.'

'What are you going to do?'

'I'll have to tell both stories, though your father won't like that, and let the readers decide for themselves which is the truth they want to believe. That's how it is in biography. It's not like fiction, where the author has to tie up all the loose ends.'

'My father will try to sue you if you implicate him.'

'I know. I'll have to word it very carefully and mention no names. At least Concetta's talking to me, and I have a feeling that now she's begun, she'll tell me more. That's one problem less.'

'There's another problem that's been bothering me,' Gianfranco said, lifting himself up on one elbow to look down at her. He was smiling. 'A much more personal one. How is it that you didn't meet anyone else after your divorce?'

Alex was startled by the change of subject.

'You're very attractive.'

She opened her mouth to protest, but he was already speaking again.

'Don't argue.' He put a finger over her lips. 'You know you are. You were living in London, there must have been lots of opportunities?'

'Oh, there were several affairs, but there was Katy, I needed a babysitter if I wanted to go out, so I didn't have much of a social life, and somehow I never seemed to meet the right person, most of them were unavailable, safely married, or just passing though.'

'Did you deliberately choose men like that?'

'Probably.' Alex had thought about it a lot in the months since Katy's death, all those waking hours at three in the morning, the ruthless dawn examinations of the conscience. 'I felt so guilty about the break up of my marriage – it was such a huge failure and I blamed myself. I somehow didn't think I deserved to be happy, so I didn't allow myself to form attachments. I focussed everything on Katy.'

'So, am I just an affair, someone passing through, or am I going to be allowed to be something more?' The tone of his voice had changed.

Alex snuggled up against him. 'It depends if you want to be.' She was thinking about what Concetta had said.

He tightened his grip on her. 'You realise neither of us has mentioned the A word?'

Amore. Alex shivered slightly, but it was impossible to tell whether it was with fear or delight. 'We hardly know each other,' she said. 'It's only a few months since we met and it hasn't exactly been easy.'

'It's not a question of time, though, is it?' He lifted his head again to look down at her. 'If someone's right for you, it's something you just know.'

'A kind of recognition?'

'Yes.'

'It's not easy.' Alex said again. 'There's so much risk involved when you embark on a relationship.'

'But if you don't risk anything you don't get anything. It's like playing jazz – you have to put yourself out there, on the line, before anything can happen.' He sounded very definite.

Alex trembled at the thought of the commitment she was being asked to make; the words that needed to be said, that she was too afraid to speak. But if she didn't let him know how she felt she would lose him and suddenly the thought of that was very bleak. 'All I can say is, it feels exactly right, and that's scary. I just need a little time to get used to it. Can you cope with that?'

'I think so. But don't mess me around, will you? I'm not as bullet-proof as you seem to think.'

One half of her was saying, I don't know if I can

do this, and the other was looking up at him and thinking how miraculous it was that someone so beautiful and *simpatico* wanted to be part of her life. Behind both there was a deep sadness, in the background now, but which would always be there.

'I won't mess you around. I promise.' Alex kissed him, gently, lovingly, trying to put everything she couldn't say into her caresses, allowing her body to say it for her. *Ti amo. Ti voglio ben.* But she was conscious of a moment of panic. The morning-after pill had been forgotten in the dash for the plane and she hadn't any contraception she could use this time either.

Gianfranco seemed to be thinking the same thoughts. He pulled away from her and said, 'I bought some condoms in the airport. Is that OK?'

'We were completely crazy two nights ago. We should have talked about it then.'

'I didn't want to ruin the moment, and then I got a bit carried away.'

'Me too.' Alex had wanted to make love to him so much, nothing else seemed to matter. 'Now we've got to be sensible.'

'When has love ever been sensible?' he asked as he kissed her.

'It doesn't seem right to be so happy,' Alex said afterwards, 'when Zenia's dead and everyone's grieving.'

'Zenia wouldn't mind,' Gianfranco said. 'She was all for people being happy. But it does seem unfair to the living. God know's what Freddi's feeling.'

I know exactly, Alex thought. As if part of her has been amputated, numb, bewildered, angry, at the centre of a black hole. 'Where is she sleeping tonight? In Zenia's room?'

'I don't know. Concetta's sitting with Zenia in the chapel.'

'I can't bear to think of Freddi alone like that,' Alex said. 'But I don't want to intrude either. Should we go down do you think?'

The chapel looked beautiful, lit by hundreds of candles and massed with white flowers; lilies and chrysanthemums and roses. Zenia was in a plain wooden coffin with wooden handles; polished chestnut that glowed in the candlelight. Concetta had draped it in an old Spanish shawl that had hung in Zenia's bedroom, peacock blue with embroidery. On the top lay a small bunch of calla lilies and a silver framed photograph of Zenia when she was young, a copy of the Man Ray image.

Concetta was sitting, stiffly upright, in a chair in the corner.

Gianfranco brought more chairs from the dining room. 'I'll go up and see if Freddi's coming down,' he said.

Concetta shrugged. 'She wouldn't come when I asked her.'

'It will be better for her if she's here with us.'

Freddi's face, when she followed Gianfranco down, was swollen and her eyes were red. She looked dazed. Gianfranco also brought a bottle of prosecco and some glasses. 'Let's drink to her,' he said.

It was cold in the chapel, despite the warmth from the candles. The chilled prosecco made Alex shiver, but she drank it anyway and accepted a refill.

'We should sing,' Concetta said. 'She always liked to sing.'

'What was that folk song she used to like?' Freddi asked. 'Something about picking olives.'

'The maid in the olive groves so fine,' Gianfranco said. 'Concetta knows it.' He looked at Alex. 'Can you sing?'

She nodded. 'School choir, not brilliant, but I can hold a tune.'

'Good. If we sing it through you'll soon pick it up.'

The words were simple:

There was a maid,
in the olive groves so fine,
the olives grew black and green
and I wished that she was mine.

The tune was less straightforward, being slightly a-tonal. It took three rounds before Alex had mastered it. Lenka would no doubt have got it in one, if she didn't already know it. But Alex was terribly glad she wasn't there; just Gianfranco's robust baritone, Concetta's alto and herself and Freddi sharing the upper register. Singing felt utterly right – Alex was aware of a slackening in the tightness of her chest, a lightening of mood despite the autumnal nature of the song.

Oh maiden fair, bind up your hair,
and we will shake the olives from the trees together
for time is short, love comes to nought
and soon enough comes winter weather.

Gianfranco's eyes smiled at her across Zenia's coffin and Alex stored the happiness it generated inside her like a guilty secret.

Alex woke early and slid out of bed without waking Gianfranco. She dressed in the sitting room and let herself out of the front door as quietly as she could. She walked up the steps, past Ludo's shack and onto the woodland path that meandered through the acacia groves and along the ridge of the hill. Alex paused for a moment beside the latched gate at the edge of the wood. The Kaštela was silent, and had a strange, almost fairy-like quality in the pale spring light. The horizon was tinged with pink where the sun was beginning to rise, but a single star was still visible out across the Adriatic. Below her the terracotta roofs of the village fanned out like playing cards, patched and piebald, held down here and there by rocks to keep them from lifting when the Bora blew hard. Alex wondered if she would ever see it like this again. If she would ever return, if, as seemed certain, Antonio inherited the Kaštela. What would happen to them all?

There was a small movement on the periphery of her line of vision. Alex turned to see better and just caught the impression of someone walking down the pathway to the car park – the flap of a jacket, the flash of a trouser leg before it was concealed by the trees. Someone else unable to sleep. Far away, she heard a car start up. The drone of its engine.

In the woods Alex looked for the flowers she had come to pick. Everyone, Gianfranco had said, must throw something into the grave with the coffin, some small offering. Zenia had loved wild flowers, so Alex sought out the woodland plants that were just beginning to come into bloom with the first warm sunlight of early March. There were pale hellebores, cream tinged with green, a clump of primroses in a sheltered hollow, a few wild narcissi exuding fragrance, a small rosette of blue hepatica, and pink and blue anemones with closed blooms that would open out in the sun. Alex picked only one or two from each clump so as not to leave the ground bare and then walked carefully back to the Kaštela. The sun was just edging over the hillside and there was a smell of coffee drifting up from the kitchen.

Ludo was there with Gianfranco and Toby, sitting round the table, a big pot of coffee in the middle and a plate of Concetta's pastries beside it. She was making pancakes on the stove, creaming the mixture across a big black frying pan with a palette knife. Gianfranco got up to get Alex a chair. 'Enjoy your walk?'

'I tried not to wake you.'

'I heard you go, but I was too tired to come with you. Did you find what you wanted?'

Alex held out her flowers. 'I'm just going to put these in water.'

As Alex came back with a small milk jug, Freddi came running into the room from the other direction. She looked distraught. 'Where's Martin? Has anyone seen him? His room's locked. I can't find him anywhere and he's supposed to be one of the pall bearers.'

It was Toby who answered. 'I saw him leaving very early, in the Fiat with Kelly, but I don't know where they were going.'

'I saw someone too,' Alex said. 'Then I heard a car. But I didn't know who it was.'

'How strange? Perhaps they've gone into Rovinj.

He isn't answering his phone.'

Toby looked unusually serious. 'Lenka says his room's been stripped out. She's in the cantina crying. She thinks he's gone for good.'

'Oh God! That's all I need.' Freddi sat down at the table as though suddenly exhausted. 'Why didn't you say something earlier, Toby?'

'Why would he go off with Kelly?' Gianfranco asked. 'Has anyone talked to Jolene?'

Toby shrugged. 'I haven't seen her.' He seemed irritated, aloof.

'Do you want me to go and find out what's happened?' Gianfranco asked.

Freddi had her head in her hands on the table. She nodded without answering.

'I'll come too,' Toby volunteered. 'I sort of knew Kelly. Not well, but she used to talk to me a bit.' He stepped out into the courtyard.

Gianfranco followed him, turning round as he approached the door.

'Alex?'

She got up and went with them down the steps below the terrace. The door of the first room was wide open and inside the cupboard doors were hanging open, hangers and garments on the floor, drawers spilling their contents, more clothes piled on the bed, shoes scattered across the rug. It looked as if it had been ransacked for the few particular things the owner wanted to take.

Jolene was sitting on the bed sobbing. Alex sat down beside her and put her arm around the woman. Her hair smelled of sandalwood and incense sticks. Toby propped himself against the door frame looking as if he'd rather be somewhere else. Alex suspected that he dreaded emotional scenes.

'She left me,' Jolene said. 'Went off with that fucking idiot.' A white ball of spit had gathered at the corner of her mouth.

'Do you know where they've gone?' Gianfranco asked.

'He used to talk about Greece a lot, driving down through Albania. Kelly's always wanted to go to Greece.' She paused for a moment, and then made a helpless gesture. 'She's my daughter. My only daughter. I don't want to lose her.' Jolene began to weep again, snorting into her hands. 'We've always been so close. How could she leave me?'

'Perhaps it's time she had her own life,' Gianfranco said. 'How old is she? Twenty-five?'

It was Toby who answered. 'Twenty-one.' Then he looked directly at Jolene. 'She said she was tired of trailing around after you.' His voice had a sharp note Alex hadn't heard before.

'She's all I have, you know,' Jolene said, tears pouring down her cheeks to soak her shirt. 'Zenia understood that.' She began to sob violently again.

What was it Zenia had said in that first interview? 'Mothers and daughters,' Alex remembered, 'The most difficult relationship.'

It was the wrong sort of weather for a funeral, blue skies, the Adriatic glittering in the sunlight and the hillsides already starred with clumps of alpine narcissi and wild crocuses, anticipating spring. It seemed that everyone from Visoko and all the neighbouring villages had turned out for Zenia's Mass. The little church was so crowded that people were standing crammed against the walls. The priest opened all the doors so that those who had packed the square outside could hear the service. Freddi had forbidden the television cameras to come into the church so they too were outside on the steps. Even so there were journalists among the mourners in the pews, clutching notebooks and cameras. Alex noted many foreign faces as she walked down the central aisle towards the family pews at the front. People who had known Zenia seemed to have come from all over Europe and beyond, including an elderly Japanese couple sitting quietly on the end of a row, a contingent of French twittering to each other like a flock of birds, and Andrew Kir scowling uneasily next to a woman in blue with a piercing Kensington accent. Alex was surprised to see Jane sitting on the other side of him, raising her hand in a discreet gesture of acknowledgement.

The cemetery at Visoko was on the lower slope of the hill above the village, with the Kaštela rising precipitously above it. A pair of honey buzzards were circling overhead making their strange cat-like cries. The graves were ranged on the hillside in steep rows, the older memorials already tilting downwards towards the valley.

Gianfranco, Toby and four men from the village carried her coffin down the steep path from the road. Antonio and Caterina stood on either side of the priest, as if to make it clear that they were in charge, that they were the only family who had a right to be there. Lenka was just behind them. Ludo, standing to one side, wept noisily, tears and mucus trickling down his chin. Concetta and Freddi stood together at a little distance, dry-eyed but stone-faced. At one point Concetta reached out and grasped Freddi's hand in her own. Freddi had her bottom lip gripped fiercely between her teeth.

'I promised Zenia I wouldn't shed any tears at the graveside,' she said afterwards, 'but it was hard, so hard. Almost unbearable.'

When the priest had read the prayers and swung the censer over the coffin, before Antonio or Caterina could move towards the grave, Concetta and Freddi stepped forward to throw in a handful of earth. Freddi dropped a small package wrapped in tissue paper and Concetta what looked like a letter in a sealed envelope. Alex had brought the bunch of wild hellebore, narcissi and hepatica picked that morning from the woods above the Kaštela and inside it, held tightly by the stems, she had placed her precious phial of ash.

It was a decision she had taken the night before, sitting in the chapel with Zenia's body. It was time to let go; to let Zenia take care of it for her *in perpetuam aeternam*. Alex stood by the grave for a few moments and thought of Zenia and wondered where her powerful presence had gone. Was everyone just snuffed out like a candle flame? Or was there something, an essential essence, that went on? When Katy had died Alex had wanted to think that, but her rational self had said no. Alex believed then and still did, that atoms were transmuted into grass and flowers and trees, an eternal part of the universe, but nothing else. She dropped her small gift into the grave and heard the glass break against the hard edge of the coffin. There was a tiny puff of cosmic dust.

At that moment, Lenka stepped forward, as if on impulse, and began to sing. Though Alex couldn't understand the words, she knew it was a lament for the dead, and Lenka sang as if all her heart was in her throat. It was powerful and primitive. The uncontrolled emotion was almost too much for Alex's fragile self-possession. Then she felt a hand on her shoulder, warm and strong. It was Gianfranco, but she didn't move away. Instead Alex turned her face into his jacket and allowed herself to weep with him.

<u>Trieste, 2006</u>

Alex is awake at 6am out of habit. It takes her a few moments to work out where she is. The unfamiliar room, with its baroque gold and maroon drapes, is on the third floor of a palazzo in Trieste, the house once owned by Zenia's father before the economic collapse of the nineteen twenties. Since then it's been an office complex and an apartment block and is currently a boutique hotel owned by a Swiss businesswoman. Since her arrival yesterday, Alex has tried to make sense of the rooms, to discover any traces of Zenia's childhood geography, but after a world war, so many alterations, and the recent ravages of a German architect, its transformation has been too ruthless.

The street outside, beyond the double glazing, is already busy. From the window Alex can look down towards the port, as Zenia must once have done. Alex can imagine her, a small girl, standing on tiptoe to see over the windowsill, wearing the white, lace-trimmed pinafores she'd worn in the photographs, a bow of ribbon in her hair, staring out at a world that was never going to be quite ready for her.

Yesterday, when driving from Zagreb to Trieste, checking her research for the final pages of Zenia's biography, Alex had given in to the temptation to take one last look at the Kaštela. Concetta had warned her, but Alex had wanted to see for herself, to make one last connection with Zenia. It had been a distressing experience. The avenue of cypress trees had been cut down and the ancient fortress had been altered beyond recognition. A large notice in red and white said, '*Proprieta Privata*' and then underneath, in Croat, '*Privatno Vlasnistvo*'. Alex thought grimly that Zenia would have approved the double languages if not the sentiment. True to Zenia's communist principles Alex had ignored the notice but was accosted before she'd even reached the terrace by a security guard with a rifle slung over his shoulder who swore at her in Croat with a strong Russian accent. He stood at the entrance, a dark threatening figure in black and green fatigues, to watch her depart. Alex knew then that she would never go back there again.

On her bedside table is a package of letters that she had begun to read last night before she fell asleep. She had been given them yesterday, summoned to the house of Angelina de Braganza by another telephone call, this time to Alex's mobile. 'If you're going to be in Trieste, you must come and see me. There's something I want to give you. Something I can't trust to our ludicrous Italian post.'

The address that Angelina gave her was a surprisingly modest apartment in the back streets of the old town, with a big loggia full of plants and basket-work sofas. The door was opened by a slim, Eastern European girl in a grey dress and white headdress like a postulant nun. Or perhaps a nurse, Alex thought, as the girl took her through to the loggia where Angelina was sitting in a wheelchair.

The *badante* brought coffee on a tray and pills in a small plastic cup which she gave to Angelina with a glass of water. Angelina was recognisably frailer than the last time

Alex had seen her. There was a faint tremor in the hand that stretched out to give her the package she held on her lap.

'Concetta sent me these, some years ago, when that American woman was poking around in the family affairs. I think Concetta thought that I was going to destroy them. It was certainly what I intended. But in the end I couldn't do it. They're not mine to destroy.'

Alex stared in disbelief at the brown, curling envelopes and the bold black script. 'These are the letters between Natalia and Zenia that Concetta took?'

Angelina nodded. 'They don't make pleasant reading. Natalia was a cruel woman and Zenia too, she was no angel. Two difficult, embittered women.' She paused to smooth her skirt over her knee. 'Still it might help you to understand their relationship. Now that you are family...'

Angelina was right, the letters make difficult reading. Alex picks up the one that she had opened last night, which had moved her so much she hadn't been able to finish it – Zenia writing to her mother;

There has never been one moment in my life, when I have known what it was to be whole – I am Gemelli, the twins, two people the same and yet different. I am not a whole woman – so how can I be a woman as you wanted me to be?

And I am not a complete man either – so I can't live as a man without believing that I am a masquerade – in fancy dress. It is only when I stand in front of a canvas and hold a brush in my hand that I can approach that feeling of One Self – believing that I can create something that contains the whole of me.

This is something that you cannot understand, and

I feel sad for you. I read once that a mother sees in her daughter the reflection of herself. But if the daughter is too different, and especially if her daughter's sexuality is different, then the mother thinks that the reflection is false. This is not her real daughter. And so the child is rejected and the mother grieves for the lost child and the daughter spends her whole life looking for the true self that was lost in the mirror. And they never come to find each other.

At seven Alex thinks she can safely telephone home. Gianfranco answers straight away and she can hear Ben chirping in the background and banging his spoon on the tray of his high chair.

'How was it? Did he sleep all night?'

'Almost. He was awake at four but I brought him into our bed and he went back to sleep. Concetta's just giving him his breakfast. Are you all right?'

'Yes, missing you both.' Missing them both too much. 'But I'll be back just after lunch if I set off now.'

'You will take care? I wish you were travelling by train. It's such a bad road.'

It's the worst road in Italy, the autostrada from Trieste to Milan, packed with Eastern European lorries, crazy Italian drivers and tourist traffic, so Alex can understand his anxiety. But the two most precious people in the universe are waiting for Alex in Vicenza and she will be driving very carefully.

And there is something else. One more reason to be careful. Over the past few days Alex has begun to realise that another small miracle is about to take place. She had been forty when Ben was born. But after the shock of his conception that night in Zenia's New York apartment Alex has discovered that her body is full of surprises. Eighteen months after what she had thought was her last gamble with fertility, it seems that Ben is likely to have a brother or a sister.

'Don't worry,' she tells Gianfranco on the phone. 'I'll be as careful as I possibly can.'

More Books By Kathleen Jones

<u>Biography</u>
Margaret Cavendish: A Glorious Fame, the Life of the Duchess
of Newcastle, Bloomsbury Publishing & The Book Mill E-book
Christina Rossetti: Learning not to be First, Oxford University
Press & The Book Milll E-book
*A Passionate Sisterhood: The Sisters, Wives and Daughter of the
Lake Poets*, Virago & The Book Mill E-book
Catherine Cookson: The Biography, Times Warner
Seeking Catherine Cookson's Da, Constable Robinson
Katherine Mansfield: The Storyteller, Penguin NZ, Edinburgh
University Press
Margaret Forster: A Life in Books, The Bookmill E-book
Norman Nicholson: The Whispering Poet, The Book Mill

<u>Fiction</u>
Three and Other Stories, The Book Mill E-book
The Sun's Companion, The Book Mill

<u>Non Fiction</u>
Travelling to the Edge of the World , The Book Mill

<u>Poetry</u>
Unwritten Lives, Redbeck Press
Not Saying Goodbye at Gate 21, Templar Poetry

<u>As Kate Gordon</u>
An Alternative Guide to Weddings
An Alternative Guide to Baptism and Baby-naming
An Alternative Guide to Funerals